THE CHALLENGE

Robert Cort

Published by Clink Street Publishing 2021

Copyright © 2021

First edition.

The author asserts the moral right under the Copyright, Designs and Patents Act 1988 to be identified as the author of this work.

ISBN: 978-1-915229-00-7 Paperback
978-1-915229-01-4 Ebook

To Bob Trinder for your friendship and encouragement.

Chapter 1

When Emma heard the telephone ring she was in the kitchen preparing her evening meal. She turned down the heat on the hob to reduce the simmering pan, wiped her hands and looked down at the telephone base unit's display screen. She immediately recognised the number. It was her husband's mobile, so she picked up the receiver. "Hello Ian, where are you?"

Ian's reply began, "Emma, you are just not going to believe this…"

"You sound excited, what's going on?"

"I'm in Monaco, in Andrei's apartment. He's left me a letter. He's… well he's gone… and left it to us!"

Ian's mind was still a mixture of excitement and bewilderment as a result of Andrei's totally unexpected surprise.

"Ian, you are talking in riddles, where has Andrei gone? What has he left?"

Ian was standing by the large panoramic glass doors which gave access to the outside balcony area of the penthouse apartment, with views looking down to the harbour and out towards the Mediterranean Sea. However, he realised that he needed to compose himself and explain properly. He moved away from the view and sat down on the white leather settee just in front of him. After taking a deep breath he slowly and more precisely tried to summarise what had happened over the last hour. Emma listened without interrupting or making any comment, however, if Ian could have seen her face he would have witnessed an extremely astonished expression.

After Ian had finished talking there was a short period of silence and then Emma said, "Well… I'm not really sure what to say. Are you saying Andrei has moved out and left the apartment to you? It doesn't make any sense. Why would he do that? Are you sure you have read his letter correctly?"

"Yes, of course. I've read it three times now. Besides, there are lots of documents on the table all signed by Andrei."

"And you don't know where Andrei is? It all sounds very odd… and a bit worrying! What are you going to do?"

"I'm not sure. My flight back to the UK is not until tomorrow. I suppose I will stay here tonight, have a good look around and… well, just have a long think. There's such a lot to take in." For the first time since he had opened Andrei's letter, Ian's was finally beginning to calm down.

"Do you want me to do anything?" asked Emma. She couldn't think of anything else to say and also needed some time to think for herself.

"No, I don't think so. I'll give you another ring if anything comes to mind."

"Okay. Look after yourself and I'll see you tomorrow. What time does your flight arrive?"

"Tomorrow afternoon, about 5.30."

"I'll come and collect you."

"Thank you. Love you."

"I love you too. Have a good night's sleep."

"Will do. Bye." Ian pressed the disconnect button and took a deep breath. He looked up from the phone and around the room. So, he thought, where do I start?

For the next 30 minutes Ian unpacked his overnight bag

in the main guest bedroom, the room he and Emma had used on their first visit. He decided he wouldn't just move into the main bedroom, Andrei's bedroom, so quickly on this visit. That would be a step too far. He then wandered through each room, but this time investigating more thoroughly. Although the beds were made and ready for use, the wardrobes were all empty. The kitchen cupboards contained all the usual cooking equipment, pots and pans, but the fridge and freezer were also empty and switched off. He was now seriously wondering if Andrei's gift was really going to work.

Having not eaten since a snack on the aeroplane, Ian was now feeling distinctly hungry and decided to try one of the bars or restaurants alongside the harbour.

As he left the apartment block, the sun was just beginning to go down, nevertheless, the air temperature was still warm. He walked along the harbourside and considered the various eating and drinking options. He decided that what he really needed first, was a cold beer, or two! Eventually he settled on Oliver's Bar.

There were a few drinkers in the inside air-conditioned bar area, but after Ian had obtained a cold glass of Peroni beer he wandered outside onto the veranda area where the only other occupants were two women. The women were sitting with their backs towards him and they were chatting in French. He sat at a table that overlooked two large yachts with the Harbour Heights apartment building in the background. He sipped his beer and looked up at the top floor of the Harbour Heights building, where he could see the black metal railings of the balcony. It was an unbelievable location.

The final rays of sunshine were still warming his face and he switched his attention to watching the variety of people as they strolled past along the harbourside. He sipped his beer and tried to reflect back on what had been a very strange and certainly an amazing day.

"Hello Ian," said a female voice, with just a hint of a French accent.

Ian looked behind him and then up to the face he instantly recognised. He stood up, smiled and kissed Marie on both cheeks. Marie was one of Andrei's lady friends, who he and Emma had met when they had both first stayed at Andrei's apartment several months ago.

"Hello Marie, and how are you?"

"I'm fine, but a little sad with the loss of my friend Andrei. However, I am also angry that he did not invite me to join him on his long vacation."

Ian smiled and remembered the comments Andrei had made in his letter. Obviously, Marie was not party to this information! "Please, would you join me for a drink… and maybe a meal later?"

"A drink, yes, but I am already committed to meeting friends for a meal this evening. Is Emma not with you this time?"

Ian spotted a waiter and called him over. Marie said she would like a glass of Chablis. When the waiter arrived, Ian decided he would have the same, and ordered two glasses. "No, I'm only here for one night and well, I thought I was meeting Andrei to discuss a business proposition."

"So you knew nothing of his plans?"

"No, nothing. I'm only now beginning to recover from the surprise."

"So you didn't know about the apartment?"

"Andrei had left a letter for me at reception. That was the first I knew about it. It was all quite a shock."

The waiter returned with the two glasses of Chablis and placed them on the table. Ian finished the last drops of his beer and the waiter collected the empty glass.

"Andrei thought a lot about you, Ian, and talked about you often. He saw in you a lot of similarities to himself at your age."

"I like Andrei a lot too. He's always exciting company."

"He'd been complaining for a while of being tired and concerned that work was the main driving force in his life. He wanted a complete change of lifestyle, and was determined to improve the quality of his life. In his own words... 'Whilst I am still fit enough'."

"I see. He did complain sometimes to me about his health, but I didn't think he was serious."

"He was very shocked and sad about the death of some friends in Moscow. That seemed to finally make his mind up."

Ian nodded and reflected back to when he had first broken the sad news to Andrei about his colleagues who had been shot in the tunnels underneath the Kremlin in Moscow.

"Did Andrei tell you about his new plans?"

"Oh yes. I also knew Andrei had other lady friends but we were both still very close. He discussed much with me and valued my opinions."

Again Ian nodded and wondered to what extent Andrei would have explained everything to Marie. In the short time he had known Andrei, he'd realised that he could be a very secretive person when he wanted to be. It was doubtful, he thought, that Andrei would have explained the details of why and how the Moscow friends' deaths had occurred. "Do you know where he is now?"

"No, except I did receive an email from him to say he had arrived in Mexico, but he would only be staying there for about five days. He did not say any more about his plans after that. He told me before he left that he just wanted to travel for enjoyment instead of business. He needed time and space to enjoy a different lifestyle. To be honest, I don't think he had any definite agenda."

"I see. He does like to make things complicated."

"Why do you say that? Did he not fully explain in the letter he left at the apartment for you?"

"Well yes, maybe, but it would have been so much nicer to have been able to discuss everything with him face to face."

"He knew you would have objected to his ideas so by putting his decision in letter form and signing all the relevant documents, you would find it more difficult to object or refuse. He also thought that Emma might take a lot more convincing and thought the explanation would be better coming from you."

Both Ian and Marie sipped their wine and Ian considered Marie's comments.

"It is fabulously generous of Andrei to do what he has done, Marie, but it puts me in a very difficult position. Emma and I both have our careers and our lovely home in England. I know Emma will not want to give them up and move to Monaco."

"You do not have to change those choices in the short term. Just use the apartment for holidays, or rent it out. Andrei thought you enjoyed working with him on his business projects."

"Oh yes, I do... did. They were exciting times, but I never envisaged being involved with his projects as a change of career, just something that was very part-time and an exciting add-on."

"He wanted to give you a helping hand or, more precisely, an opportunity to make a lot of money and improve the quality of your two lives." Marie was surprised that Ian was not grasping this wonderful gift with both hands.

"I would have loved to have had this conversation with Andrei directly because, if I'm not careful, this could all blow up in my face... and I may lose Emma. I would do anything to avoid that!"

Marie drank the remains of her wine and stood up and put her hand in her handbag. After a couple of seconds, she produced a card and handed it to Ian. Ian also stood up.

"Here are my contact details. I would love to meet Emma again. Please email or telephone me to let me know when you will be next in Monaco. I will make sure I'm available for you both to visit for a meal."

Ian took hold of the card and briefly read the details before putting it into his jacket pocket. "Thank you, Marie, it's been great talking to you again. I know Emma would love the opportunity to meet up with you again."

"Excellent. I must go now, my friend, Chantal, is waiting for me." Marie pointed to where she and Chantal had been sitting two metres away.

Ian now realised that Marie and Chantal were the two women sitting with their backs to him when he first arrived on the veranda.

Marie continued, "Please give my regards to Emma." Marie closed her handbag and leaned across towards Ian and gently kissed him on the cheek.

Whilst Ian was registering this affection, Marie and Chantal made their exit. Ian sat down again on his seat and sipped his wine. He gazed out into the harbour and thought back to the opening line of Andrei's letter:

'Hello my good friend and welcome to your new world!'

Chapter 2

It was just before 10 pm when Ian re-entered the apartment. After he had finished his wine at Oliver's Bar and paid the bill, he'd walked back along the harbourside to the nice-looking restaurant that he'd spotted earlier. It had been reasonably busy but the waiter said he could fit him in. Ian had ordered red snapper and another glass of Chablis and spent most of the evening watching the other customers whilst they were eating and chatting. Everyone seemed to be in couples or groups, and he definitely felt jealous. He didn't enjoy eating alone and was definitely missing Emma's company.

Ian awoke the next morning just before seven o'clock local time. The sun was already streaming through the gap in the bedroom curtains. He got up, shaved, showered and was dressed before eight o'clock. He entered the kitchen and switched on the kettle. After his meal the previous evening he'd called at a late-night grocery store and purchased a few items for his breakfast. He made himself a mug of tea and a large bowl of muesli, which he carried over towards the large glass doors. After opening one of the doors he stepped outside and onto the balcony. He placed his meal on the metal table, sat down and watched the activity in the harbour below. He immediately began to feel the warming early morning rays of sunshine on his face and arms. However, he still had mixed feelings towards Andrei's gift.

Whilst he ate his meal, he continued to watch the activity below. He identified Oliver's Bar and the veranda where he had a drink with Marie. He had to admit this was still a stunning view and a fabulous setting. He could see for many miles out into the calm blue waters of the Mediterranean Sea. His eyes shifted and focused on a large white yacht that was slowly emerging from its mooring at the harbour-side. He was very impressed with the manoeuvrability of the yacht and the skill of the captain to exit from such a tight area of space, especially as it was surrounded by a number of other boats and large luxury ships. Five minutes later the yacht was heading out of the harbour and away towards where? Ian pondered, yet another warm and sunny destination possibly? Certainly on a journey that only the mega-rich could afford to take! This was definitely, most definitely, a different world!

Ian planned his morning activities and hoped he could achieve them before his taxi was due to arrive at 12.30 pm. He firstly washed, dried and returned all the breakfast items he'd used and then telephoned security. It was Bates who answered the call and Ian explained that he wanted to enter Andrei's… no his… security vault. Bates agreed to meet him at his apartment in ten minutes. Just enough time, thought Ian, to pack my bag ready for my departure later.

True to his word Bates arrived at the Penthouse suite apartment just ten minutes later and pressed the doorbell. Ian opened the door and invited the uniformed security guard into the apartment. When he had first introduced himself to Ian yesterday, Ian thought Bates' size and appearance was probably the epitome of what a security guard should look like. Tall and strongly built, certainly not the sort of person one would choose to have an argument with!

"Good morning, Mr Caxton. I hope you have settled in well."

"Good morning, Mr Bates. I'm just beginning to find my way around the apartment, but I would now like to visit the security vault."

"It's just Bates, sir. All the security guards are just known to the residents by their surname. Now to get you into the vault I need to inform you of some of the security procedures."

"Okay."

"We have your hand prints on file from yesterday, so we don't need to do that again. The vaults, as you probably remember from your earlier visit there with Mr Petrov, are situated in the lower basement, which is the lowest floor within the building. That is two floors below the car parking area."

Ian nodded and was trying to remember some of the other security requirements he had experienced with Andrei.

Bates continued, "When the lower basement floor button in the elevator is pressed, this also notifies our security team in the vault area that a keyholder is arriving shortly. You will hear an extra buzz in the elevator when this button is pressed. When you arrive at the lower basement floor and step out of the elevator, you will be met by two uniformed guards who will not let you proceed further until you produce your personalised keycard pass." Bates put his hand into his pocket and produced a plastic pass key which was about the size of an average credit card. "This is your keycard, sir." Bates handed it over to Ian. "It has all been uploaded with all the required security information I obtained from you yesterday and you will notice your photograph also appears on it."

Ian looked at the card and commented, "Not overly flattering, is it?"

Bates ignored Ian's joke and continued.

"Although the guards usually know each of the vault key-holders by sight, this procedure has to be followed every time! All activity is recorded 24 hours a day on several hidden security cameras. When we get down to the vaults, I will show you how to use your card. Are you ready to go now, sir?"

Ian placed the pass keycard into his jacket pocket and replied. "Yes, let's go."

The two men left the apartment and walked towards the elevator where Bates pressed the request button. The down arrow lit up. A few seconds later the door opened and the two men were greeted by the elevator attendant.

"Good morning, Mr Caxton," said the uniformed lady.

"Hello, Louise. It's nice to meet you again," replied Ian. Although Louise was not on duty yesterday, he remembered her from his previous visit.

"Lower ground floor," said Bates, and Louise duly pressed the required button. Immediately Ian heard a distant buzz and he looked at Bates and nodded.

When the elevator arrived at the lower ground floor the doors opened and Louise stepped out, allowing the two men to pass by her. Ian once again noticed the long corridor with 12 strongroom doors along each side. There were no windows, but the air was still cool and fresh, just as he had remembered. Two large, uniformed guards blocked their way. Ian didn't think he remembered these two particular individuals from before. They appeared to ignore Bates and Ian produced his newly acquired pass keycard. They both viewed the card and waved Ian and Bates through.

"Thank you," said Ian, and the guards both nodded.

Bates pointed down the corridor and the two men walked on. As they proceeded Ian looked at each door, which he decided were identical except for a different number printed at roughly eye level. Bates stopped outside number 14. There were no handles on the door, just a metal plate and a small horizontal slot.

Bates pointed to the horizontal slot. "Insert your card in here, sir, with the photograph this way up." Bates now had his own card in his hand and pointed to it.

Ian followed Bates' instructions and inserted his card into the slot. Immediately a green light flashed above the door. Ian turned and smiled at Bates.

"Now, sir, put your left palm on the metal plate." Ian duly followed instructions and the green light flashed again.

"Okay, nearly there. One of the guards now has to place their hand on the metal plate. The door will not open without this last task," said Bates, and he duly placed the palm of his hand on the metal plate. The green light flashed for a third time and Ian looked at Bates and wondered why the door had not opened.

"It usually takes about ten seconds for the door to…"

Suddenly the door clicked and slowly began to move. As the door opened, three internal lights automatically came on.

"The guards are not usually allowed into the vaults unless invited by the keyholder or there is an emergency. At this point the guard normally goes back to his station near the elevators. Do you want me to come into the vault with you and explain all the other measures or do you want me to explain it out here?"

"Please, do come in. I certainly don't want to lock myself in!" Ian smiled but Bates kept the serious expression on his face.

"You can't do that, sir. I'll explain."

The two men entered the vault and Ian stared around the room. The vault was about 4 x 4 x 3 metres in size. Ian remembered at the far end of the vault there was a group of individual safes of varying sizes, all with their doors slightly ajar. Against one of the bare concrete walls there were stacked, Ian counted, six framed paintings. A lot less now than when he had first visited with Andrei. He was eager to see what the pictures were, but waited until Bates had finished his instructions.

"Now, to close the door, sir, you press that yellow button next to the door." Ian walked over and pressed the yellow button. Gradually the thick metal door quietly closed, but there was no click.

"Okay, so the door is now closed but not locked. The guards check every ten minutes. When they put a hand on the outside metal door plate, that white light flashes." Bates now pointed to an LED light bulb near the door. "You then press the blue button, over there next to the yellow button. You have to press the blue button within 20 seconds." Bates pointed again. "The guards will then go away for another ten minutes. If you do not press the blue button, within 20 seconds, they will enter to investigate."

"Okay." Ian shook his head in disbelief. He wondered if he was really going to remember all this.

Bates continued. "Now, the safes are the easy bit. Due to all the other security measures here, each safe is secured by just a four-digit number. You can use the same number for each safe, but we would not recommend that."

Ian wandered over and looked inside three safes at random where their doors were slightly ajar. All were empty.

"We suggest that any safe not being used should have its door left slightly ajar. That way they will remind you which safes are actually being used."

Ian nodded and thought that made sense.

"Now, to exit and lock your vault, all you have to do is the same as the entrance procedure but in reverse. You firstly press the yellow button and the door will slowly open.

Once outside you put the palm of your hand on the metal plate and the door will close. You then insert your keycard into the slot and you will hear a click noting the door is locked. At the same time the green light above the door will flash. If the green light does not flash the door is not locked and you should call one of the guards."

As Ian was about to reply to Bates the white LED light flashed. Without instruction, Ian walked over to the door and pressed the blue button. The LED light immediately went out.

"Good," said Bates. "Do you want some more time on your own? I'll wait outside and check with you when you are finished."

"Thank you. Yes, I would appreciate that."

"Okay, so I will press the yellow button to exit and then you press it again to close the door." Ian nodded and Bates pressed the yellow button. Slowly the vault door opened and Bates stepped out and into the corridor. Ian pressed the yellow button and watched as the door slowly closed. Once this was completed he looked into the other safes and checked that they were all empty. Which they were. He then walked across to the stack of six paintings and picked them up, one at a time. For the next few minutes, he inspected each picture very carefully. As he picked up the fifth picture he saw the white LED light flash above the door and so walked over and pressed the blue button. The white light, once again, went out and he continued his inspection. Once he had finally looked at all six paintings and replaced them back against the wall, he stood back and whispered under his breath. 'Thank you, Andrei, you are so full of surprises.'

Ian pressed the yellow button once again and the vault door slowly opened. When he stepped out, Bates was waiting for him and watched whilst Ian placed the palm of his left hand on the metal plate. The door slowly closed. Once it was fully closed, Ian inserted the keycard and heard a click. The green light flashed for about two seconds.

"Okay, sir. All locked again. Our computer has now registered both your entry and your exit. Any time you want to check our records, just contact security and this can be arranged. Similarly, if you forget any of these procedures that I have shown you this morning, please check with one of the guards, but you must have your pass keycard with you first. If you do happen to lose the card then we will immediately invalidate that card and issue you with a new one."

"Thank you very much, Bates. That was all very useful and much appreciated." Ian inserted the keycard into his pocket and wondered where he was going to keep it securely in the apartment.

"No problem, sir. That's what we're here for."

The two men walked back towards the elevator. When they arrived at the door, Ian pressed the request button but Bates announced he needed to speak with his colleagues. So when the elevator door opened, it was just Ian who stepped in.

"Top floor, please, Louise."

"Penthouse suite, Mr Caxton," she reminded him with a smile and pressed the button marked 'Penthouse Suite'.

Back in his apartment, Ian checked his wristwatch. Ten minutes before 12 o'clock. Okay, he thought, I've not got time to do the couple of the jobs I'd planned but I can do them once I get home. He walked over to the dining room table, sat down and decided to go through the paperwork and documents Andrei had left. He started by splitting them up into two piles. One pile he would take back to England to read more thoroughly and discuss with his solicitor. The other pile was just useful details and information, which he decided could be left in the apartment and dealt with at a later date.

Ian then walked over to the office and found an empty cardboard folder which was just big enough for the documents he wanted to take home. Back at the dining table, he inserted the files and papers into the new folder and then placed the folder into his overnight bag.

Suddenly, he remembered his security pass keycard for the vaults was still in his pocket. He picked it out and wondered where would be a safe enough place to hide it... and not to forget it! He wandered back into the office and looked under the desk, behind pictures and in cupboards, but he could not find a home safe. But why would Andrei need one, he pondered, because he already had Fort Knox downstairs in the vaults!

He was just about to give up when he had one final thought and quickly went through to Andrei's bedroom and opened the three cupboard doors in the walk-in wardrobe. Hidden at the back, on the bottom shelf, he spotted a small safe similar to those often installed in the bedrooms of the better-quality hotels. Without intentionally looking for it, he would never have spotted it tucked away, especially if shoes or similar clothing were hiding it from immediate view. He lay on the floor and saw that the door was slightly ajar. On the front of the door was a keypad. Ah, ha, he thought. I just wonder. He pushed the door into the closed position with one hand, then typed in the numbers of the day and month of Emma's birthday and then pressed 'enter'. The safe pinged and briefly displayed back the same code before disappearing. The safe was locked. He then re-entered the same code again. The safe pinged once more and the door swung open. "Jackpot," shouted Ian, to himself. He quickly removed the keycard from his pocket, placed it in the safe and locked it again with the same code. As he got back to his feet he checked his wristwatch. 'Five minutes, I'd better check everything else is locked and all okay'.

Once this was all done, he picked up his overnight bag and took one final look around the lounge area and walked towards the door. Suddenly the telephone rang.

When Ian picked up the receiver and answered the call, he listened to the receptionist advising him that his taxi had arrived. He opened the door and stepped outside pulling the door to. When he heard the initial click, he placed his left palm on the metal door plate. The door made a final click and was secured in the fully locked position.

So, he thought to himself, it's now back to Emma... and the real world!

Chapter 3

Ian's plane landed at London Heathrow airport and once in the main terminal building, he rang Emma's mobile phone. After three rings she answered his call.

"Hi Emma. I've just arrived at Terminal 5. I should be through passport and customs in about 20 minutes."

"Okay," replied Emma. "I'm on the M25 and should be with you in about 30 minutes. See you then."

It actually took a little longer than Ian had anticipated to finally emerge into the daylight outside the terminal building. Although he only had his overnight cabin bag, the delay in passport control was much longer than he had anticipated. Apparently two large groups of passengers, one from the USA and another from Mallorca, had arrived just before him. As a result the 'snake' of human beings trying to get to the passport control desks was longer than usual. Still, he had now emerged from the building and looked amongst the rows of taxis and cars for Emma's red BMW. He wandered past travellers getting into vehicles and exiting from others, but no sign of Emma. When he got to the end of the row of parked vehicles, he turned and started to walk back, suddenly he spotted Emma's car approaching. He waved and the car pulled in. He threw his bag onto the back seat, quickly climbed into the front passenger's side and sat down. He immediately leaned across and they both kissed before Emma put the car into first gear and they were away. Ian clipped on his seat belt, sat back and gave a long sigh.

It was Emma who was the first to speak. "So who's had a surprising weekend?"

"It was incredible, Emma. It was all such a shock, so unbelievable. I still don't really know what it's all about!"

"So, what have you decided?"

"Decided? Well nothing at the moment. We need to have a long conversation."

"We certainly do."

The rest of the journey was spent with Ian talking about what he had been doing in the apartment, arranging his security pass, visiting the vault, the chance meeting with Marie and their subsequent discussions about Andrei.

As Emma's car exited the M25 motorway at junction 10, she was still thinking about Ian's comment on the 'chance meeting' with Marie. She was not as convinced as Ian was that it was just a chance meeting.

It was later that evening when they agreed to discuss the Monaco apartment and Andrei's 'opportunity'. They had just finished their meal and were still enjoying the remains of a very nice bottle of New Zealand chardonnay.

"What are your thoughts on the apartment then?" It was Ian who began the discussion. He was eager to know Emma's initial thoughts.

"I've been thinking about it ever since you telephoned. I really don't understand why Andrei has, well, almost abandoned such a valuable asset. It doesn't really make too much sense... but, of course, it's still a fabulous gesture! But we can't really afford the upkeep costs, can we?"

Ian was certainly pleased that Emma had not thrown the whole idea out of the window at the first opportunity.

"Andrei said in his letter that he will be providing some money each year towards the upkeep."

"But will that be enough?"

"Three million Swiss francs a year for the next ten years."

"What?!" cried Emma in surprise. "Wow, this is all so mind-blowing."

"Yes I know. You had better read his letter." Ian had already brought his Monaco folder of papers and documents into the dining room in preparation for this discussion. He picked it up, pulled out Andrei's letter and handed it across for Emma to read.

Whilst Emma put on her reading glasses and began reading, Ian topped up their wine glasses until the bottle was empty. Four minutes later Emma put the letter down. "He doesn't really trust me, does he?"

"I think he knows that you have never fully been in favour of our business dealings."

"Well that's certainly true, but only because I saw it as a potential threat to your career, your wellbeing and ultimately our relationship."

"I never saw it as a threat to any of those things but, gradually, I did realise that I was getting sucked in deeper and deeper. But the truth is, I still found it exciting and ultimately it's been financially very rewarding. I never saw the activities taking over my life, just something extra to everything else."

"That's not Andrei's understanding from the tone of his letter. He's saying he is giving you, or us, a big opportunity to change everything."

"Mmm. I know and deep down I'm not sure I want to do that. Do you know what Somerset Maugham said about Monaco?"

"No," replied Emma, surprised by Ian's question.

"He said Monaco was a sunny place for shady people!"

Emma smiled and thought Andrei probably fitted that description. "Well, we do not need to make any massive decisions today," she replied. "Let's keep talking about it and discuss it in more detail again later. We also need to find out what our solicitor thinks."

"We've suddenly become very rich, Emma. The apartment is still not technically ours but the paintings in both the apartment and in the vault are ours. I estimate their market value to be close to £6 million!"

"Ian, what have you got us into? I'm really quite afraid now!"

It was 8.30 the next morning when Ian sat down at his desk at Sotheby's. Although it was only about 60 hours since he had last sat there, so much had happened in those hours. He felt he'd been away for a whole week!

Penny, Ian's PA, had requested a day's holiday and so his outer office area was very quiet for a Monday morning. Just as Ian was going to get himself a cup of coffee, he had a surprise visit from his boss, Michael Hopkins. It was very rare for Michael to do this. It was usually Ian who was summoned to Michael's office. Ian sat back down in his chair as his boss walked over and sat on the chair opposite.

"Good morning, Ian. Did you have a good weekend?"

"Yes, thank you, Michael. Busy catching up on things." Although Ian's answer was somewhat vague and he tried to keep the smile from his face, he knew he could not even begin to explain exactly what he'd really been up to. "And you?"

"That's what I would like to have a chat with you about. We went to a small dinner party on Saturday night at our neighbour's house. Nice people, John and Anne Baldwin, new to the village, so we did a lot of exchanging of information about each other. Anyway, when I mentioned my role at Sotheby's, John and Anne immediately looked at each other. They both had surprised looks on their faces. For a few seconds, I wondered what I had said to offend them. However, it transpired that John got in touch with Sotheby's some months ago when we were promoting the Turner and Constable paintings joint auction. He telephoned us to say that he had two Turner paintings and would we be interested in including them in our auction. It seems as though John might have spoken with young Vic from how he was describing the person he discussed the matter with on the telephone. John gave Vic the titles of the two paintings, outline descriptions and details of their provenances. Vic apparently suggested that Sotheby's could be interested but he would have to investigate further and get back to him. Two days later Vic telephoned John back with the bad news."

Ian sat up in his seat and was wondering where Michael was going with this story and also, if Vic had been involved, why had he not mentioned it to him. "Bad news?" asked Ian.

"Yes," continued Michael. "Vic had checked the picture descriptions in the Turner catalogue raisonné and found that both pictures had been removed and reclassified as not genuine Turners in 1956."

"Ah. That can happen sometimes, especially if the provenance is challenged or the picture is proved to be a copy or a fake," replied Ian, pleased that Vic had followed the correct procedure. "Expert opinion can change with often catastrophic consequences to the value of a painting."

"I know and apparently that's what Vic explained to John. The interesting point that John raised with me at the weekend was that he understood both these paintings had been in his family's ownership right back to the time when they were purchased directly from Turner when the artist was living in Margate. John said he had no idea that the paintings had been delisted in 1956 and therefore both now rejected as being original pieces of Turner's work."

"Mmm. Interesting. Obviously something does not quite stack up here. What are you suggesting?"

"Speak to Vic, would you, Ian? Find out his side of the story and maybe get him to delve a bit deeper. Ask him to investigate what happened in 1956. If we can prove that the 1956 decision was flawed and the pictures are subsequently reinstated as genuine Turners, then John has promised us two paintings to sell. He's a bit upset and untrusting about the art world!"

"Okay. I have a meeting with Vic this afternoon, so I'll raise it with him then. We'll keep you informed of his findings."

"Good." At that Michael rose from his seat and started to walk towards the door. However, before leaving, he stopped, turned around and continued, "Any developments on that flat you were talking about some weeks ago?"

Suddenly Ian briefly stopped breathing with shock. He knew he had not mentioned the Monaco apartment to Michael. In fact, nobody at Sotheby's knew anything, except the small amount that Vic knew and it was extremely unlikely that he would have said anything to Michael.

Michael was confused with Ian's queried look, "You told me that you might have to look for something closer to the office during the week, remember?"

"Oh yes, sorry, Michael. I'd forgotten that we'd had that conversation." Ian was relieved and started to breathe again. He remembered that he had told Michael he was pondering on the possibility of buying or renting a weekday flat to reduce the time spent commuting. "No. I did look a little into the possibility, but the prices are out of my league and, when I suggested it to Emma, she was not that keen. So it's the daily commuting life still for me."

Michael smiled. "The women like to know where their men are, Ian. Probably a wise decision." At this, Michael left Ian's office.

Ian leaned back in his chair and gave a deep sigh. He then said to himself, 'So Vic, what have you been up to?'

Ian's and Vic's meeting was scheduled for two o'clock. They were meeting to discuss a forthcoming private sale of three of Sir Alfred Munnings paintings. Viktor explained that the sale would be completed later this week and the buyer, who was from Saudi Arabia, had agreed to pay the asking price for all three paintings.

"Okay, Vic, that's good news and well done. Good call of yours to remember the Saudi client's interest in any quality painting depicting horses. Now, moving on. Michael Hopkins came to my office this morning and mentioned to me that you may have spoken to Mr John Baldwin. Mr Baldwin apparently wanted Sotheby's to include his two paintings in the Constable and Turner auction we had some months ago."

Viktor wrinkled his brow in thought. The name did not immediately mean anything to him.

Ian continued, "You discovered that both paintings had been removed and reclassified as not genuine Turners in 1956."

"Oh yes, I remember now," replied Viktor. The incident was all coming back to him. "Yes, that was a strange one. According to the Turner catalogue raisonné, the two paintings had both been deemed no longer to be genuine works by Turner. I explained all this to Mr Baldwin at the time. He was extremely surprised and said he would investigate further himself. I never heard any more from him again. I think it was when you were in Moscow, otherwise I would have mentioned it to you at the time. Have there been some new developments?"

Ian repeated the story that Michael had told him. After Ian had finished, Viktor looked across at his boss and said, "When do you want me to start?"

"Finish off dealing with the Munnings sale first and then do a bit of delving, would you? I've got a feeling we are going to find out some very interesting details. Turner was quite a character and a controversial figure in his day so it's my bet that not everyone is going to come out of this smelling of roses!"

Chapter 4

Later that same day, Ian telephoned his former university, the London Courtauld Institute of Art, where he had obtained his Master's degree. He left a message saying that he would like to speak with Professor Jackson. Professor Jackson was Ian's former tutor and is recognised as one of the foremost experts on the life and paintings of Joseph Mallord William Turner.

It was just after Ian and Emma had finished their dinner that Emma answered a telephone call. It was Professor Jackson and he said he was returning Ian's call.

Ian smiled as Emma announced the caller's name and he was quick and eager to take the receiver. "Richard. It's great to hear from you. Thanks for returning my message."

"Hello Ian. It's been such a long time. How are you doing? Are you still at Sotheby's?" replied a strong authoritative voice. Nobody would be in any doubt that this was the voice of a confident and well-educated man.

"I'm doing very well, thank you and still at Sotheby's, but in London now. And you? I see you are still a very important part of the Institute."

"Not for very much longer, Ian. I've been offered a fabulous research opportunity at Yale, in America, so I am moving there for three years until my retirement."

"That sounds very interesting, Richard. I was hoping we could meet up before you disappear from our shores."

"I'm not moving until the end of the year, so yes, it would be lovely to meet up again."

"That's good. There are two reasons I would like us to get together again. Firstly, it would be nice just to catch up again but, secondly, I would like to bring one of my graduate trainees along so that he can pick your brain about Turner."

"Okay. How much detail do you want me to provide?"

"We all know about Turner's famous paintings, but I would like you to tell us more about the controversies and problems that both his life and work has caused in the art world."

"Interesting. That will take longer than a lunch break."

Ian laughed, he knew what the professor was hinting at. "What about dinner at a restaurant of your choice?"

"That sounds excellent. When were you thinking of?"

"To fit in with you, Richard. I know how busy you are, but as soon as possible please."

"Just a moment." Ian could hear paper being rustled at the other end of the line and assumed Richard was checking his diary. "I can do next Thursday. Is that okay?"

"Yes, that would be excellent."

"Good. I'll book a table for three at the Bistro2 in Covent Garden, for 7 pm. I'm sure you will both enjoy it. It's a favourite of mine."

"Thank you, Richard. It should be a good evening."

Both men said their goodbyes.

The next morning when Ian arrived at his office desk, he telephoned Viktor's extension. When Viktor answered, Ian told him about the dinner meeting arrangements. He also suggested that in the meantime, Viktor should do as much swotting up on Turner as possible. It would be unprofessional not to respect such an opportunity with the eminent professor.

After finalising the sale of the three Munnings paintings to the Saudi client, Viktor set about trying to understand just why Turner was considered such a controversial figure. He knew a lot more about Turner's paintings following his earlier involvement with Sotheby's Constable and Turner auction and he was especially aware of the high prices that could be demanded and achieved, for some of Turner's more famous works. In particular, the paintings completed during the earlier part of Turner's career always seemed to generate the largest amount of interest in the art world, even to this day. But, Viktor wondered, why was that so?!

Viktor accessed the internet and found that there were many websites devoted to Turner's life and works. He established that from quite a relatively young age, Turner had gained the reputation of being one of Britain's greatest landscape painters of his day, especially through his special ability to be able to capture the drama of wild sea storms and ships in distress. He had a unique talent for mixing paints and producing almost surreal, atmospheric seas and skies, long before some of the 20th century artists such as Dali, Picasso and Miro made Surrealism a cultural movement.

Viktor gradually realised that Turner was obviously well ahead of his time. However, despite the artist's special talents, Turner didn't appear to be able to command the respect these abilities evidently deserved. Why, he wondered, was Turner not always fully accepted by his peers or indeed, by those in higher authority, during his lifetime?

What he really needed to do now, he decided, was to get a much better understanding of why, during the last 200 years, such a range of different opinions of Turner's work existed. It was obviously a more complex subject than he had originally thought and, whilst he was eagerly looking forward to hearing what the professor would have to say, he needed to try and find out for himself some of the basic reasons for all the controversy. Indeed, he wondered if any of these reasons had contributed to the 1956 decision with regard to the two Baldwin paintings.

Ian and Viktor arrived by taxi just before seven o'clock for their meeting at the Bistro2 restaurant. When they entered through the main entrance, they found a cosy and welcoming atmosphere. They were quickly spotted by a waiter and, after Ian announced they were expected by Professor Jackson, the waiter led them into the main restaurant area and towards a small side alcove. Professor Jackson was already seated and was reading a copy of the menu. As Ian and Viktor approached, the professor rose from his chair, gave Ian a big smile and held out his hand. The two men shook hands firmly and greeted each other warmly.

"It's so good to see you again, Ian. It's been what, eight years?" Professor Richard Jackson was 60 years old, with a thick mop of grey wavy hair.

"Yes, I think it must be," replied Ian, trying to remember. "That was at the last reunion meeting that I could attend. I missed the others because I was either in Hong Kong or New York."

"Poor excuse," said Richard, and both men laughed.

"Let me introduce you to my colleague, Viktor Kuznetsov. Viktor, this gentleman is my favourite tutor from many years ago, Professor Richard Jackson."

Both men shook hands and Viktor announced, "I'm very pleased to meet you, sir."

"Now, first things first. I'm Richard. Please, gentlemen, sit down."

During the next 30 minutes, the three men ordered their drinks and selected their food. Ian and Richard discussed what had been happening in their lives since they had last met and Richard was very pleased to hear that Ian was now married. Viktor sat quietly and listened to the conversation.

When they had all finished their main course, Richard raised the subject of Turner. "So, Viktor, I gather you want to know about Mr JMW Turner, warts and all, so to speak, with the emphasis on the warts!"

"I understand his career was somewhat shrouded in controversy and this has carried on until the present day," replied Viktor, wanting to demonstrate he had at least a little knowledge.

"I will give you a potted summary and will then point you in the direction of some useful reading."

"Thank you."

"Well, and as they say in all good stories, let us start at the beginning. Born on the 23rd April 1775, Turner was a child prodigy, enrolling at the Royal Academy of Arts when he was just 14 years of age. Intensely private, eccentric and something of a recluse, he was a secretive person and a controversial figure throughout his career. Even after his death, on the 19th December 1851, many of these controversies still continued to surround one of Britain's most famous artists." Richard stopped talking to have a sip of wine before continuing. "There are probably three main areas of controversy connected with Turner. The later part of his career, Mrs Sophia Caroline Booth and his prolific collection of non-landscape sketches and watercolours."

"I thought Turner was just a landscape painter," interrupted Viktor.

"Well, that's what he is mainly famous for and the serious art hierarchy has tried it's best to highlight just this area of his work. They have also tried their very best to hide, or censor, what some people would describe as the 'dark' side of his work. Especially his watercolours, sketches and drawings of a rude and erotic nature."

Ian and Viktor looked at each other. Both raised their eyebrows and Ian smiled at Viktor's surprised look.

"Just before Turner died, he bequeathed all of his unsold works of art to the nation. From his London studio it was estimated that there were in the region of 300 oil paintings and 30,000 watercolours, sketches and drawings. What was also included within this collection were most of his sketchbooks. At least 300 of these contained the so-called sordid depictions. It is fair to say that this was a serious shock to the art authorities, especially the Royal Academy, as they pompously stated 'This is just not what one would have associated with a landscape painter like Turner.' Almost overnight his image became tainted – and still is today!"

It was Ian who had noticed that the chardonnay bottle was almost empty and suggested another bottle. Richard agreed and Ian called the waiter over and ordered another bottle of the same Australian wine. When Ian asked if anyone required a dessert, Richard said he would be content with the wine and probably a coffee later. Viktor agreed and so no desserts were ordered.

"To make matters worse," continued Richard, "a certain Mrs Sophia Caroline Booth came to the public's attention when Turner left her 150 guineas a year in his will. Again demonstrating the secret nature of Turner's lifestyle, he had apparently been having a relationship with this Margate boarding house landlady for some 18 years!"

"Quite a character!" interjected Ian.

"Indeed," continued Richard, "and so was Mrs Booth! Apparently on becoming aware of her legacy, she decided to sue Turner's executors for more! She cited the fact that Turner had lived in her boarding house for about six months every year, for the last 18 years of his life … and had not contributed one penny towards his board and lodgings."

"I didn't know this," exclaimed Viktor. When he looked

at Ian, Ian just responded, "Oh there's a lot more still to come!"

The waiter arrived with their new bottle of wine and Ian topped up all three glasses.

Richard continued. "Mrs Booth also stated that when Turner lived at her property, he kept his anonymity by calling himself Mr Booth. Needless to say, once this information about their relationship became public knowledge, it caused a massive scandal in the art world. The Royal Academy especially, were up in arms and thought it was a disgrace and against all the normal standards of respectability."

"Wow. I guess morals have changed a bit since those days," replied Viktor, taking a sip of wine from his refreshed glass.

"Hypocrisy hasn't changed much since those days," interrupted Ian. "Margate was notorious for where the London upper classes used to go to let their hair down and have their dirty weekends away from their partners and the prying eyes of London's society. Turner was no exception, he just got caught out, but fortunately for him, only after he'd died!"

"So Turner's reputation was now totally shredded," continued Richard, "but, of course, he was dead and could not defend himself any longer. Still, I'm sure he would have been watching and smiling to himself from his grave in St Paul's Cathedral. He would have loved to see the outrage he had caused within the art nobility. These people were a faction that Turner could never really get on with. He thought the hierarchy of the Royal Academy, for example, were, at best, both snobbish and snooty!"

"So now we have the third controversy," said Viktor. He was really enjoying all these revelations and was eager to hear more.

"Well young Viktor, not so eager. We have still not

finished with Mrs Booth!" Richard checked his watch. "Mmm. My train leaves in 40 minutes so I had better speed up. Mrs Booth had been married twice before Turner came on the scene and her first husband was named Pound. They had a son, who they named Daniel John. Now there is nothing unusual about that, but I'll come back to this person later."

Richard sipped his wine and continued with his story. "When Turner was staying in Margate, you may know that he made many sketches from which he used to paint lots of his most famous pictures. Despite painting in many different European locations, he always said that the reason why he kept returning to the Kent coast was because of the skies. He said they were the loveliest in the whole of Europe. His earlier work demonstrated this so clearly. He also really enjoyed painting the special light, the wild seas and storms. So now we have established that Turner completed lots of his work during his relationship with Mrs Booth in Margate. Therefore when he died a number of his paintings were still residing in his room at the boarding house. If you remember earlier, I said that Turner had bequeathed all his unsold collection of work to the nation – now largely residing in the Tate Britain incidentally. Well this is where the plot thickens."

Viktor sipped his wine and leaned forward. He was engrossed and listened eagerly to every word of Richard's tutorial.

"Turner's will had been somewhat vaguely written and not specific at all about the intentions of the paintings residing at Margate. Mrs Booth argued that these were given to her by Turner. The Royal Academy argued that if Turner had wanted Mrs Booth to have these paintings then he would have said so in his will. However, there was no real proof one way or the other and in the end it was decided that only those works of art in his London studio were his bequest to the nation. Mrs Booth kept her paintings, but, from then onwards, they were always surrounded by allegations of either fraud or theft. They were certainly tainted by their association with Mrs Booth!" Richard paused briefly and asked Ian if he could have a cup of coffee. Black, no sugar.

"Of course, Richard. I'll call the waiter." Ian established what Viktor wanted and gave the order to a passing waiter.

Richard finished his glass of wine and refused a top-up. He continued, "We now move on to 1865. In that year a number of Turner's paintings, owned by Mrs Booth, were auctioned by Christie's. However, this is where we begin to see the involvement of one Daniel John Pound. Remember I mentioned him earlier?"

Viktor nodded vigorously, not wanting to stop Richard's flow.

"Well, by now Daniel Pound had become an extremely skilled picture engraver and was developing a good career. However, because he was linked with Mrs Booth, lots of questions were raised. Could Mrs Booth's collection of paintings not be the work of Turner after all, but fakes created by the hand of her son? The experts of that time did not have the technical aids of today, so a lot of Mrs Booth's paintings were challenged by the art authorities. However, there was still a growing art industry. People just wanted to buy Turner's work, tainted or not. Galleries and auction houses still sold as many 'real' Turners as they could, sometimes with not necessarily full and accurate provenances. Unsuspecting wealthy buyers just wanted a real Turner to display in their homes. So it all became a very murky world, even more so when a number of good and not so good fakes also began to be sold as genuine Turners. The result was that in later years new experts began to review earlier decisions and decided to reject a number of long-established Turner paintings as either being fakes or copies. In many cases with financially disastrous consequences to the owners!"

"Yes, we are looking into two Turner paintings that were rejected in 1956," replied Ian.

The cups of coffee arrived and Richard looked at his watch again before continuing.

"So, finally, we come to the third area of controversy, Turner's later years. During most of his adulthood, Turner was extremely wealthy, but as we have established with his involvement with Mrs Booth, he was also a very mean man and was becoming more and more eccentric. He had very few friends, never married and after his father died he suffered bouts of depression. His style of work was changing too and this caused much unease in the art world and again much controversy. Some critics thought he had lost his mind and cited the fact that his mother had died in a lunatic asylum. Another critic commented that his work *Schloss Rosenau* was 'the product of a diseased eye and a reckless hand.' Much of his later paintings became far more abstract, impressionistic and wild. A few people said his new work had become more innovative, but many more thought they had lost the quality of his much earlier work. Many of these later Turner paintings were not even catalogued and as time went by new experts questioned a number of these paintings and simply rejected them out of hand. They stated that this period of his work did not have the correct and usual Turner style. They concluded, therefore, that they must be fakes!"

Richard looked at his watch, drank the last of his coffee and said, "I must go in a few minutes, but…" He put his hand in the inside pocket of his jacket and pulled out a typed sheet of A4 paper, which he then handed to Viktor. "Here is a list of some useful reading. The best one is the first on the list," he said, with a small grin on his face.

Both Ian and Viktor looked at the sheet together. Both smiled when they noticed the first entry was one of Richard's own books!

"To finish," continued Richard, "I hope you can now understand why Turner's work, his life and his place in art history, has always been surrounded by controversy and speculation about the genuineness of much of his work. I also know a little about the 1956 decision you mentioned earlier. I am fairly sure that the committee, at that time, must have been looking for reasons to reject any previously authenticated Turner paintings. That was the easy option. Fortunately we now have advanced technology available to us and maybe modern buyers are more forgiving and less judgmental about Turner's morals and tainted history. My guess is most buyers today are only interested in one thing, whether their picture is a genuine Turner... or a fake! Thankfully now, it's modern technology and not just dubious opinions, which helps the experts come to their final decision."

At this, Richard stood up and held his hand out towards Ian. "Lovely evening, Ian. I hope I have been of some use. Look forward to seeing you at the next reunion."

Both Ian and Viktor shook Richard's hand and Viktor thanked him for his time. Viktor finished by saying it had been a fascinating and extremely useful evening.

When Richard had walked away Ian and Viktor sat down again.

"Well," said Ian, "I hope you found that interesting?"

"Yes I did, it was fascinating. Did you learn anything?"

"Whenever I speak with Richard I always learn something. I am sure you will enjoy reading his book too. It's a new one, so I would love to read it after you."

"Of course. I will try and get a copy tomorrow."

"So Vic, where do you go from here with regards to the two Baldwin paintings?"

"Having listened to everything that Richard has said this evening, I am even more convinced that both these pictures could well be genuine Turners and I am going to do my utmost to prove that this is the case!"

Chapter 5

Ian arrived home from the dinner meeting with his former tutor and Viktor just before 11 o'clock.

Emma had already retired to bed, but called down to Ian when she heard him come through the front door. "Ian, I'm upstairs."

"Okay". Ian locked the front door, swapped his outside shoes for his slippers and went upstairs to their bedroom.

"Did you have a good evening?" asked Emma. She was sitting up in bed and had just put her book down when Ian walked into the room.

"Yes, it was really good to meet up with Richard again. He's been offered a research project at Yale University, so he's off to America at the end of the year."

"That sounds interesting. So how did your meeting go?"

"It was really useful for Viktor. I've got him working on a project about Turner's paintings and their impact on the art market. So I think listening to Richard has really stimulated his interest."

"I've never met Richard. What's he like?"

"Well, in some ways he is your typical archetypal professor, very knowledgeable, single minded and just a little bit wacky. However, he is a really nice man who I have a lot of time for. His lecture presentations were always interesting and stimulating. As my tutor he had a massive impact on the grade of my Master's degree."

"He sounds like a really nice man. By the way, Oscar telephoned from Hong Kong. I told him you were out for the evening so he said he would ring you at your office tomorrow morning."

"Okay. Thank you." Ian left the bedroom to go to the smallest bedroom, which he used as a dressing room. After all, he was well aware that there was no wardrobe space available in the main bedroom! Even Emma could not get all her clothes in there! As he undressed and then went into the bathroom, he wondered what Oscar wanted. It had been a few weeks since he had last spoken with him.

Next morning, when Ian walked into his outer office area, Penny was already at her desk. After they both exchanged good mornings, Penny asked how the dinner meeting had gone.

"It was a good evening, thanks. It was great to meet up with my old tutor again and I thought Vic thoroughly enjoyed the experience. I'm expecting an in-depth investigation report from him about the Baldwin paintings." Suddenly the telephone began to ring in Ian's office. "Excuse me, Penny, I'm expecting Oscar to ring from Hong Kong." Ian strode briskly into his office, put down his briefcase on the desk and picked up the receiver.

"Hello, Ian." Ian recognised Oscar's voice immediately. "How's things in the UK?"

"Fine thanks, Oscar, and how's Hong Kong?" replied Ian, now sitting down in his chair as he spoke.

"Yes, fine too. It's been a little quiet here lately, but things may be brewing in Beijing. May Ling telephoned me yesterday. She is coming to Hong Kong on Monday and wants to meet me to talk about obtaining some Munnings paintings. I'm not aware of any possible Munnings sales coming up soon and wondered if you had any knowledge of anything likely to be happening in the UK?"

"No, not at the moment. We have just completed a private sale of three Munnings paintings to a client in Saudi Arabia, but I'm not aware of anything else due to be coming on to the market here. Have you checked with Christie's?"

"No, but that's my next call. Thought I would try my old buddy first."

"Sorry. I'll let you know if I do hear a whisper."

"Thanks. Must chat again soon. Bye for now."

"Goodbye Oscar." Ian put down the receiver and called Penny.

Penny walked into Ian's office and as she moved closer to his desk, Ian asked, "Are you aware of any Munnings paintings coming up for sale shortly?"

"Munnings? No. Vic dealt with the three that went to Saudi Arabia, but I'm not aware of anything else."

"Mmm. Okay. If you do hear anything, can you let me know please."

Penny nodded and went back to her desk.

Ian opened his briefcase and pulled out his laptop computer. After switching it on, he accessed a series of familiar art websites that he often searched for paintings that would shortly be coming onto the market via auctions. As he viewed each site he inserted the search name of 'Sir Alfred J Munnings'. When nothing of any note came up advertising a probable sale, he sat back in his chair and tried to think about other possible options. Suddenly a broad grin began to emerge on his face. 'I just wonder' he thought.

Viktor had arrived at Sotheby's office slightly earlier than usual. He wanted to find a supplier of the book *The Complex Life of JMW Turner* by Professor Richard Jackson MBE. After accessing the internet on his computer, he inserted the book's details into the websites of the local bookshops and stores. Nobody locally seemed to have a copy immediately in stock, but nearly all said the book could be obtained. Waterstones said they could get him a copy within 48 hours, so he decided to order with them there and then. Within seconds he had received an email confirming the book could be collected in two days' time.

Whilst his computer was still open, Viktor googled the names of the two paintings belonging to Mr Baldwin, *Margate at early dawn* and *Margate beach and seascape.* He remembered doing this when he had first spoken with Mr Baldwin some months ago. Unfortunately the results this time took him back to the same websites that he had visited before. Some gave more details than others, but none revealed any new or more up to date information. The two paintings were still categorised as 'rejected'.

He next tried to find any information connecting the two paintings to the 1956 committee investigation. He eventually found one particular report that was light on detail but did list some general pointers as to why a number of Turner's paintings had been rejected by the committee: poor provenances; pictures were not good enough; didn't look like the hand of Turner; obvious copy or fake; the painting was possibly started by Turner but finished by another artist; the painting had been cut down from a much larger painting; obvious inconsistencies with Turner's usual style.

Mmm, reasoned Viktor, so these are the key objections I've now got to overcome, especially if I'm going to have any chance of convincing the experts to overturn the earlier decisions. Also, he now realised, even if he was able to put together a really strong case, if either of the two Baldwin paintings did have any historical connection with Mrs Booth, as the 1956 experts had alluded to, then it was almost certain that they would still be unfairly tainted.

Another issue was, of course, could he find any modern-day Turner expert who would be prepared to put their reputations on the line and overlook such outdated snobbery? Okay, he thought, I like a challenge!

Ian looked through his private telephone book which contained the names and contact details of the important art connections he'd met and recorded during his career. When he got to the letter 'M' he ran his finger down the listing until he got to Munnings Art Museum, Dedham, and the name of David Wardley, chief trustee. He dialled the museum's number and when the call was answered Ian advised his name and asked if Mr Wardley was available.

"I'm sorry, Mr Caxton, but Mr Wardley is not at the museum today. Can I give him a message?"

"Yes please. That would be very kind." Ian gave the lady his full name, Sotheby's title and mobile telephone number.

"I'll make sure Mr Wardley gets this message."

"Thank you," replied Ian, and they both said their goodbyes. A bit of a shot in the dark, thought Ian, but you never know.

It was later that same afternoon when Ian's mobile phone rang. He was still in his office and looking through a forthcoming Christie's auction catalogue. Always useful to know what the opposition is doing! He put the catalogue down and answered the call.

"Hello, Ian. Long time no speak. David Wardley."

"Hello, David. Thanks for phoning me back. How are you?"

"Very well, thank you. So, what can I do for you?" replied David. He had a strong, clear voice and Ian held his phone a few centimetres away from his ear.

"I remember from when we previously met, that you told

me the Munnings trustees tried to keep a comprehensive record of the ownership and whereabouts of all Sir Alfred's paintings."

"Yes, that's still the case. Well it's the intention anyway. Some private sales can cause a headache."

"Yes, I can see that. But tell me, do you get to know of possible future sales in advance?"

"It depends. Sometimes potential buyers may try to check out provenances with us. Sometimes sellers may do the same to make sure their records are correct, particularly where pictures are inherited. Why do you ask?"

"I have a keen buyer who is eager to purchase any of Munnings pictures and I was wondering if you knew of any possible sellers?"

"It is funny you should ask that because there is a family in the High Street, here in Dedham, that might be tempted. The husband was asking my thoughts only last week about the two pictures he owns. Would you like me to ask him if he wants to speak to you?"

"That would be very kind of you, David. You can also tell him that I would be prepared to drive up to Dedham."

"Fine. I will pass on your offer. If you do come up to Dedham, let me know and we can meet here at the museum. There have been a number of changes since you last visited us."

"I certainly will."

Both men said their goodbyes and Ian put his phone back in his jacket pocket. A trip up to 'Constable country', thought Ian, now that would be a really nice day out.

He opened up his laptop and started writing an email to Oscar.

Chapter 6

It was two days later, during his lunch break, that Viktor visited the local Waterstones bookshop and collected his ordered copy of *The Complex Life of JMW Turner* by Professor Richard Jackson MBE.

When he arrived back at his desk he immediately opened the book at the 'Introduction' and started reading and writing lots of notes in his new 'Turner' notebook. By the time he was ready to go home he had reached Chapter 15 and by the time he had switched off his bedroom light, later that evening, he had reached Chapter 29. Much of the book's content followed the same information Richard had summarised at their meeting, but the book did go into a lot more detail and gave Viktor a number of ideas and possible next steps to take. He also pondered on the paradox that here we have two paintings that were currently worth possibly just a few hundred pounds, but in just a few weeks' time they could be worth maybe millions! Could this only happen in the art world!?

By the time he settled down to go to sleep he was even more convinced that he would be able to prove that the Baldwin paintings were genuine Turners.

When Viktor arrived at his desk the next day, and although

he had not yet finished reading the whole of the professor's book, he had already formulated a number of ideas in his head. However, before heading off and speaking directly with Mr Baldwin, he decided he would like to discuss these thoughts with Ian first.

Penny arranged an appointment for Viktor to see Ian later that afternoon. Ian had also suggested that it might be useful if Penny joined them too. So when Viktor arrived in the outer office just before 3 pm, Penny was waiting with her notebook and pen.

"Ian's just finishing a call at the moment," said Penny, as Viktor walked towards her desk. "I don't think he is going to be too long. So how's the Turner research going?"

"It's really quite fascinating and it has made me even more determined to prove the Baldwin paintings are genuine."

"It's so difficult to get experts to agree to change their opinions. They will need lots of compelling evidence."

"Mmm, I know, but by the time I'm finished they will just look like fools if they do turn me down."

Penny smiled. She liked Viktor's determination and knew he would not leave any stone unturned. "Ah, Ian's off the phone now. Let's go in."

Both Viktor and Penny entered Ian's office and Ian told them both to sit down.

"So, Vic, what have you got to tell us?" asked Ian as he tidied his papers and then sat back in his chair to give Viktor his full attention.

"Since our meal with Richard the other evening, I've obtained a copy of his book and I'm about three quarters of the way through. I've now got a number of ideas that I wanted to pass by you before I go back to Mr Baldwin."

"Okay," replied Ian.

"I know we have not actually seen these paintings yet 'in the flesh', so to speak, but all my ideas are based on the fact that when we do we will be convinced that they are not copies or fakes. After all, they were considered genuine works completed by Turner right up until 1956. So I think our first move is to speak to Mr Hopkins and get his agreement to approach Mr Baldwin."

"I've already spoken with him this morning. He says that Mr Baldwin is expecting us to telephone him."

"Excellent," replied Viktor. "I'll do that straight after this meeting."

"Before you do that, Vic," interjected Ian, "I suggest you speak with Mr Hopkins first and outline your findings to him as well. Also tell him what your approach will be when you do speak to Mr Baldwin and also list the next steps you propose to take trying to prove they are genuine Turners. He is very keen to be kept in the loop and he might just give you some extra advice."

"I see," said Viktor. He was not too sure whether Mr Hopkins' keen interest was a good or bad thing.

"Anyway, so what are you proposing?" Ian was keen not to give Viktor the impression that he and Mr Hopkins were going to curb Viktor's enthusiasm or try to catch him out.

"Firstly, I want to establish the correct provenance. I remember Mr Baldwin saying when I originally spoke to him, that he understood the two paintings were purchased directly from Turner! This obviously conflicts with the expert's report which says that Mrs Booth was the owner, so I want to establish which statement is correct. Secondly, I would like to speak with Professor Jackson again and seek his help in trying to get both paintings subjected to all the latest technological advancements and forensic investigations at the London Courtauld Institute of Art. Finally I would like to approach Tate Britain to get some comparisons of the paints used in our pictures compared to similar Turners in the Tate."

"Sounds as though you are going to be busy," said Ian. "What do you think, Penny?"

"I agree. It's certainly a big challenge, but I'm confident Vic will provide the correct answer – one way or another."

"Just make sure, Vic," said Ian, "that the evidence does stack up. If you have any doubts, come and discuss them with me. Otherwise, good luck!"

Next morning Viktor discussed his plans with Mr Hopkins. Mr Hopkins said he was happy with Viktor's approach and then added, "John and Anne Baldwin are expecting a telephone call, so I suggest you ring them today. I have seen the paintings for myself and as far as I can see they are excellent pieces of work, but I'm not one of the Turner experts that needs to be convinced. The Baldwin's have also agreed for the paintings to be subjected to forensic tests, but please be careful, these paintings could be worth several million pounds."

"Thank you, sir," replied Viktor. "I will be extremely careful and will also keep you and Ian informed of all developments."

After the meeting, Viktor went back to his desk and telephoned the number he had been given by Mr Hopkins. It was Mrs Baldwin who answered the telephone and she told Viktor that Mr Baldwin was not at home at present. However, they both agreed to a meeting at ten o'clock in two days' time. Mrs Baldwin said she knew her husband would be available then.

Viktor finished reading the last two chapters of Professor Jackson's book and pulled together all the sheets and notes he had written to date. Five minutes later he received a telephone call from Penny. "Vic, I would like to give you some help with your Turner investigations. I've also got some extra information that might help you."

"Okay. That would be great. Thanks."

"I'll pop down to your desk in about ten minutes."

Whilst Penny was away from her desk, Ian received a telephone call from David Wardley at the Munnings museum. David advised Ian that his colleague in Dedham definitely would be interested in seeing someone from Sotheby's. David asked if Ian would be available to attend a meeting next Monday at 6 pm. Ian quickly checked his diary and confirmed this was convenient for him. David gave Ian the seller's name, address and telephone number. He also said that if Ian travelled up to Dedham earlier in the day, then they could meet at the museum beforehand. Ian agreed that this was a good idea and suggested he would arrive at the museum about three o'clock.

When Ian had finished his telephone conversation, he opened up his laptop and accessed his email inbox. He was pleased to see that Oscar had replied to his earlier email.

'Hi Ian, I had a useful meeting with May Ling. She has a new client in Beijing who is a keen collector of Munnings paintings. Apparently he already has six and would like another four. He is especially interested in the early gypsy period of Munnings' work. Hope you can help. Cheers, Oscar.'

Ian replied to Oscar telling him of his planned meeting in Dedham and that he would get back to him when he had more information.

Penny arrived at Viktor's desk and sat down. "This is a big job you've decided to take on, Vic."

Viktor looked at his pile of notes and said, "Yes, just a bit daunting, but it's a great opportunity."

"I might be able to help. My cousin works in the conservation department at Tate Britain and I think that if I ask her she may be able to assist you with the analysis and forensic work you need."

"Wow. That would be great. Can you speak to her?"

"I'll telephone her this evening," replied Penny. She knew Viktor had helped her in the past and she was anxious to try and repay at least one of the outstanding favours.

"I've got a meeting with the Baldwins at their home in two days' time, so I'll get to see the paintings for the first time then."

"Just be careful, Vic. Don't get your hopes up too high. There are lots of Turner fakes out in the market and some are excellent and they have even fooled the experts! Also opinions in the art world are so hard to challenge and change. Reputations and years of experience would be put on the line."

"Yes, I know. That's what Ian's professor, Richard, told me. I've also got to make sure I'm not putting my own career on the line either! Both Ian and Michael Hopkins will be watching me like a hawk!"

Chapter 7

Viktor arrived at the Baldwin's home just before ten o'clock and parked at the top of their long driveway in front of the double garage. When he got out of his car he looked at the sizable front garden which was mainly planted with rose trees that were just beginning to show their new leaves. The house, Viktor guessed, must be Victorian. It also had a mature wisteria covering much of the lower part of the front red brick facade.

Mrs Baldwin answered the door and Viktor introduced himself. Mrs Baldwin was probably in her mid-60s, Viktor guessed, but she was still quite attractive, especially when she smiled and welcomed him into the house.

"John is upstairs, so I'll give him a call. Do go into the lounge." Mrs Baldwin pointed to an open door leading off from the hallway. From the bottom of the stairs she called her husband.

Viktor walked into the lounge and immediately noticed it's large size and the open log fire crackling away in the fireplace, despite the mild weather. He quickly spotted a number of paintings on the walls and wandered over to inspect what Viktor thought might just be a Stubbs.

Mrs Baldwin entered the room and announced that her husband was just coming. She also asked if Viktor would like a cup of tea.

"Yes please. That would be very nice," replied Viktor, walking back towards the centre of the room.

At that moment Mr Baldwin arrived through the doorway and wandered across to shake hands. Viktor thought Mr Baldwin was probably in his late 60s but had not worn quite so well as his wife. He obviously enjoyed his food and wine!

"Good to meet you at last, Viktor. Did you have a good journey?"

"Yes, thank you, sir. Mr Hopkins gave me exact directions."

"Nice neighbour is Michael. We've not known him for very long. We've only been here for what, six, no it must be seven, months now. Time really flies when you get to our age."

Viktor smiled.

"So you have come to look at our Turners. They are both in the dining room so we'll pop in there after you've had your tea. Ah, here's Anne."

Anne Baldwin carried a loaded tray and put it down onto a coffee table next to where Viktor was standing. She bent down and removed the teapot, milk jug, cups, saucers and a small collection of biscuits. "Now then, Viktor," she said, "How do you like your tea?"

"Milk and no sugar please, Mrs Baldwin,." Viktor and John Baldwin watched in silence as Mrs Baldwin poured the three cups of tea and handed one to Viktor.

"Please help yourself to a biscuit," she said.

Viktor spotted a chocolate digestive and put it on his saucer before sitting on a sofa chair. "Thank you," he said.

John and Anne both collected their cups and sat down together on the settee.

"You have a very nice house," said Viktor, wanting to break the silence.

"Thank you," replied Mrs Baldwin. "We didn't think we were going to be able to buy it, did we, John? Another couple were looking at it too, but we were renting at the time so had the money in the bank. That seemed to make a difference."

Viktor nodded and ate half of his biscuit.

"So, what have you found out about our Turners then, Viktor?" announced Mr Baldwin, wanting to get on with the main reason for the meeting.

Viktor summarised what the professor had told him and the extra information he had picked up from the internet. He finished by saying, "So as you can see we probably still have a few hurdles to cross before we can convince the art market that your paintings are true Turner's."

"Mmm," replied Mr Baldwin. "If you want my opinion, I think the whole thing is very fishy! These so-called experts just want to pick up paintings on the cheap and then get them authenticated as genuine. That way they make their millions!"

"Fortunately the art market does not usually work that way, but I can understand the point you are making," replied Viktor. He had already learnt, despite his very brief career to date, that the art market was definitely not perfect. It was also a world where not only 'caveat emptor', 'buyer beware', applied, but also 'seller beware' too!

"Right," said Mr Baldwin, standing up and putting his empty cup back on the tray. "Let's show you these Turners."

Viktor stood up and replaced his cup and saucer on the tray and followed Mr Baldwin out of the lounge, through a section of the hallway and into the dining room. On the opposite wall, behind the dining table, hung the two Turner pictures. Viktor immediately walked over and inspected each painting and noted the two small brass name plates attached to the middle bottom of each frame. One said

Margate at early dawn, JMW Turner. 1841. and the other said *Margate beach and seascape, JMW Turner. 1841.*

Margate at early dawn displayed a beach in the foreground in semi-darkness, with a gradually brightening, golden, calm sea leading to the horizon. Here the sun was just emerging. The sky was filled with billowing white and grey heavy clouds. *Margate beach and seascape* was of a similar scene but set much later in the day. All the paint colours were much brighter, but the composition was much more abstract, impressionistic and wild.

After about ten minutes, Viktor stood back and said, "Do you mind if I take some photographs?"

"No, no, my boy. Do carry on."

Viktor took both paintings off the wall and laid them carefully on to the dining room tablecloth covering. He removed his mobile phone and a tape measure from his jacket pocket and took four different photographs of each painting, including some of the reverse sides. Whilst each painting was face down, he measured the back of the painting's size inside the frame. He made a mental note that both were approximately 100 centimetres high x 130 centimetres wide. When he had finally finished, he returned each picture to its original position on the wall. He stood back again and checked that their positioning was correct. "Well, they look like good examples of Turner's work to me but, unfortunately, it is not me who has to be convinced."

"Quite. So what are Sotheby's suggesting?"

"I think we need to start with the paintings' provenances. I gather you disagree with the experts' statement that they were once owned by Mrs Booth."

"Yes I do! I inherited these paintings about 20 years ago from my father and with them came various documents which showed that the pictures were bought directly from Mr Turner himself!"

"Have you still got these papers, Mr Baldwin?"

"Yes I have. The original copies are in the bank, but I have a set of photocopies in the lounge. I brought them downstairs when you arrived."

The two men walked back into the lounge. Mr Baldwin picked up a green folder and handed it to Viktor, who then sat down and removed several sheets of A4 photocopies. He spent the next few minutes inspecting and carefully reading each individual sheet. Finally he said, "I can see where the paintings have been passed down through your family's generations, but the earliest paper states that the two paintings were purchased from an agent."

"Yes, but my understanding is that the agent was employed directly by Turner to sell his paintings."

That's not quite the same as buying directly from Turner and having the receipt to prove it, thought Viktor. "Do you mind if I take photographs of these papers?"

"No. Carry on. I hope they can help to prove our case," replied Mr Baldwin, who was now a little less sure of the value of his claim.

Once again Viktor removed his mobile phone out of his pocket and photographed each sheet. Whilst he did so, he noted that there was no obvious reference to any previous ownership by Mrs Booth. However, it was still possible that the agent could have purchased the paintings directly from Mrs Booth! So, unfortunately, it was not quite as straightforward as Mr Baldwin had initially suggested!

Viktor put the papers back in the folder and handed it back to Mr Baldwin. "At some stage we will need to borrow the paintings to complete some forensic testing. Will that be alright?"

"What exactly will that entail? Michael said that you might need to do this sort of investigation. I don't want the paintings damaged."

"No. It just sounds worse than it is. Essentially each painting is firstly x-rayed. In the past, experts could only use their eyes to look at a picture. Nowadays x-rays can look through all the layers of paint that the artist has applied. Sometimes older work or changes made by the artist are found on the boards or canvas. Secondly, the paints used to produce the picture are analysed against other similar confirmed examples of Turner's work. Microscopic flakes of paint can now be analysed to establish the exact paint type and its chemical composition. These results are then cross referenced against other Turner paintings of that same period. These modern advancements and techniques have revolutionised how experts now look at paintings. A number of paintings once thought to be genuine have more recently been proved to be fakes using these methods. For example, these microscopic flakes can also identify whether the paints used were even in existence at the time that the painting is supposed to have been painted!"

"I see. So when would you like to borrow them?"

"Firstly we'll need to do some more provenance investigations and then make appointments for the forensic testing. I will ring you when I have these results. In the meantime, I recommend you speak to your insurers as they will need to know of our plans."

Twenty minutes later Viktor was driving back towards London. His mind was still reflecting on his meeting with the Baldwins. Both pictures, he was convinced, looked every bit a Turner, but what was it that was now niggling him? There was something, but at that precise moment, he couldn't quite put his finger on it!

Chapter 8

On the following Monday afternoon Ian was driving his car northwards through Essex on the A12. He saw the turning for Colchester and checked his watch. 1.45 pm. Not far now, he thought, I should be in Dedham by two o'clock. Five minutes later he was leaving the main road and turning onto the B1029. The signpost sited at the junction said 'Dedham 1 mile'. As he followed the country lane, he was reminded of the story relating to John Constable who had grown up in the nearby village of East Bergholt but went to school in Dedham. Some years after Constable had moved away from the area, to live in London, he had travelled back to Dedham one time to visit his sister. As the stagecoach and horses were travelling along a nearby road one of the passengers, not recognising the celebrity fellow passenger on board, announced, "We are now entering the countryside where John Constable had grown up and where he's supposed to have painted many of his famous paintings." Another passenger had duly responded, "So this is 'Constable Country' is it?" It is believed that Constable himself had never heard the phrase 'Constable Country' before, but was extremely pleased nevertheless!

As Ian's car crossed the bridge over the River Stour, the county boundary between Suffolk and Essex, he glanced out of the window to his right-hand side. There he saw a large red brick block of apartments overlooking the river. On this site, he remembered, once sat a large water mill that was owned by John Constable's father, just one of several mills that he owned in the area. This Dedham Mill subsequently became the subject of a number of Constable's early paintings.

Just a little further on the left-hand side was an impressive large cream-coloured house. Ian recalled that he had read somewhere that this property was where John Constable's sister once resided.

A few metres further on and he came to a 'T' junction with the High Street. The large 15th century St Mary's church was straight in front of him. He turned right and after about 200 metres he signalled to turn right again to enter through a tall cartway. Years ago, this would have been the entrance for travelling stagecoaches and their horses. As Ian drove through, he was immediately reminded that this was, after all, the 21st century. This area beyond was now the car park and a beer garden for the Rising Sun inn. The Rising Sun, for many hundreds of years, had been a coaching inn. Now the coaches have been replaced by motorcars, but the clientele is still a mixture of travellers, tourists and local villagers seeking rest and refreshments. This was to be Ian's home for one night.

After booking in and being shown to his bedroom, Ian decided to stretch his legs and go for a walk. He had been to Dedham before on business, but he had not had time to explore the main sights in this most picturesque village. He had just under an hour before he was expected by David Wardley at Munnings museum. He crossed over the High Street and stood in the main gateway to the churchyard and looked up at the old church building. A notice nearby had stated that the church had been completed in 1492. Ian remembered that this was the same year that the Pilgrim Fathers had set out on their adventure to America. He then turned around and could see quite a lot of the length of the High Street. He knew that many of the substantial properties are either Grade 1 or Grade 2* listed buildings and were originally constructed in and around the 15th and 16th century, but are probably more famous now for the Georgian timber-fronted upgrading completed many years later.

Wandering down the High Street towards the large war memorial, Ian entered Royal Square. Opposite was a large red brick house which was once the old grammar school which John Constable had attended. He stood for a few moments and generally admired the view all around him. He wondered how much had changed since Constable's day. He then thought how strange it was that two of Britain's most famous artists should have had connections with such a small village. But even stranger still, that Dedham was also formerly the home to yet another artist that was probably, in Ian's opinion, one of the greatest British art talents of the 20th century!

Ian turned around and walked through a creaking, black metal railing gate. This was a side entry into St Mary's churchyard. His aim now was to try and find the grave of that particular talented artist.

Searching amongst many old gravestones, some with their engraved details now quite indistinguishable, he eventually found what he was looking for, the final resting place of one Thomas Patrick Keating. To his surprise, however, the gravestone was a simple affair. It just stated 'Tom Keating'.

Keating, Ian knew, was originally an art restorer, but, latterly, more famously remembered as a very skilled 20th century art forger. He claimed to have faked more than 2000 paintings during his lifetime and was able to copy the styles of over 100 different artists! Nobody really knows how many of his paintings are still in the art market with forged signatures. But whilst he never became wealthy himself, his fake work, or 'Sextons' as he called them, are estimated to have a total value of many millions of pounds. Interestingly, and as a taunt to the commercial art world, he often planted what he called 'time bombs' in his pictures. For example, he sometimes wrote a message onto the blank canvas using 'lead white' before starting to paint. He knew x-rays would later reveal that the picture was not a genuine painting by the said artist. He also teasingly added semi-hidden unique features within a composition that would only have been known about, or invented, within the 20th century. Such additions were only obvious to a very keen eye and a number of Keating's fake 19th century and earlier pictures have still not yet been unmasked to this day!

As Ian stood and stared at the simple engraving, he smiled as he remembered reading about how Keating spent much of his time ranting and fighting against the art establishment. He stated that he had only created all his forgeries as a protest against all the art dealers and traders who became very rich at the artist's expense. He always refused to list all his many forgeries and in 1977 he was arrested and accused of 'conspiracy to defraud and obtain payments through deception amounting to £21,416'. He pleaded not guilty on the basis that he was never intending to defraud anyone! However, the charges were later dropped due to Keating's poor health. Public opinion warmed to him as they thought he was 'just a charming old rogue'. His health did improve for a while, but he died in 1984. During his later years, he presented a series of television programmes demonstrating the special painting techniques of the old masters. What a truly talented artist, thought Ian.

As he started to walk away from the grave, Ian still had a smile on his face. Despite the fact that both he and many of his colleagues in the art industry had been seriously challenged in the past by some of Keating's fakes, he nevertheless had a soft spot for this special character. Indeed, to Ian, he would always remain a very talented and special old rogue!

It was a warm afternoon so Ian decided to walk the short distance to Castle House, where the Munnings museum was based. The museum building was once the home of Sir Alfred Munnings and his wife. It was always Munnings' wish that the property should be preserved for the public to be able to visit and see his work.

Ian arrived on the gravel driveway approach just before three o'clock. He recognised the building immediately, although the dominant pink painted outer walls had been changed to a much calmer shade of yellow.

He passed through a small white porchway and entered the reception area where he was greeted by a pleasant smiling lady sitting at a reception desk. Ian announced his name and that he had an appointment with David Wardley. The lady rose from her seat and disappeared into the main building. When she returned shortly after, she was accompanied by a tall middle-aged man that Ian immediately recognised.

"Hello, Ian," said the man as he greeted Ian with an outstretched hand. "It's so good to meet you again."

Ian shook David's hand and replied, "And you too, David. It's always a pleasure to come here."

"Come. I'll give you the tour and show you all our recent changes." David stepped out of the way to give Ian room to pass by and enter the large hallway.

After a few paces, Ian stopped and looked all around him. Munnings' paintings and sketches, unsurprisingly, adorned the walls downstairs and above the dark wooden staircase. He also knew there were further display rooms upstairs.

"Still as impressive as ever, David."

"Thank you. We try to keep the display interesting and

fresh for our regular visitors. We can make subtle theme changes each year utilising our storage collection and also by temporarily exchanging with other collections. Come, let me show you around."

About an hour later the tour had been completed and the two men now sat in David's office with a pot of tea and some biscuits. "Tell me," said David, "Are you looking for a particular period of Munnings' work?"

"Yes. There is a potential client in China who is particularly keen on increasing his Munnings collection. He's especially interested in the early gypsy period."

"China, eh? Well Bob Robins, who you will be meeting later, has two nice Munnings paintings and two sketches. Only one painting is from the gypsy period, the other is a horse racing scene at Newmarket. The two sketches are both small working drawings of horse's heads."

"Mmm. And you think he wants to sell them?"

"I don't think he's sure. All four pictures have been in the family for many years, but he's not really a collector. I think he would sell if he could get a good price. He wants to pass on some money to his two children and grandchildren now, so hopefully that will reduce his inheritance tax liability in the future."

"Okay. What about the museum? Are you looking to raise any extra money sometime soon?"

"Not at the moment, Ian. Financially we are very sound, but one never knows. I'll let you know if things change."

"Thank you." replied Ian. He knew it was always useful to keep Sotheby's name in the minds of all potential buyers and sellers.

"Bob Robins has asked if I would join you at this meeting. I hope that's okay?"

"Yes, fine." replied Ian. "I'm sure Mr Robins will feel more comfortable with your presence. Is he a friend of yours?"

"More of a colleague really. We both play golf at the same club in Colchester."

"I see. Do you have any plans between now and the meeting?"

"No, not really. But what are yours? Are you planning to travel back home this evening?"

"No, no. I've booked into the Rising Sun, in the High Street, for one night."

"Good idea. I'll buy you a pint then. Bob Robins' house is only about 50 metres away from the pub."

The two men spent the next hour talking more about Sir Alfred Munnings, his paintings and the art market in general. It was just before they set off to the museum's car park to collect David's car that Ian mentioned Tom Keating and that he had been to visit his grave.

David was surprised that Ian referred to Keating as a likeable rogue as he knew Keating's work had caused all manner of problems in the art market. Ian just laughed and said that he wished he had been born with just half the man's talent.

"My father knew him quite well," replied David, to Ian's surprise. "There was a group of men in the village who liked to drink in the pubs and, although Keating was a bit of a recluse, he was apparently interesting company when he had a pint of beer in his hand! I vaguely remember meeting him when I was a youngster. If you talk to the older locals who did know him, I think you will find that most of them feel the police were desperate to put him behind bars!"

The two men got into David's Mercedes car and they sped off down Castle Hill for the three-minute drive to the Rising Sun. David parked his car next to Ian's BMW and they entered the front bar. It was still relatively early, but there were already three men standing with drinks at the bar. David nodded to them and they acknowledged him back.

Ian insisted that he was buying the drinks and two pints of beer were ordered. Ian looked at his watch. It was a little after 5.30. Just enough time, he thought, to have a relaxing drink before the serious business started.

At one minute to six o'clock, David and Ian arrived outside Mr Robins' home, one of the old impressive High Street houses that Ian had admired earlier that afternoon. David leaned forward and pressed the front door bell.

Chapter 9

"So, how did your meeting with the Baldwins go?" asked Penny, as Viktor walked up towards her desk.

"It went quite well. I've got copies of the provenances and photographs of the two pictures. They look like Turner's work to me, but…"

"But! What does 'but' mean?"

"It means that there is something I've noticed, but I'm not sure what. I just cannot put my finger on it at the moment. I know Mr Hopkins and Ian are going to watch me like a hawk, so I want to get this one right."

"Is it something to do with the paintings, or something else?"

"You warned me before I went to the meeting. I took your advice seriously, despite feeling that there was nothing to worry about, so I was on my guard," replied Viktor. He was anxious to investigate more fully all the information he had obtained, but was concerned now that it all might just be a waste of time.

"Maybe it will come back to you soon. In the meantime, what are you going to do next?"

"I thought maybe I would speak to Ian first. I really don't want to put my foot in it with Mr Hopkins and his neighbour."

"Ian is visiting Dedham…"

"Where?"

"Dedham. It is a village between Colchester and Ipswich. John Constable went to school there and Sir Alfred Munnings used to live there."

"Oh, okay. But why has Ian gone there?"

"He thinks there might be a number of Munnings paintings available for sale and he is also taking the opportunity to visit the Munnings museum."

"I've heard about the Munnings museum but I didn't realise it was in Dedham!"

"Anyway, he will not be back in the office until tomorrow afternoon."

"Okay. I suppose I could start looking a bit deeper into the conflicting evidence over the provenances relating to these two Turners." Viktor was unsure that he should proceed with his investigations until he had spoken with Ian, but, as Ian was not available, he decided to try and use his time more productively.

"By the way, I have spoken to my cousin, Susan, at Tate Britain and she said she could arrange an appointment for you to take the paintings in for the forensic paint sampling."

"Oh great! Thanks. If we can get that far with the early investigations, I'll certainly take up that offer."

"Come on Vic, this negativity is not like you. You were so confident just a few days ago." Penny was concerned that her earlier comments to Vic to 'be careful' had deflated him a little and he was probably now looking for problems that maybe didn't really exist.

"I know. It's just… well, I'm sure there is something I'm missing."

When Viktor got back to his desk he removed from his file the eight photographs of the two paintings he had taken with his mobile phone. He had printed these copies after chatting with Penny. They were all A4 size and he slowly examined each individual print very carefully. After about 20 minutes, he still could not find anything out of the ordinary. He refiled the prints back into the folder and removed the photographs of the provenances that he had taken. He read through the details of each sheet once again and decided the first thing he needed to do was to understand why the experts in the past had suggested that there was a Mrs Booth ownership connection.

Penny decided she would try to help Viktor and was searching the internet for any Turner painting that had been originally deemed a genuine Turner, but had subsequently been reclassified to being a fake. She also wanted to identify if any of these same fakes had now been reclassified back to being genuine... and why!

Later that same day Penny telephoned Viktor. "Vic, I think I've found something that may be of interest to you. What do you know about The Davies Collection at the National Museum of Wales?"

"Err... well, nothing. Why?" Wales, thought Viktor. What's that got to do with Turner?

"I suggest you visit their website and read about the bequeaths of the Davies sisters. In summary, these two wealthy sisters had a large collection of valuable paintings and in 1951 they decided to bequeath them to the museum for the benefit of the Welsh nation. However, in 1956 – ring a bell? – a group of Turner experts decided that three of the donated Turners were actually fakes and the museum had no choice but to take these pictures off display! In 2012, however, a BBC television programme investigated fully the history and composition of these three paintings. They were eventually able to prove that all three paintings were genuine after all! You really need to check out this story. It may help you with your own investigations."

"Wow, that's great Penny. Thanks. I'll look at it now."

Viktor was suddenly remotivated. He accessed the BBC news website for 2012 and found the story to which Penny had referred. Sixty minutes later he was not only motivated, but very excited! The television programme did indeed have a serious impact in proving that the experts' decisions made in 1956 were incorrect. With the benefit of modern technology and more up to date forensic analysis, there was little doubt that the three blighted Turners were not fakes after all. Viktor could not see the sense of these paintings going from a value of many thousands of pounds before 1956 to then being almost worthless for the next 56 years and then in 2012 these same pictures suddenly had valuations well into the millions of pounds! The monetary valuation of a painting, he concluded, was apparently not solely dependent on the quality of the composition, but mainly whether the artist had personally signed the painting as his own creation! Welcome Viktor, to the crazy world of the art market!

Just before 5 pm, Viktor telephoned Penny and discussed his findings with her. To say thank you, he offered to take her for a drink at The Grapes, their usual watering hole. Penny agreed and an hour later they were both entering the familiar public house on Maddox Street.

Viktor ordered and paid for the drinks and they both went over to a nearby vacant table and sat down.

It was Viktor who opened the conversation. "That television programme was a real eye opener. Can you believe how ridiculous the whole art world really is? These three pictures were painted over 200 years ago, they were not damaged or changed at any point in all that time, but their monetary value went from initially, many thousands of pounds, then down to virtually nothing, and finally worth many millions of pounds! It's just absurd! How is that a true reflection of the quality of the painting and the expertise of the artist?!"

"Well it isn't, is it?" replied Penny, who was now off on her personal hobby horse. "You also know my feelings about modern art. Where is the quality of the painting and expertise of the artist here? Many of those paintings are just rubbish, so how do they get their value? Take a wooden board, for example, cover it with randomly thrown paint, which you, I, or even a child could do blindfolded, it would rightly be deemed worthless, but if the same picture has, say, a proven, genuine Jackson Pollock signature, well, then it suddenly becomes worth millions! Isn't that crazy too!? No wonder there are so many fakes about."

"The good news though is that this all helps me, and hopefully, the Baldwin's case!" replied Viktor, with just a hint of smugness on his face. "I do not have to prove that their two paintings are genuine after all!"

Penny looked at him wondering how Vic had come to this devastating conclusion.

"No, I just need to find enough evidence that shows they are **not** fakes!" Viktor picked up his glass of beer, sat back, sipped his drink and smiled at Penny.

"Isn't that the same thing?" Penny peered at Viktor with a quizzical look.

"No, not at all. Just think about it. What I need to do is just shoot down every one of the reasons the so-called experts decided, in 1956, that the paintings were fakes. Once I have done that, they will not have a leg to stand on and will have to agree that the paintings should never have been deemed fakes in the first place! They will then have to reinstate them back to their status before the 1956 decision! It's very doubtful that any of today's experts will put their reputation on the line and state absolutely that they are genuine Turners. But my argument would then be, okay, if they aren't fakes, then they must be genuine!"

"I'm not so sure. How are you going to do all this? What are your plans?"

"The provenances are my first attack. After that, I think I might just have a few surprises for everyone!"

Chapter 10

When Ian and David arrived at the Robins' home, night-time was just beginning to set in. There were no street lights in the High Street and very few in Dedham generally. What little light that did exist was escaping from the front windows of a few houses and the local Co-op supermarket. To Ian, it all felt a little Dickensian.

Whilst they waited for the front door to be opened, Ian stood back and admired the facade of the property and smiled at the way fashion had changed the appearance of these High Street properties during the Georgian period. The flat facades were built directly on to the front of the existing houses. This resulted in many of the frontages now being much closer to the road.

The hallway light suddenly shone through the small window above the dark wooden door. After the sound of the click of the lock being undone, the door was slowly eased open emitting a low creaking sound. A middle-aged lady stood at the entrance and immediately smiled as she recognised David. Both men were invited into the house.

They were then led into a large sitting room where a roaring log fire was ablaze in the grate. Most of the wall space was covered in pictures. Mostly paintings, but also quite a collection of what Ian assumed were photographs of the Robins family.

"Hello, David," announced a voice from the far end of the room. "Just trying to get this damn light to come on. Ah, there we are." The bulb on a tall free-standing lamp-stand had suddenly lit up the far end of the room. Ian could now see a small grey-haired man, probably in his late 60s, walking towards them.

"Hello, Bob. Let me introduce you to Ian Caxton from Sotheby's. Ian, this is Bob Robins and his wife Barbara." They all shook hands.

It was Barbara who was first to speak. "Would anyone like some tea?"

"No thank you, Barbara. Very kind of you, but we have just had a quick drink at the pub." Ian nodded in agreement with David's comment.

"So, you would like to see my Munnings' artwork?" asked Bob. "They are in the dining room. Follow me."

Ian and David followed Bob across the hallway and into the dining room. Although Bob switched on the main lights, the quality of lighting to inspect the paintings was not very bright. Ian knew from experience that a lot of paintings were kept out of strong light so he always carried a small torch in his jacket pocket.

"Here we are gentlemen." Bob pointed to two oil paint-ings hanging on the wall immediately at the side of the door they had just entered through.

Ian and David moved further into the room and stood back to look at the overall compositions. Both paintings, Ian guessed, were about 60 centimetres high by 90 wide. They were very colourful representations, but of very dif-ferent subjects and certainly painted at different periods of Munnings' career. Ian stepped forward and took a closer look at the first picture. It was painted during the early part in Munnings' life and depicted a group of five male gypsies sitting around a bonfire. In the background, slightly out of focus and in the gloom of early evening, were the silhouettes of two women, two horses and three gypsy wagons.

Ian pulled out of his pocket a small torch and switched it on to inspect the painting much closer. Munnings, he thought, was at his best during this period. He had captured the atmosphere of the bonfire and the red glowing faces of the gypsies perfectly. This particular picture, Ian knew, was painted when Munnings was actually living and travelling with the gypsies. He was young and not very wealthy at that time, yet still had ambition and was passionately striving to achieve the best possible piece of work.

After looking at this first picture in more detail for another minute, he then moved on to the second painting. He saw that this picture depicted a close up of the faces and heads of a group of jockeys and their horses whilst they eagerly awaited the starter's instruction to race. Ian thought Munnings had definitely captured some of the atmosphere and anticipation of the race, but the painting somehow lacked the same heart and quality as the first one! By this stage of Munnings' career, he was much older and had made a name for himself as a revered painter of horses. However, Ian's opinion of the artist was that he had become a little lazy and his work now lacked the same level of commitment and desire. It was slightly more abstract and lacked the previously seen depth of quality and detail. He wondered if, at this stage of his life, Munnings thought just his name attached to a painting would sell whatever work he produced? Ian also wondered if, like with Turner, success had reduced the need for quality in favour of quantity!

Ian stood back and resumed his position standing at the side of David. It was David who was the first to speak. "What do you think?"

"I think the gypsy painting is excellent and will surely generate a lot of interest. The racing scene is more difficult to judge. It's a much later time in Munnings' career and a lot of collectors feel the quality is not as good. However, I am still confident both will sell, but I would put a much larger reserve on the gypsy painting."

David turned around to speak with Mr Robins, who was standing behind Ian. "What do you think, Bob?"

Bob Robins had been quiet up to this point as he wanted to hear the professional's comments first.

"Interesting. I am not a great fan of Munnings work, but my late father loved both these paintings. I have to decide whether, for sentimental reasons, I keep them, or be more practical and sell them. The money would come in very handy for my children and grandchildren. Hopefully I can then live for another seven years and they will then avoid having to pay extra inheritance tax when I finally do pop my clogs! What do you think they are worth, Ian?"

"That's always a difficult one, Bob, because there are so many variables. However, I would think you should be thinking about a reserve at auction of £500,000 for the horse race painting and maybe £5 million for the gypsy painting."

"Wow!" exclaimed Mr Robins, who suddenly disappeared from the room and could be heard shouting in the hallway as he headed for the kitchen. "Barbara! You'll never believe this!"

From the dining room, David and Ian could not fail to hear Bob's shout. They looked at each other and smiled. They had both witnessed this level of excitement many times before.

"Didn't you say there were also two sketches?" asked Ian as he began to look at some of the other pictures in the room.

"I think they are both in Bob's office at the back of the house. I'll ask him when he gets back."

Ian walked around the dining room table and inspected another painting. Nothing of significance he thought. He then looked at a small collection of photographs and relished the thought of sometime in the future having a collection of photographs of his own children and grandchildren.

Bob Robins reappeared and David asked him about the Munnings sketches. Bob beckoned to the two men to follow him into his office. Once there, he pointed to two small framed and signed pencil drawings about 40 centimetres high by 30 wide. Each drawing depicted part of a horse's head.

Ian walked across the room and leaned over the desk to take a closer view. These drawings were typical of Munnings' sketch-work depicting horses. Munnings had always been fascinated by a horse's physical construction and had sketched many hundreds of drawings showing different sections of the horse's anatomy. Munnings knew it was so vital for him to understand both the bone and muscle structure and also the interdependent relationship between the two.

"Good examples of Munnings' eye for detail and technical accuracy," said Ian, as he stepped back. "Unfortunately, there are so many similar examples in the art market today that I think you should keep these for the time being. More a longer-term investment."

"So, do you think they are worthless then, Ian?" asked Bob, a little deflated after the earlier more positive news on his oil paintings.

"Good god no," replied Ian. "You may get possibly £2000, maybe £3000 for each, but if it was me, I would keep them. They are still nice pieces of work, and I suspect they will only increase in value over time."

"Nice to keep so that you can hand them down to your children, Bob," said David. "Anyway, they are interesting examples of Munnings' early study work. We've got quite a few similar illustrations at the museum."

"Mmm," replied Bob. "Okay, so I just need to make up my mind about the two oil paintings. At the moment I'm thinking that selling the gypsy painting is probably the best option and then decide on the other one depending upon what price is achieved for the gypsy. By the way, the name for the gypsy painting is *The winter bonfire gathering*. The race scene's title is *Calling them up*.

David and Ian stayed for another hour. During that time Ian explained to Bob the selling process and the options and benefits of either a private sale or by an auction. He also advised that the painting would need to be fully examined, cleaned and provenances checked. For a painting worth potentially £5 million everything had to be correct.

When Ian and David finally left the Robins' home, Bob promised he would speak with his children, but his personal preference was to sell *The winter bonfire gathering*. "I will let you both know my final decision, probably by the end of the month."

After their meeting with Bob Robins, David had accompanied Ian back to the pub. There they chatted, ate a lovely Mediterranean-style meal and drank several pints of the local beer. Just before 11 pm, David informed Ian that he had better make a move and head home. He said he only lived about five minutes' walk away and was going to leave his car in the car park. He hoped the fresh air would also help to sober him up before he had to face his wife! Ian had laughed at this comment and wished him the best of luck! David promised he would let Ian know as soon as Bob had told him of his final decision.

Chapter 11

Whilst Ian was away for the evening in Dedham, Emma had decided to take the opportunity to investigate more fully the paperwork attached to the Monaco apartment. She also wanted to know what exactly she and Ian could and could not do with it, bearing in mind the strange provisos Andrei had insisted on.

Ever since Ian's telephone call from Monaco and his surprise bombshell, Emma had been quietly considering what this all really meant for their future. Initially she was certainly frightened. Frightened at the potential financial implications, the possible impact on their careers, for their personal relationship and indeed, for the continuing indirect control Andrei still seemed to have on Ian's life. However, once Ian had explained that Andrei was promising and setting aside more than enough money to pay for the usual upkeep costs, her worries over the financial implications began to diminish. Nevertheless, she was still concerned about the other issues. Still, even she had to admit that, if one looked at the gift in isolation only, it was a fabulous gesture and the more she thought about it the more she tried to put all the other worries out of her mind.

It was just after midnight, and after three large glasses of chardonnay, that Emma decided to call it quits for the evening. She had read through all the papers Ian had brought back from Monaco twice and three times, the thick report that their own solicitor had produced. Yes, Emma concluded, the whole thing was definitely strange and unusual, but legally probably faultless. They knew that Andrei could walk straight back into the picture and demand his property back, but in the meantime, they could treat the apartment as their own. What was there to worry about? That was Ian's response. But for Emma, she still had to be fully convinced. This was not what she had planned for when she agreed to marry Ian. A nice home, maybe children in time, good careers and a comfortable and stable lifestyle. Where in that scenario was the potential 'ownership' of a multi-million-pound apartment in Monaco!?

When Emma finally got into bed, she found it difficult to switch off and go to sleep. The apartment was still playing on her mind. She knew Ian was keen to fly out there again and very soon. He wanted them to be able to enjoy a special time there together. She on the other hand had mixed feelings. Yes, she had enjoyed a lovely few days with Ian as a guest of Andrei, but now she felt that to visit again, in these new circumstances, would be a different and possibly an uneasy experience. She worried that they would never fit in and people would probably talk about them behind their backs. But, of course, Ian was only suggesting another visit, not a permanent move. It was a lovely holiday home. Yes, that was it! Let's just look at it like that, a holiday home! No commitment, leave the responsibilities to Ian and to take it all a day at a time. Gradually Emma started to relax and began to think of the positives of the situation. Yes, she could revisit the apartment for, say, a weekend. Enjoy the weather, the balcony and its fabulous views. What would the harm be in that? She pondered more on these new thoughts and finally concluded that she would speak with

Ian tomorrow evening and let him know her new feelings. Now, in a far more relaxed frame of mind, she was able to snuggle under the duvet and accept the small smile that was appearing on her face. It was just a few minutes later, when her brain had finally surrendered for the night and she fell into a long and deep sleep.

Ian took full advantage of his stay at the Rising Sun, enjoying a lie-in until 7.30 am. Also, the benefit of a lovely cooked breakfast waiting for him when he arrived downstairs was a further bonus.

After his breakfast, Ian sent a quick email to Emma and a separate catch-up email to Viktor and Penny. He also said he would not be in the office for the rest of that day, but would travel back home that afternoon and continue working from there. He had other plans for the rest of the morning.

Ian had earlier dressed in his casual clothes and after checking out and paying his bill, he put his suitcase in the car boot. He put on a pair of old trusty walking boots that he always kept in the car. His aim was to walk the two miles to the hamlet of Flatford. The area around Flatford, Ian knew, was the setting for a number of John Constable's paintings. The location of probably his most famous painting, *The Haywain*, could, apparently, still be seen to this day at Flatford Mill.

When Ian left the car park, he walked through the cartway and turned left and back along the High Street, the route he had walked the previous evening. He crossed over Mill Lane and continued to the far corner of the road, where the road took a sharp turn to the right. This direction led up the hill to Munnings museum, but this time Ian turned left and walked down a track towards the fields in the distance. Ian knew that when Constable was a young boy, he walked the three miles from his home in East Bergholt to school in Dedham each day, probably following some of this same route. A lovely walk in the summer, but in the dark and cold winter days, he thought it must have been quite a challenge. Today it was a lovely clear day, with hardly a cloud in the sky. Just a gentle breeze to rustle the new leaves on the willow trees along the river bank. Constable would have struggled today, thought Ian, as he was famous for his skies with great billowing clouds.

It was not long before he saw the River Stour ahead of him and he passed through a wooden gate and stood on a small bridge. This, he knew, was the site of Constable's painting, *The Leaping Horse*. To his left, and for the last 250 years, the diverted River Stour flowed along this route. Directly under the bridge and to his right, was now just a small ditch, but this was once the original course of the River Stour. Today, however, it still remained the official county boundary. After two steps Ian had left Essex and had now entered the county of Suffolk.

He continued to follow the path alongside the river noting Fenn Bridge set back on his left-hand side. This was a relatively new wooden bridge, but for several hundreds of years there had been a number of other wooden bridges at this spot allowing a crossing of the river. One of the earlier bridges is thought to have been one of Constable's crossing places to and from school. In the distance, across the lush green meadows, Ian could just make out the lone building known as Bridge Cottage. This cottage, or sections of it, also appear in several of Constable's compositions.

Ian continued along the path, which now took him slightly away from the meandering river. He stopped briefly to observe the 'large skies', as Constable had recounted when he had painted some of his famous scenes. The very flat water-meadows with just a few trees and some cattle in the distance was still a similar view that Constable would have recognised. Yes, Ian thought, there certainly is a lot of unbroken sky to see.

As he crossed the river via another wooden bridge next to Bridge Cottage, he started to enter the hamlet of Flatford. He briefly stopped and looked closer at the small thatched cottage, which he noted was now mainly occupied on the ground floor as a museum. As with most of the properties in Flatford, it was owned by the National Trust.

The hamlet and the surrounding area, Ian observed, had changed very little since Constable's day. He was convinced that if Constable came back today he would recognise immediately where he was. He walked around the side of Bridge Cottage and into a narrow lane with fields on the left-hand side. After about 50 metres he stopped at a gate on his right-hand side. He placed both arms on the top of the five-bar wooden gate, leaned forward and stared at the view. In the distance there were a few trees and the green meadows, but as his focus moved closer, he could see the river cutting across from right to left. In the immediate foreground there was a special excavation in the ground with separated parallel wooden sleepers covering the whole of the floor area. This was once the old dry dock where repairs and maintenance could be made to the local boats and the famous Stour Lighters. This dock was used over 200 years ago and has now been preserved by the National Trust. It was the site of yet another John Constable painting, this time, *Boat building near Flatford Mill*.

Carrying on walking down the lane, Ian spotted the first views of the large red brick building of Flatford Mill coming up on his right-hand side. Like Dedham Mill, it too was once owned by John Constable's father. As he carried on, he finally saw what he had mainly come to see, the site of Constable's famous painting *The Haywain*. The view from in front of Flatford Mill across the millpond to Willy Lott's House was still virtually the exact picture that Constable had painted all those years ago. Ian wondered if any other 200-year old setting was still so unaltered or so wonderfully preserved.

Just behind him, against the wall of the mill, Ian spotted a wooden bench. He sat down and looked again at the view. His mind began to drift and consider the fact that within this very tiny area of Flatford, Constable had sketched and painted several hundreds of pictures and drawings! Quite amazing.

As he continued to sit and ponder, he noticed that there were no modern traffic noises or pollution, just the occasional splash of a duck in the millpond or the distant warble of local songbirds. A peaceful and serene part of the world. Flatford is certainly a wonderful place, he thought, for walkers, nature lovers and of course, landscape art historians. Ian smiled, it was certainly a completely different world to the contrasting concrete jungle of skyscraper buildings and the many billionaires living in Monaco!

Ian looked at his watch. Despite the idyllic and peaceful moment he decided it was time to leave. Back to the real world. The world of hustle and bustle, commuting and the buying and selling of works of art. The complex world that the likes of Constable or Willy Lott could never have imagined. Back to decisions about the future, his future, his and Emma's future. Was he, or indeed how was he, going to take advantage of what Andrei had described as … 'your new opportunity'? This, he decided, would have to be his next challenge.

Ian arrived back home just after 3 pm. The house was quiet and Emma had left a note to say she would probably be home about seven o'clock. She also suggested that Ian took the casserole out of the freezer for tonight's meal.

After unpacking his overnight bag, Ian took his laptop into the home office and switched it on. Whilst he waited for it to warm up, he went into the kitchen and made himself a cup of coffee. He removed the casserole from the freezer and set it aside for heating up later. When he returned to his computer it was ready to be used. He checked his email inbox and replied to some queries from Penny. He sipped his coffee and then set about drafting a detailed email to Oscar in Hong Kong, advising the full details of the two Munnings paintings owned by Bob Robins.

It was just after Ian had pressed the send button on the email to Oscar that his inbox pinged with another incoming message. This time it was from Viktor. Viktor's email outlined a serious problem he had encountered with one of the Turner paintings owned by John Baldwin. Could he speak to Ian tomorrow morning? Ian immediately wrote back. "10 o'clock, in my office."

Chapter 12

The previous afternoon, Viktor had taken the printed photographs of the Baldwin paintings and provenances home with him and studied each photograph in minute detail. This time with the added use of a magnifying glass, he was searching for any tiny bit of extra evidence that supported his new view that *Margate beach and seascape* was, possibly, a fake after all!

During his earlier investigations, Viktor had searched the internet for any information relating to these two paintings, but when he found large colour photographs of both pictures in a 1932 catalogue, he thought his earlier suspicions might just have been confirmed. The catalogue photograph of *Margate at early dawn* looked exactly like his own photograph, but with *Margate beach and seascape*, there were two very small and subtle differences! Viktor used his home printer to print copies of the two catalogue pictures. He then compared them with his Baldwin photographs. It was only by putting the two separate photographs next to each other, that he was really able to notice the differences.

Next morning Viktor arrived at Ian's outer office at 9.45. Penny was sitting at her desk and she looked up when he entered the room. "Good morning, Sherlock. I gather you have found some interesting new information," greeted

Penny, sitting back in her chair. "Ian's on the telephone at the moment."

"Good morning to you too. Yes, I think maybe one of Baldwin's paintings could well be a fake after all. I need to chat this through with Ian as the last thing I want to do is upset Michael Hopkins," replied Viktor, sitting on the edge of Penny's desk. "It would be useful if you came into the meeting with me when I discuss this all with Ian."

"So, you want your hand holding do you?" teased Penny, laughing at what she'd just said.

"It would be very useful for you to hear my findings too. I would really appreciate your thoughts as well."

"Well thank you kind sir... Ah, Ian's finished with his call. Shall we go through?"

Viktor followed Penny into Ian's office, where Ian was sitting behind his desk, but looking out of the window and obviously in thought. When he heard them come in, he swivelled around and said to Penny, "Can you remind me to talk to you about Munnings later. Now then Viktor, what's this mystery you've unravelled?"

Penny and Viktor had already sat down and Viktor removed, from his folder, the printed photographs he had taken at the Baldwin's home. He firstly began to explain the details of his meeting with Mr and Mrs Baldwin and his subsequent discussions with Penny. Ian asked some questions which Viktor answered.

"When I started my investigations," Viktor continued, "I felt that there was something about one of the paintings that was just not right. I had intended to look into the conflicting provenance comments about the Mrs Booth connection first, but instead tried to find out as much information as I could about the two paintings. I told Penny that I thought something was not quite right." Penny nodded and Viktor continued, "The more I investigated the more I was convinced that the *Margate beach and seascape* painting was a fake. I subsequently found two large colour photographs of both paintings, firstly on the internet in a 1932 Turner catalogue and then we had a copy of that same catalogue in Sotheby's library. When I put my photographs next to the ones in the catalogue the two *Margate at early dawn* matched exactly, but with the *Margate beach and seascape*, I began to spot some small and very subtle differences! Only by putting the two photographs next to each other, was I really able to spot these differences. Both pictures have a small boat on the horizon, but one boat is slightly larger than the other. Also, the angle of the same boat is different. Finally, I noticed that there are several groups of small rocks on the beach and one group is not quite in the same position."

Viktor put his Baldwin photograph and the one he had subsequently printed from the internet side by side and passed them over for Ian to inspect. Penny got up from her seat and moved to her boss' side to view the same pictures. Ian lifted a plastic ruler out of his top drawer. He measured the length of the two boats and sure enough one was three millimetres longer than the other. He then checked the ratios against other objects and they proved to be similar. Penny pointed to the obvious slight difference in the angle of the boat and the small cluster of rocks.

"Well done, Vic," said Ian, putting his ruler back into the desk drawer. "Okay, so we have a problem. My first question is, which is the correct Turner? Baldwin's or the catalogue's? Probably the catalogue, but we cannot be absolutely certain."

Penny sat back down again on her seat and said, "If Baldwin's painting is a fake, or a very good copy, that puts a question mark against Baldwin's provenances. Maybe one of the family sold the original painting and had a copy made to replace it? What does the catalogue say about the ownership of its picture?"

"It doesn't," replied Viktor. "It only includes the photograph and the title… and, of course, that it was painted by Turner."

"Okay," interrupted Ian. "We can easily find out if Baldwin's is the fake by continuing with the forensic investigation exercise as soon as possible. Let's just keep this information to ourselves for the time being. No point in worrying Michael, or the Baldwins, for the moment. At least not until we know all the facts."

"I will telephone John Baldwin this morning and see when we can collect the paintings," said Viktor. He was relieved that Ian was fully aware of the situation and the responsibility was not just resting on his shoulders.

"I will telephone my cousin and see when we can get Tate Britain to carry out the forensic paint sampling work," suggested Penny.

"Okay," replied Ian. "Excellent job, Vic. I can contact the London Courtauld Institute to arrange the x-rays, but let's get the Tate to do their work first. Wouldn't it be interesting if the Baldwin picture was the real painting and the one in the catalogue was the fake?! Wouldn't that put the cat amongst the pigeons?!"

All three smiled.

When Penny and Viktor rose from their chairs to leave, Ian called Penny. "Penny, can you hang on, I want to speak to you about some Munnings paintings."

Penny sat down again. Viktor left the room blowing a huge sigh of relief as he went.

"As you know," said Ian, "I was in Dedham the last two days. Whilst I was there, I had a long chat with the head trustee of the Munnings Museum, David Wardley. He's a very interesting and knowledgeable man when it comes to Munnings the person and his career. The museum has a large collection of Munnings' work and not all of it is on display. David did mention to me that occasionally, depending on demand, they run a two-day in-depth course and they have one lined up for the week after next. I thought you might like to attend the course and learn a bit more about Munnings and his life and work. If you think it is worthwhile then we can send Vic on the next one. He's got too much on his plate at the moment to go this time."

Penny was pleased but a little surprised. "It sounds very interesting. Which days are they?"

"Thursday and Friday. Is that alright?"

"Yes, I think so. Yes, I'm certain it is. Thank you."

"Good. You might want to stay over on Friday night as well. We'll pay for the accommodation. You can use your time on Saturday looking around Dedham and Flatford. You will pick up a lot of information about John Constable there too."

"I've never been to Dedham, so it should be a very interesting stay."

"I'll email David and tell him that you'll be joining them on Thursday morning. Book yourself in at the Rising Sun for three nights to include Wednesday night."

"Thank you, Ian. Vic might just be a tad jealous."

"If you think the course is worth it, then his turn will come."

After Penny left Ian's office, Ian emailed a brief note to David Wardley telling him that Penny would be joining them on the two-day course. Later that afternoon a member of David's team emailed back enclosing the joining instructions and a summary of the course programme.

When Viktor arrived back at his desk, he telephoned John Baldwin and it was agreed that Viktor would collect both of the Turner paintings in two days' time.

After Penny's meeting with Ian, she booked herself three nights' accommodation at the Rising Sun and then telephoned Susan, her cousin, at Tate Britain. An appointment was set for seven days' time for the forensic investigation. She then emailed Viktor and Ian to confirm the appointment had been made.

Viktor read Penny's message and whispered under his breath… 'Yes!' However, for the next few days he also made deliberate detours avoiding the possibility of bumping into Michael Hopkins. If anyone should speak to him at the moment, it should be Ian. All Viktor wanted to focus on was establishing if either of the two Baldwin paintings were genuine works by Turner. He was now fearing that not one, but both, might just be fakes!

The previous evening Emma didn't get the chance to discuss with Ian her new thoughts about the Monaco apartment. She had been delayed at work and then a serious motor accident on the M25 had meant that her and Ian's evening was completely disrupted. She decided that an extra 24 hours would not make a great deal of difference. Tonight she was home earlier than Ian and was certainly more prepared for the discussion that started soon after they had finished their meal.

Now sitting relaxed in the lounge with their cups of coffee, Emma opened the conversation. "Ian. I think I would like to go back to the apartment in Monaco soon, but only for a weekend, or maybe three days. I've been thinking a lot about it lately and… well… it might work as a holiday break just now and then."

"Right," said Ian, suddenly attentive and very surprised. "Why have you changed your mind?"

"It's a lovely apartment and a fabulous setting and if we just treat it as… well… just a treat, a sort of holiday home, then it might just work. I'm willing to give it a go."

"Okay." Ian sat up and looked at Emma. "When should we go?"

"I've got an opportunity in two weeks' time from the 25th, so how does that fit in with your diary?"

"I'm not sure. I will need to check it out but I cannot think of anything at the moment that is more important. If I have forgotten something, I'm sure I can change it or get Penny to attend in my place. Do you want me to book the flight tickets?"

Emma was quiet for a few seconds before she announced. "I think that would be a lovely idea."

Chapter 13

Viktor met up once again with John and Anne Baldwin as arranged. He cautiously removed the two paintings from the hooks in the dining room and carefully packed them using polythene bubble wrap, thick cardboard sheets, strong tape and a wooden frame. He carefully placed his parcels into the boot of his car and walked back to their front door where Mr and Mrs Baldwin were standing watching him. Their faces were full of apprehension and a little sadness. Come on, thought Viktor, this was not their children going off to university for the first time. Get real!

"Please don't worry," said Viktor trying to change their mood. "The paintings are in good hands and will be properly looked after. You will soon get them back, undamaged, I promise!"

Anne Baldwin smiled at Viktor, but John's expression did not change.

"Better get back before the rush hour," said Viktor, trying to sneak away.

"Please keep us informed," said John, with just a hint of emotion in his voice.

"Of course," replied Viktor. "I will let you know as soon as we have any news." He was anxious to pick his words carefully.

Viktor said his goodbyes and got into his car. He wanted to drive off quickly before the Baldwins changed their minds, but decided just to cruise slowly down the driveway. In his rear view mirror he saw only Anne Baldwin waving. John had disappeared indoors. Viktor waved back and then turned out of their driveway and into the narrow lane. Once out of view he accelerated away, back in the direction of London.

He arrived safely at the rear of Tate Britain after following Susan's precise instructions. He parked the car and immediately telephoned her number. Within two minutes Susan and a male colleague joined him in the car park. Viktor was surprised when he saw the lady, probably in her late 30s, emerging from the building. He had assumed that being Penny's cousin, she would have been much closer to Penny's age. They exchanged greetings and Viktor opened the boot of his car. The male colleague picked up both paintings as though they were of no weight at all and disappeared back towards the building.

After a brief chat Susan then said, "It should be two days. I will telephone you with the results."

"Thank you," replied Viktor. He was already fairly sure that one painting was likely to be confirmed as a fake, but he was now wondering if the experts back in 1956 had been correct after all. Were both paintings going to be confirmed as fakes? Was he indeed, just wasting everybody's time?

It was a week after the meeting with Bob Robins that David Wardley telephoned Ian. David explained that Bob had discussed the pictures with his children and it was generally agreed to try and sell *The Winter bonfire gathering*.

"Does he want to sell by auction or by private sale?" asked Ian.

"He recognises that he might get a better price by auction,

but if you could achieve £5 million privately, he would take that level of offer," replied David. He had already agreed in his own mind that if Ian could achieve that price then he would recommend the sale to his friend.

"I think I might have a possible buyer, but there is another agent involved so there would be extra commission to pay. Would Bob be happy with that?"

"I've not discussed the finer sale details with Bob, but as long as he gets around the £5 million net of all costs, I'm sure he would be happy."

"Okay, I understand," replied Ian. He mentally calculated what sort of gross price he should be putting to Oscar. "I'll let you know as soon as I have any feedback or do you want me to speak to Bob directly?"

"I think you should go back to Bob directly, Ian. I'm really only a colleague of Bob's, not his agent or advisor."

"Okay, David. Leave it with me."

After Ian had replaced the telephone receiver, he typed an email to Oscar explaining the details of the painting and where to find a photograph of the painting on the internet. In the final paragraph he suggested that an offer in the region of £6 million would probably be accepted.

Viktor was still anxiously awaiting the results of the forensic testing on the Turner paintings. Susan had said she would send him the results within two days. It was now the third day since Viktor had delivered the pictures to Tate Britain. Not knowing the results was frustrating. He wanted to telephone and chase the answer, but he also thought that there must be a good reason for the delay and he would only be told they would get back to him when they were ready! Patience was not one of Viktor's strengths.

He decided to ring Penny to see whether she had heard anything from her cousin. Penny, however, was not answering her telephone, so that increased his frustrations further.

He decided to calm down by going to collect a cup of coffee from the drinks machine. When he returned to his desk there was a red light flashing on his telephone indicating a message. He quickly put down his coffee, snatched the receiver and pressed the 'retrieve message' button. It was a female voice and the message simply said, "Viktor, Susan Heslop, Tate Britain. Will you ring me and we can discuss the Turner results?"

Viktor switched off the message and immediately dialled Susan's number. It rang three times before it was answered. "Hello, Susan Heslop speaking."

"Hi Susan, Vic Kuznetsov from Sotheby's, returning your call."

"I presume you want to know the results," teased Susan.

"Yes, please." Viktor was trying his best not to signal his exasperation.

"Firstly the *Margate at early dawn* painting. We were able to take very small fragments of paint and compare its chemical composition with our records of similar paintings accepted to have been painted by Turner about the same time. The good news is that they largely match. We can therefore safely say that your painting was probably painted about 1841."

"So, does that mean it was painted by Turner?"

"I'm sorry, Viktor, but we cannot absolutely say that. All we can say is that the paint used does tie up with similar paints used in Turner's work about 1841."

"Oh," said Viktor. Just a small word but it did convey his big disappointment.

"Now *Margate beach and seascape*," continued Susan. "I'm sorry to say that this painting is a good copy and it was not painted by Turner. Fragments of paint examined from this painting put the picture at the mid-20th century, certainly not 1841. Sorry."

"Mmm, well you have only confirmed my thinking, so I'm not surprised. Thank you for your help. When can I come and collect the pictures?"

"I will put our two reports in writing for you. They should be ready by Friday, so if you call in then you can collect the paintings and the reports at the same time."

"Okay. Thank you," replied Viktor. They both said their goodbyes and Viktor switched off his call. He sat back and thought about Susan's comments. He was disappointed but not surprised. The good news was that *Margate at early dawn* might not be a fake after all, but the bad news is that it would definitely not be accepted as a genuine Turner, just on this evidence. A lot more investigation is certainly still required! As for the *Margate beach and seascape* picture, how was he going to tell the Baldwins that their painting is definitely a fake?

Viktor now decided that he needed to explore the provenances and to see what surprises they were going to produce. Firstly, however, he put a short email together for Ian and Penny which summarised Susan's reports. He concluded by saying that all was not lost with *Margate at early dawn* and he was now going to investigate the provenances. Until he had a better idea of these then there was little point in pursuing any further technical investigations.

Next morning Ian had only been seated at his desk for a few moments when his telephone rang.

"Hi, Ian." Ian recognised Oscar's voice immediately. "Received your email about the Munnings painting. Thanks. I have spoken with May Ling, who says she has spoken with her client. In summary, the client is interested in the painting, but not at £6 million. He would, subject to the usual satisfactory viewing, be prepared to offer about £4.5 million. How flexible do you think your seller would be?"

"Ideally he is looking for a net amount of £5 million, after costs. I can go back to him and inform him of the £4.5 million offer but I'm fairly certain he will not sell unless he can get in excess of £4.5 million net of costs. The alternative is for him to go down the auction route."

"Okay, Ian, I will pass on this message. How's things generally?"

"Fairly good thanks, Oscar, and you?"

"I'm thinking of taking a few days off for a holiday. Three of the guys here in Hong Kong are chartering a boat for the annual fishing trip around the Fijian islands. I think I might join them this time. What about you? Do you fancy joining us? It's been a while since you last came with us on our fishing trips."

"Not this time, Oscar. Thanks." Ian smiled at the thought. At one time he would have jumped at the opportunity. Nowadays he has more responsibilities to consider. "Emma and I have a break lined up in Monaco next week."

"Okay. Have a good time. I will get back to you when I have spoken with May Ling. Cheers."

"Bye, Oscar. Thanks for the call." Ian put his phone down and switched on his computer. He looked through the new emails in his inbox. Most were business related until he came to the one sent from Marie in Monaco. He clicked it open and read the contents:

Hello Ian,

I hope you and Emma are well. I am fine.

I received a brief email from Andrei a week ago. He said he had left Mexico and had flown north (not sure where to). He planned to stay there for about 3 months. No mention of an invitation for me to join him!

Have you any plans to come to Monaco soon? It would be lovely to meet up with you and Emma again. You would be most welcome to come to dinner and meet some of my friends.

Kindest regards,
Marie xx

Well, thought Ian. What do I do about that!? He pondered the options of telling Emma or not. If he didn't and they all bumped into each other in Monaco, it could all be very embarrassing. But if he did tell Emma, he was sure she would not want to meet up with Marie, especially after Emma's reaction when he had told her of their chance meeting the last time Ian was there. Mmm, tricky!

Ian's thoughts were broken when Penny appeared at the door. "Good morning, Ian."

"Ah, hello, Penny. Good morning."

"I'm leaving at lunchtime to travel up to Dedham. Is there anything you want me to do before I leave?" Penny walked further into Ian's office.

"Come and sit down for a minute would you." Penny duly sat down on her usual seat on the opposite side of Ian's desk. Ian continued. "Have you seen Vic's email about the Turner paintings?"

"Yes. Are you going to speak to Michael Hopkins?"

"No, not at the moment. If he asks, I'll just say that investigations are progressing. Hopefully Vic may have some more news in the next couple of days. What do you think?"

"Me? Difficult isn't it? I think we are now sure one of the paintings is definitely a fake, but there's not enough evidence yet to be able to challenge the current expert opinion on the other one. I think we ought to wait until we have more definite news on the second picture."

Ian nodded his head. "I'm trying to let Vic follow this one through on his own. All good experiences, but if you think he may need some help, can you let me know?"

"Of course. I'm still working a little bit with him on it anyway."

"Good. Right, one other thing. Emma and I are having a few days holiday next week so you will be on your own from Monday. I should be back on Wednesday. But if there is anything urgent, I can be contacted via my usual email address or on my mobile."

"Okay. Going anywhere nice?"

"Yes, we are flying out on Saturday to spend a few days in Monaco again."

"How lovely. I hope you both have a wonderful time."

"Thank you. I also hope you have an interesting time in Dedham. Did you book in at the Rising Sun?"

"Yes, for the three nights as you suggested. I hope that's okay?"

"Yes, yes. No problem there. I look forward to hearing your comments about the course. We can talk about it when I get back from Monaco."

Chapter 14

It was early Friday afternoon when Ian and Emma's flight landed at Nice airport. Once they had collected their suitcases and emerged from the terminal, they looked for the taxi queue. Fortunately, it was quite short and within a handful of minutes they were being whisked off towards the Principality of Monaco.

Emma was quiet and stared out of the window at the passing buildings and the countryside. She was still not totally convinced that she had made the right decision. Even more so after Ian had informed her about the contents of Marie's email. However, after she and Ian had discussed all the options, it was agreed that Ian would invite Marie to Andrei's... correction... *their* apartment, for dinner. Ian duly replied, inviting Marie to join them on Saturday evening. He did however, jokingly, warn Marie that the meal would not be anything like the standard previously produced by Andrei's part-time chef, Claude. Marie immediately responded to say that she was very pleased to hear from Ian again and was really looking forward to meeting both him and Emma on Saturday evening.

The taxi continued its journey. Ian was also quiet and looked out of his side window. He was pleased to be back, excited but also a little nervous to be revisiting the apartment once again. He was happy that Emma had finally seen the positives of the short break, but he was even more surprised when she suggested the meal with Marie... but only on their own territory! He just hoped that the few days break would all work out nicely for everyone and this sort of trip could eventually turn into a more regular occurrence.

Once the taxi had passed through the usual security procedures and delivered them to the apartments' reception area, Ian paid the fare including a tip. He collected both their suitcases, which fortunately were on wheels, and they entered the building.

"Welcome back to Harbour Heights, Mr and Mrs Caxton. The Penthouse Suite apartment has been prepared for you and here is your post," said the young lady with a nice smile. As she handed over a number of letters to Ian she asked, "Do you require any assistance with your baggage?"

"Thank you," replied Ian, taking the letters and passing them on to Emma. "We are fine with our own luggage."

"I hope you have a most enjoyable stay."

Emma smiled at the receptionist and they both headed towards the elevator, Ian pulling the two suitcases. Seconds later the door opened and it was Louise's turn to welcome them back.

"Hello, Louise, how are you?" asked Ian, pulling the cases through the door.

"I am fine, thank you, Mr Caxton." Louise pressed the button for the Penthouse Suite. "Welcome back Mrs Caxton."

"Thank you," said Emma as the elevator quietly accelerated upwards.

Within just a few seconds the elevator had stopped, there was the usual arrival 'ping' and the doors opened. Ian and Emma stepped out into the short corridor and walked the few steps to the front door. Ian heard the elevator doors close behind him. He put his left hand on the metal plate next to the door. Emma was surprised when, after only about two seconds, the door clicked and moved slowly ajar. Ian stood forward and pushed it further open.

"How did you do that?" asked Emma, as she watched Ian enter the apartment.

"It's all part of the security. We will have to speak to the security team tomorrow and get them to arrange for your hand profile to be able to open and close the door as well."

Ian pulled the suitcases into the apartment and Emma followed nervously. Once she had stepped into the main entrance area, she put down the letters on a small table next to a telephone unit. She just stared around the space and remembered most of the area's details from her only previous visit.

"It's still very impressive, Ian. A little less personal than last time, but very tidy. Did you leave it like this?"

"No. Andrei had arrangements so that when he was away the apartment was thoroughly cleaned and ready for his arrival back. We seem to have picked up this benefit too."

"That's nice. Can we have the same in England?" said Emma, slowly walking towards the kitchen area, noting how pristine all the surfaces were.

Ian decided to ignore Emma's comment. "It does feel very welcoming."

He pulled the suitcases towards the guest bedroom, but then stopped and asked Emma. "Where do you think we should sleep? I slept in the guest bedroom last time. It just felt odd to move into Andrei's room."

"Let's have a look." Emma walked towards Andrei's old bedroom but stopped at the door. "Have you been in here?"

"Yes. I went into every room when Bates, one of the security men, was here with me. I wasn't sure what I would find. But there is no evidence now of Andrei's presence at all," said Ian, walking across to join her.

Emma hesitantly pushed the door open and walked in. Ian followed her. It was a large room with cream painted walls and two pictures. There was still a hint of the aroma of paint, so Emma assumed any previous picture hooks and holes had been repaired and the walls all repainted. On one wall, opposite the huge king-size bed, was a large window with views partly down to the harbour and partly towards the Palace. The other main wall, to the right of the bed, had two internal doors. When Emma investigated and pushed through the first door, she walked into an enormous en-suite bathroom which had a double shower and huge corner bath. The second door led her into the largest walk-in wardrobe she had ever seen. "Wow," she said. "At least I've got somewhere to hang my clothes!"

"So, you are moving in now, are you?"

"I think we should use this bedroom, Ian. It's sheer opulence! Andrei said 'Use the apartment as you see fit.' I think we should take him at his word."

Ian went back to the entrance to the guest bedroom and pulled the suitcases into their new bedroom. There he found Emma lying on the bed.

Two hours later, they had unpacked and Emma was trying out the shower. Ian, meanwhile, was in the kitchen searching for the teabags he had left from his last visit. After filling the kettle and setting it to boil, he realised that they didn't have any milk. However, when he opened the fridge door, more in hope than expectation, there was a two-litre carton of fresh milk. In addition, there were three bottles of champagne and three bottles of chardonnay!

Wow, thought Ian, how did they know we were coming? When he then looked in all the other cupboards he also found three bottles of pinot noir. Mmm. Andrei certainly had his priorities right!

Ian made two mugs of tea and carried them on a tray

towards the balcony. He sat the tray down on a nearby coffee table and opened the large glass door leading out onto the balcony. When he turned around, he found that Emma had joined him and she had picked up the tray. They both stepped out onto the balcony and sat next to the small table. They were both temporarily quiet and just stared at the wonderful view. The sun was hot and strong and they both shielded their eyes with their hands. They stared down to the harbour area and out to the Mediterranean Sea in the distance.

"It is just as fabulous as I remember it," said Emma. "Why would Andrei want to leave such a fabulous spot?"

"He obviously had his reasons. His loss is our gain!" said Ian, lifting his mug of tea and toasting his absent friend. "Cheers Andrei… and thank you. You are still amazing my friend, truly amazing!" Ian smiled at the thought of his friend. He realised, again, how much he missed Andrei's presence and the excitement he brought to his life. How was he ever going to live up to Andrei's 'opportunity'?

Emma continued to watch the activity below in the harbour. Ian could not fail to notice the lovely relaxed smile on her face.

For the rest of the afternoon, they discussed what they would cook for Marie's meal. Ian reminded Emma that he had already warned Marie that it would not be up to the high 5* standard that Claude had provided. However, they both agreed they should still try to produce a really nice and interesting meal. Maybe something that she would rarely eat in France and Monaco.

That evening they found the supermarket just behind the harbour area that Ian had used previously and a separate small vegetable store. From these two shops they managed to source all the ingredients for the next evening's meal.

After they had carried the food back to the apartment,

they returned to the harbourside to find a venue for this evening's meal. Eventually they found a small and quiet restaurant with lovely views across the harbour. As well as having a wonderful setting, it also attracted Ian and Emma as it's advertising board said it specialised in Mediterranean fish and seafood meals. When they returned to the apartment later that evening, they both agreed that the Blue Marlin had been an excellent choice and they would certainly return and eat there again.

The following morning, Ian telephoned the security team and was pleased when it was Bates who answered the call. After exchanging pleasantries Ian said he would like his wife to be able to access the apartment. Bates suggested that if Mrs Caxton came down to the security room before noon, when he would be going off duty, he would make all the necessary arrangements himself.

It was just after 10.30 later that morning when Emma and Ian arrived at the security room. Bates took Emma through the same process that he had done previously with Ian and then accompanied them back to the Penthouse Suite to check everything was working correctly. Emma stood quietly waiting for Bates' instructions.

"Will you place your hand on the panel, madam, please?" asked Bates. "Either hand should work."

Emma lifted her right hand and placed the palm onto the metal plate. After two seconds the door clicked and moved slowly ajar.

Bates pulled the door closed and they heard a click. "Place your right hand on the metal plate again and the door will then be securely locked."

Emma followed the instructions and they all heard the door click again.

"It all seems to be working okay, but let's try with the other hand, to make sure," said Bates.

This time Emma placed her left hand on the metal plate. Again, there was a brief delay of about two seconds before the familiar click and the door slowly opened.

"Good," said Bates. "It looks as though all is working fine. If there are any problems just call us on your internal phone system. Dial 124… 24 hours."

Emma and Ian both thanked Bates who then wandered back to the elevator where Louise was waiting with the doors open.

Emma, still standing in the corridor, decided to check she had got everything right. She pulled the door to its closed position and then secured the door properly again. She then changed hands, placed her hand on the plate and waited for the two seconds for the click. After two seconds the door clicked and moved slightly ajar. She smiled at Ian and pushed the door wider and re-entered the apartment.

During this exercise Ian had remained silent, but had a smile on his face. He was very happy that Emma was becoming more and more positive with their new surroundings. Softly, softly catch your monkey, he thought!!

Chapter 15

After Ian had helped Emma with the preparations for the Saturday evening meal, he left her in the kitchen. He suddenly spotted the letters on the table where Emma had left them the previous day. He walked over and picked them up. There were five letters in total, one addressed to Ian, but four addressed to Andrei. Mmm, he thought, what am I going to do with these? He eventually decided to see what Marie might suggest and put them back on the table. The letter addressed to him had a post date of two days ago and a local postmark. He ripped open the envelope and unfolded the sheet of A4 paper that was inside. The typed letter read:

Hello my friend!

I hope you and Emma are well and are enjoying your new world! I am very pleased you are taking advantage of your new apartment. I hope Emma is 'coming around'. Is that the correct English phrase?

I am thoroughly enjoying my lazy new lifestyle. Mexico was fabulous. The food was superb and I met a lovely Señorita in Guadalajara and …

Must get back to the gym to lose some of the extra pounds I have put on!

*Have you started to make use of 'my opportunity' yet? Drop
me an email from time to time.*

*Hope you have a lovely evening with Marie. She is a very
special person.*

Best wishes, my friend.

Andrei.

Ian stared at the letter and read it again. What! How on
earth did Andrei know we were in the apartment? How did
he know we were entertaining Marie? Ian thought hard and
was rather concerned. Was the apartment bugged? Were
people watching them? Were the Russian Mafia trying to
catch up with Andrei? Finally, he decided this was stupid
and he was being paranoid. Marie must have contacted
Andrei and told him of our plans to visit Monaco and
about her invitation for the meal. Nevertheless, it did feel as
though 'Big Brother' was watching! He knew Emma could
not see him from the kitchen area, so he quietly folded the
envelope and letter and put them in his back pocket. Picking
up the other letters again, he wandered back to the kitchen
and spoke to Emma. "The post we received yesterday."
Ian waved the four envelopes. "All these are addressed to
Andrei. Any suggestions on what we should do with them?"

"Are they bills?"

Ian looked at each envelope. "I'm not sure. The envelopes
all look similar. See what you think." Ian passed them over
to Emma who looked at them individually.

"They are not really any of our business, Ian. We could
ask Marie what to do or just post them on to Andrei's legal
people. The ones that did the legal paperwork for the apartment transfer, I suppose." Emma passed the letters back to
Ian.

"I don't think, on reflection, that we should involve
Marie," said Ian. He walked into their bedroom and put

the letters in one of the bedside set of drawers. He was also thinking that maybe he had already said and discussed far too much information with Marie in the past. This 'Andrei's latest letter' could well have been typed and sent by Marie! After all it was all typed, had no written signature and was posted locally. Okay, if that was the case, why? The more he thought about it the more it did not make any sense. The only sensible action now was not to tell Marie anything.

Ian telephoned reception to advise them that they were expecting a guest about seven o'clock that evening. He gave them Marie's full name and brief description. The lady on reception said thank you and confirmed that she would advise security and ring him when his guest was in the elevator.

By seven o'clock the meal was almost ready and Emma and Ian had dressed ready for their guest.

Ian poured two gin and tonics for themselves and carried the drinks over to the balcony where Emma was sitting.

"Do you know, Emma, I've been thinking," said Ian, passing over her drink.

"Well, there's a first!" teased Emma.

"Seriously. I have been thinking about Marie. We really do not know that much about her. Andrei always kept her at arms' length. I'm now concerned that I might have discussed far too much with her in the past. I think we ought to keep our discussions this evening on more general subjects."

"What's happened to make you think this way?" replied Emma, wondering if Ian knew more than he was letting on.

"Who told reception to clean and prepare the apartment and stock the fridge with milk and wine? Why is she so keen for us to keep in touch and for us to join in with her group of friends? Maybe it's all just a coincidence, but maybe it's not!"

"Are you telling me everything Ian?"

"Yes! … Look, let's chat some more after she goes. Let's just see what she has to say this evening and take it from there."

"Okay," said Emma. She was now really unsure and concerned about what Ian's real motives were. Just then the telephone rang.

Ian got up and walked back into the lounge and picked up the telephone.

Emma heard Ian say, "Thank you."

"That was reception. Marie is in the elevator."

Ian opened the front door and stepped into the corridor just as Marie was emerging from the elevator. When she saw him, Marie gave him a big smile and then a strong kiss on his cheek. "Hello Ian, so lovely to see you again, and Emma?"

"It's lovely to see you again, Marie. Come in. Emma is on the balcony."

Marie entered the apartment and immediately looked around. "It's the first time I have been back here since just before Andrei left. It's a little bare now without all the paintings."

Emma walked into the apartment from the balcony and over to Marie. They briefly kissed on both cheeks and greeted each other.

"Would you like a drink, Marie?" asked Ian. "We are drinking gin and tonics."

"A gin and tonic. Yes, that would be lovely, please, Ian."

"Come on over to the balcony," suggested Emma. "It's still lovely and warm out there. Ian will bring your drink." She was keen to get Marie into a conversation whilst Ian made the drinks.

Over dinner and during the rest of the evening, Marie did not bring up any potentially contentious issues. Ian was unusually careful not to talk about his relationship with

Andrei or the apartment and Emma decided to spend most of the evening just listening and observing. It was all a rather strange evening and it was clear that all three of them were pleased when Marie said her driver would be waiting for her downstairs to take her home. Marie thanked them for their hospitality and the lovely evening. She also suggested that they must meet up again soon. A lot of talk and little said was how Ian summarised the evening.

After Ian and Emma had tidied up and loaded the dishwasher, they sat down in the lounge area and began to relax for the first time since Marie had arrived. Ian was the first to speak. "I really did not enjoy that at all. What did you think?"

Emma sat back on the sofa, kicked off her shoes and stretched her legs so that her bare feet rested on a small grey pouffe. "I am sure that Marie is up to something. I don't know what and I don't know why. If I was going to guess, I would say she desperately wants this property! She said so when I was here last time and she hinted the same again this evening."

Ian knew better than to challenge Emma's 'female intuition' on such matters. He had listened to what Marie had said, but Emma listened to what was not said. It always baffled him!

"Do you think that is all it is? Even if we wanted to sell, she knew we couldn't... at least not until Andrei had died." There was a pause in the conversation until Ian continued. "You don't think Marie knows more about Andrei's situation than we do, do you? The whole thing is becoming more and more bizarre by the minute."

"You know, Ian, I am warming to this apartment. It is fabulous and beyond my wildest dreams. Totally unreal and mind boggling, but ... it all still makes me feel nervous. However, there is no way that this woman is going to interfere in our lives or try and pressurise us to move out or, indeed, sell it to her! If Andrei had wanted that, then that's what he would have done!"

Ian gulped and wondered what to say. Once Emma was in this frame of mind, he knew it was time to just take a back seat and wait for the right time to add any further contributions. At this precise moment he was just pleased to know that Emma was on his side! Added to that, of course... she had said it herself... 'I am warming to this apartment.' Don't rock the boat, Ian. Time for bed.

Next morning Ian was awake just before seven am. He quietly got out of bed and showered. When he returned to the bedroom, Emma was just stirring. He went through to the kitchen and made two mugs of tea, taking them both back into the bedroom. Emma was now sitting up in bed. Ian placed her mug at the side of the bed and sat down on Emma's side.

"Do you know, I've been thinking," said Ian, whilst holding on to his own mug.

"What, again?" teased Emma.

"Seriously. The situation with Marie and the apartment. What do you think we should do now?"

"I'm not sure I understand what you mean," replied Emma, who had now leaned over to pick up her drink.

"Well, do you think I should write to Andrei? I do have his email address."

"And say what exactly? I don't think this is Andrei's problem. We need to decide what we are going to do with the apartment and also avoid any further contact with Marie."

What Emma was more concerned about was that Marie could just become a serious threat to her relationship with Ian. She had watched how Marie had looked and acted towards Ian. Fortunately, Ian had seemed to think her advances were just typical French overfriendliness. Yes, we need to keep this woman well away!

Chapter 16

After leaving Emma with her cup of tea in the bedroom, Ian went to Andrei's office and switched on his laptop computer to access his emails. He immediately spotted an entry in his inbox from Oscar and started to read its contents.

Hi Ian.

I have been discussing the Munnings painting with May Ling. Her client is now offering £5.2 million, but that is the maximum he is prepared to pay (he is keen for it not to go to auction). All costs associated with the purchase will have to be borne by the seller. If this is acceptable, he will want his UK representative to fully inspect the picture before any money is transferred.

Let me know your client's answer asap.

Going fishing in 10 days' time!

Cheers buddy,

Oscar.

Ian smiled at Oscar's final few lines. He opened his mobile phone and selected the calculator app. For the next five minutes he roughly calculated the costs associated with the purchase. Finally, he concluded that the net benefit to Bob Robins would be in the region of £4.4 million.

Hopefully, he thought, that might just swing the deal. He opened his client notebook and looked for Bob Robins' details. He found both Bob's mobile telephone number and his email address. He decided to email him immediately and typed the following message:

Dear Mr Robins,

Good morning. I have just been advised by our contact in Hong Kong that a private buyer is prepared to offer you £5.2 million for the painting 'The winter bonfire gathering' by Sir Alfred J Munnings. This would net you, after all costs, approximately £4.4 million. This offer is subject to the buyer's UK representative being able to both inspect the painting and provide a satisfactory report. The buyer has stated that this offer is the maximum he would be prepared to pay.

If you decide not to accept this offer please advise me whether you would rather the painting be sold at auction.

Yours Sincerely,

Ian.

Whilst Ian was dealing with his emails, he decided to also send a catch up note to Penny and concluded by saying that he hoped she had enjoyed her course at the Munnings museum and also found 'Constable Country' and Dedham interesting.

It was just after he had pressed the send button that Emma appeared from the bedroom. She was still in her dressing gown. "Did you know there is a safe in the bottom of the wardrobe?"

"Is there?" Suddenly Ian remembered that that was where he had placed the vault key for safe keeping. "Oh yes, I remember now. I locked it the last time I was here."

"Is there anything in it?"

"Er…." Ian was careful not to drop himself into deep water. Better come clean. "Just the vault security key. I thought it would be safer to be locked in there."

"What's in the vault then?"

"Just some pictures that Andrei left. I told you about them before."

"Oh yes," said Emma, but she could not really remember if Ian had told her or not.

Ian was anxious to change the subject. "Do you fancy going for a walk? It's such a lovely day. We could walk around the harbourside and stop off for breakfast somewhere."

"Okay. Give me five minutes to get ready."

Five minutes, thought Ian, that would be a new one!

Twenty-five minutes later Emma was ready.

Back in the UK, Viktor was at home. It was Sunday afternoon, but he was still trying to establish the correct provenance for the Turner painting *Margate at early dawn*. He could not understand why the experts had decided, back in 1956, that the painting was a fake. He had read, several times, the rationale they had given, but he was sure there must be something more sinister going on. His frustrations were increased after he had read, only yesterday, an article in an art magazine written by the 'Fine Arts Expert Institute' where they suggested that more than half of all paintings in circulation today are fakes! Wonderful, he thought, that gives a great deal of confidence!

Despite all his efforts, he could not find any evidence that either proved or disproved that Mrs Booth was connected in the sequence of ownership. But, even if she was, what the hell! Surely it should just be based on the painting itself – was it painted by Turner or someone else!? He really needed to find some extra evidence that said Turner had directly employed this agent to sell the painting and the agent had directly sold it on to one of Baldwin's ancestors. What he needed was paperwork or any evidence that supported this situation.

Viktor continued to scan through the internet for any morsel of positive information. Suddenly, a different report, headed 'da Vinci seized', caught his attention. It was a translation from an Italian newspaper which stated:

A hugely valuable painting, believed to be the work of Leonardo da Vinci, has been seized from a Swiss bank in the southern canton of Ticino on the orders of the Italian police. The police had suspected the painting had been moved out of Italy illegally. On Tuesday, Italian prosecutors said that a portrait painting of the Renaissance noblewoman, Isabella d'Este, had been taken from a vault in Lugano, near the Italian border.

At the time of the seizure, negotiations were being concluded on a private sale of the painting. It was thought that the painting was owned by an Italian family, now living in Switzerland. It was rumoured that a price had been agreed equivalent to about £100 million!

One leading Leonardo da Vinci expert stated that he believed the work was a completed oil version of the Mona Lisa, the sketch of which now hangs in the Louvre in Paris! Other experts, however, have cast doubts on whether the painting is really the work of da Vinci at all, suggesting that maybe it could have been done 'in his style' and based on the Louvre sketch. Alternatively, it might have been started by da Vinci but completed by one of his students!

Typical, thought Viktor. How am I supposed to sort out my painting if all these so-called experts cannot even agree on one da Vinci painting! He carried on reading the rest of the article, which frustrated Viktor even further:

Italy has one of the largest collections of artistic heritage in the world and is a serious target for art thieves and traffickers. In January alone, police seized over 5,000 ancient works of art after dismantling a Swiss- Italian trafficking ring.

Viktor sat back on the settee and laid his laptop on the seat cushion next to him. He stared out of the window, but his mind was not focusing on the view outside. He began to wonder why he had ever decided to be involved in such a corrupt and maybe dangerous career. He knew his father, and especially Andrei, had seriously profited from this world, but was this really what HE wanted?

He closed down his computer and decided to go out for a walk.

Penny, meanwhile, on the same Sunday afternoon, was travelling back towards London along the A12 in her rental car. After leaving Dedham yesterday afternoon, she had called on an old university friend, Amy, who was living in Witham. Amy had persuaded Penny to stay the night and they spent most of the evening drinking and reminiscing about their university days. Now Penny was back on the road and on her way home. Living in London, she did not need to use a car very often, so this trip was also a novelty from a driving point of view. As she proceeded, she reflected on her three days in Dedham. The Munnings art course had been a fascinating insight into the man and his work and, as a result, she now had gained a much better understanding of his paintings. She particularly noted the gradual changes in his style as he grew older and wealthier. However, she was staggered to find out that in his twenties, Munnings had been accidentally blinded in one eye and therefore she was doubly impressed by the quality of his subsequent work, despite this impediment.

Penny especially enjoyed the visit to Munnings' garden studio. Lots of his artist tools and working sketches were on display there, plus an old skeleton of a horse and many drawings of all the muscles in a horse's body. It was explained to Penny's group that Munnings had spent many, many hours trying to understand how and in what way, all the moving parts of a horse worked and were joined together. Without this understanding and detailed knowledge, Munnings is reported to have said, he would never have been able to accurately paint and perfect such a true likeness of any horse.

The course had certainly reaffirmed Penny's appreciation of the classical style of the likes of Munnings and other similar artists such as Constable. She thought that this category of paintings was much more interesting and also demonstrated a far greater depth of the artist's talent. So much more so than the 'splashings' of modern art, which, generally, she had no time for.

The extra day in Dedham, recommended by Ian, was also a success. She had purchased, from a local shop, a map with specified walks of Dedham and the surrounding area. This map also covered Flatford and highlighted a number of the sites that Constable had used as a viewing point for his paintings.

She had also remembered to bring with her from home, a Constable book which contained many photographs of his paintings. So, after her last Full English breakfast at the Rising Sun, she spent most of Saturday morning following the map's suggested route to Flatford. She found many of Constable's viewing locations and compared them with the paintings in her book. Ian had been right, she thought, despite the nearly 200 years difference in time, she was able to identify the views and the exact spot where Constable would have sat to sketch or paint. Quite amazing that during that period very little had really changed.

After visiting the first five locations and comparing the view to the paintings in her book, Penny quickly realised that Constable was a regular user of 'artistic licence'. She joked to herself that Constable must have put St Mary's church in Dedham onto wheels and moved it around the countryside! This was because the church so often appeared in the distance of a number of his pictures purely to balance and enhance the view! She now realised that whilst Constable's paintings were generally a good representation of the landscape view at that time, they were not totally a 'photographic' record of what the artist was actually seeing!

It was just after 2pm when Penny parked her car and entered the communal ground floor area of her apartment building. After being engrossed for three days in the world of Munnings and Constable, it was now back to the real world once again. Her partner Harry was away in Paris on a work colleague's 'stag weekend' and she remembered there were still lots of clothes to be washed and ironed before Monday. A quick trip to the supermarket was certainly required and of course, Ian was also away from the office, until, what was it… Wednesday? Oh well, she thought, I guess that's the rest of Sunday taken care of!

On the Monday morning in Monaco, Ian was up early and made himself a mug of tea. Emma was still asleep, so he moved quietly around the apartment. He went over to the office and opened up his laptop. He started by checking the previous days' UK football results. The season was coming to an exciting climax and after yesterday's results, three teams could still potentially win the title with only one game still to go! After reading some of the match reports, he decided to access his emails. He was pleased to see that Bob Robins had swiftly made his decision:

Dear Ian,

Thank you for your email. I have discussed your client's offer with my wife and three children. We all agree that the offer, giving us a net sale price of £4.4 million for 'The winter bonfire gathering' painting, is accepted.

If your client's representative would contact me, we can then agree on a date and time for the required viewing and inspection.

Many thanks for your excellent services. We are all very pleased with the outcome.

Kind regards,

Bob Robins.

Excellent, thought Ian to himself. He quickly drafted an email to Oscar advising him that the gross offer of £5.2 million had been accepted by his client, as had the client being responsible for the commission and costs. He continued and suggested that the buyer should instruct his UK representative to contact Ian and he would then set up the appointment for the painting's inspection.

Next, Ian drafted a further email, this time to Penny, attaching a copy of his email to Oscar. He also told Penny the full details of the proposed Munnings sale and instructed her to inform the rest of the Sotheby's team first thing Tuesday morning. He would advise her in due course the contact details of the buyer's agent when he knew who they were.

After sending these two emails, Ian finished drinking his tea and went back to the kitchen area to brew a new cup. Whilst he waited for the kettle to boil, he reflected on a good morning's work. Also, he thought, it had all been achieved from the apartment… in Monaco! Such was the modern world of technology and business. Not that many years ago all similar communications would have been done by telephone, fax or post. Now it was so much easier and very much quicker. But, what about in five or even ten years' time, he wondered? How will communications have developed in just that short period of time?

"Are you making me a cup of tea?" It was Emma calling from the bedroom doorway.

"Just coming," replied Ian. He walked over to the cupboard to collect another cup.

"I'm just going to have a shower." Emma had already disappeared back into the bedroom and was heading for the en-suite bathroom.

On Tuesday morning, Viktor telephoned John Baldwin and suggested that they should meet so that he could update him and his wife with his findings. It was agreed that Viktor would call at their house again at 11 o'clock, the next day.

At approximately the same time as Viktor was making his phone call, in Monaco, Ian and Emma were climbing into their taxi for their return journey to Nice airport. Ian was thoroughly pleased with the overall outcome of the trip to the apartment. Whilst Emma had not yet said so, he felt she had probably enjoyed the trip as well. Possibly better than she had anticipated? Hopefully. However, he didn't want to push his luck, but he now hoped that this trip would be the start of more regular visits. After all, a lot of his work could easily be done from the apartment. A bigger challenge, however, was to convince Emma that she too could do some of her own accountancy work from Monaco. Yes, with proper planning and good organisation, he was convinced that they could both carry on working from the apartment without too many problems.

Emma continued to look out of the passenger window as the taxi left Monaco and re-entered France. She was pleased that her fears about returning to the apartment had been unfounded. She was also content now that she had been able to persuade Ian that Marie was probably someone not to be trusted. They had agreed not to keep in contact with her anymore. Emma definitely thought Marie was a threat to her and Ian's future together. Even more so now that she had discovered, that very morning, that she was probably pregnant! One of her first jobs when she got back to the UK was to make an appointment with her doctor. In the meantime, she decided not to tell Ian, not just yet. Afterall, she thought, until she had a more positive answer, it could still be a false alarm!

Chapter 17

In a small apartment, very close to the Harbour Heights building in Monaco, a man was in the process of composing an email to his boss:

Dear Mr Sokolov,
  They have now left the apartment. They have enjoyed their stay, although the dinner meeting with Marie was a strained affair. Mrs Caxton does not trust Marie and they are unlikely to communicate with Marie again. You might have to think about a new contact.
  Mr Caxton already suspects all is not right and that somebody may be watching their activities.
  Julian.

Julian, previously Andrei's driver and assistant, was now employed to organise both Andrei's continuing travel arrangements and to watch over the apartment and also to report on Ian and Emma's activities when they were in residence. He was also expected to keep in contact with Marie and pass on to his boss any new information.

Five minutes later Julian's computer made a 'ping' sound and he accessed his email inbox. The incoming email was from Mr Sokolov:

Julian.
> *Thank you.*
> *Suggest you replace Marie's activities and offer your own services to the Caxtons.*
> *Sokolov.*

Julian smiled at Andrei's reply. He would email Ian Caxton later that week.

On the aeroplane back to the UK, Ian began to think about Andrei again. He had still not resolved in his mind the issue of receiving the strange letter from supposedly Andrei. If Andrei was now in Canada, the USA or wherever, how could he have posted a local letter just a day before their arrival in Monaco? How did Andrei also know we were in the apartment? How did he know they were entertaining Marie? How did the apartment management know he and Emma would be visiting when they did? So many questions. It all still felt very sinister… and needed to be resolved … and quick!

He decided not to discuss these concerns with Emma unless absolutely necessary. He certainly did not want to sow any potential seeds of doubt into Emma's mind, especially after she now appeared to have overcome her initial worries of returning to the apartment.

Back at Sotheby's, Penny was holding the fort in Ian's absence. She had liaised with a number of colleagues in the office, putting them on warning about the Munnings painting sale. Now everyone was just waiting for Ian to advise details of the buyer's UK representative so that all the final tasks could be completed.

In Ian's absence from the office, Viktor had been discussing the issues surrounding the two Turner paintings with

Penny and, in particular, what he was going to say to the Baldwins. He told her that he was worried about potentially upsetting Mr Hopkins and that ideally he would have preferred to discuss the situation with Ian first. Nevertheless, as he also had a high regard for Penny's opinions, he decided to broach his concerns with her instead. After a good deal of discussion, Viktor finally decided to follow Penny's suggestions. He walked away from the meeting in a happier and more positive frame of mind.

On Wednesday morning, Ian arrived at his desk with a spring in his step. The Munnings sale was progressing and he was also happy that Emma was a lot more positive about the apartment. On the aeroplane she had even made two suggestions as to how they could improve the internal layout. Things were on the up.

It was just a couple of minutes later that Penny arrived at her desk and, hearing Ian moving around in his office, she immediately joined him.

"Did you have a nice time in Monaco?" Penny asked, as she walked towards Ian's desk.

"Hello, Penny. Good morning. Yes, thanks," replied Ian. "It was a lovely break. Emma enjoyed it too."

"And yet, you still managed to find time to get an agreement for the Munnings painting. Have you heard anymore as to who the UK representative is going to be?"

"No, not yet. I'm hoping Oscar will get back to me sometime today. Anyway, how have you been whilst I've been away and how did the Munnings course go?"

Penny sat down on her usual seat and gave Ian a brief summary of the course and her tour of 'Constable Country'. She concluded by saying that the course was extremely useful and informative and she would certainly recommend it for Viktor. She then told Ian about the discussion she'd had with Viktor and her suggestions about the Turner paintings.

She also outlined the strategy Viktor was going to employ in his meeting with the Baldwins, later that morning.

"Sounds as though you didn't need me anyway," replied Ian, pleased that Penny and Viktor were working well together and making good business decisions.

"We'll see when Viktor gets back," replied Penny, hoping Ian's optimism would be justified!

Viktor pulled up outside the Baldwin's house at just after 10.45 am. He double checked he had all his paperwork and notes and then took a deep breath. He got out of his car, walked around to the back and opened the boot lid. He picked up the wrapped painting of *Margate beach and seascape*. After closing the lid, he walked up to the front door and rang the doorbell.

It was Mrs Baldwin who opened the door and after both people exchanged greetings, Viktor was invited into the lounge. Mr Baldwin rose to his feet from the settee, shook Viktor's hand and invited him to sit down on the chair opposite. Mrs Baldwin joined them, sitting down next to her husband on the settee. They both looked at Viktor.

After Viktor had sat down, he put the painting at his side and removed his notes from the file. He then started to speak. "We have had some initial forensic investigative work done on the two paintings using the experts at Tate Britain. They were able to take very small fragments of paint from both your paintings and compared the chemical compositions with their records of similar paintings accepted to have been painted by Turner about the same time. With *Margate at early dawn*, the good news is that they largely match. Tate Britain has therefore confirmed that it is likely that this painting was probably completed about 1841."

"Well, that's good news then isn't it, John?" said Mrs Baldwin, looking at her husband.

Mr Baldwin was not moved by this positive news. "I've got a feeling that Mr Kuznetsov is now going to tell us there is a BUT."

"Yes, there is a but, I'm afraid. This is because, on its own, it does not prove categorically that this picture was painted by Turner. All Tate Britain will say is that the paint used does tie up with similar paint used by Turner in 1841. The picture could still have been painted by another artist about that time, maybe a pupil of Turner's, or the painting could have been started by Turner, but completed by someone else. I have also checked out the provenances you gave me and, at this stage, they do not confirm that Turner sold the picture directly to your ancestors. I have been trying to find out if the agent named in the purchase note, 'Bigby & Co.', had any direct dealings with Turner. So far, I have not been able to find any evidence that this is the case with *Margate at early dawn*. Nor, incidentally, have I found any records that suggest prior ownership by Mrs Booth, but obviously, I will continue my investigations. Until we can solve these issues, there is no point in carrying out further forensic tests at this stage. I'm sorry."

"I see," said Mr Baldwin.

"Oh dear," said Mrs Baldwin. Her earlier enthusiasm had now evaporated.

"Is there any possibility that there could be some additional paperwork anywhere in your father's files that just might produce more evidence?" Viktor knew he was clutching at straws, but wanted to get Mr Baldwin to try one further search.

"There are some boxes in the attic which have a number of old papers in them. I've been meaning to get around to sorting them out, but I'm sure they are more to do with my father's own personal files."

"Probably now would be a good time for us to go through

them, John," said Mrs Baldwin. She had been keen to get rid of all this rubbish for years and now she saw this was a good opportunity.

"Mmm," replied Mr Baldwin. "I'll have a look tomorrow." Mrs Baldwin smiled.

"Now with regards to *Margate beach and seascape*, I'm afraid that Tate Britain says this painting is a good copy. It was definitely not painted by Turner. Fragments of paint examined from this painting put the picture at the mid-20th century, certainly not 1841. I'm sorry."

"Oh dear," said Mrs Baldwin. John Baldwin's face was impassive as ever.

"I have returned the picture though." Viktor tapped the parcel at the side of his seat. "The real question is, if the provenances for this picture are true, then at some time in the mid-20th century, the original painting appears to have been swapped and replaced by this copy! Have you any thoughts or ideas as to how this could have happened?"

With this news, Mr Baldwin's expression suddenly changed to one of surprise. "Now that is very interesting. You know, I have some old black and white photographs of a 1951 Christmas lunch with a gathering of my father, mother and four others. In the background I'm sure that the *Margate beach and seascape* painting was hanging on the wall. When I inherited this picture, I remember comparing it to these photographs. The strange thing is I thought at the time that my picture had been altered. The boat on the horizon had changed slightly. I thought a minor repair must have occurred. Not really knowing about paintings, I didn't think any more about it … well, that is, until now."

Viktor smiled and explained that he had found an old 1932 art catalogue which had a photograph of *Margate beach and seascape* and, not only did he spot the boat issue, he also noticed that there appeared to be several changes to the groups of small rocks on the beach.

"Oh well," said Mrs Baldwin, "I still think it should go back on the wall. I still quite like it."

John Baldwin did not say a word.

"Of course, we still have the mystery," replied Viktor. "Which painting was shown to the experts in 1956 and what happened to the original? Was it sold, stolen, damaged? If it was stolen, then you still have legal ownership and are entitled to its return." Viktor was now trying his best to lift the Baldwin's spirits.

"I really do not know the answer to that one, young man," replied Mr Baldwin. "However, I just wonder if Uncle Tom can recall anything. He was in those photographs of the 1951 Christmas lunch. He and my father were brothers, so…"

"Uncle Tom," interrupted Mrs Baldwin, "is in a home. He's 92 and very frail. I'm not sure he's likely to help."

"He still has all his marbles!" retorted Mr Baldwin, annoyed at being interrupted. "I will go and see him tomorrow!"

Mrs Baldwin was just about to remind her husband that sorting through those boxes in the attic was already earmarked for tomorrow, but she reluctantly decided to let it pass – for the time being.

It was later that evening that Ian received the email from Oscar. He was in his home office when he heard his computer ping. Oscar's email said that the contact details for the inspection of the Munnings picture was going to be Mr Joseph Zhang, the person May Ling had previously used with the Baxter paintings. Ian smiled as he remembered Viktor's comments when he had escorted Mr Zhang to view the Baxter collection.

Ian immediately emailed Penny with these details, but decided, this time, he would personally deal with making the arrangements with Bob Robins.

Ian was just about to close down his computer when he noticed a new email had arrived in his inbox. It was from someone called Julian Jefford.

Chapter 18

Ian stared at the title of the email, 'Harbour Heights'!
What's this all about, he wondered. He opened the email
and read the contents:

> *Dear Mr Caxton,*
>
> *You probably do not remember me, but I was Mr Petrov's
> personal chauffeur in Monaco.*
>
> *Now that Mr Petrov does not need my services any more,
> I was wondering if you require a driver when you are stay-
> ing in Monaco?*
>
> *I can provide full or part-time arrangements or just a
> personal transport service to and from Nice airport.*
>
> *Yours Sincerely,*
> *Julian Jefford.*

Now that is very interesting, thought Ian. How does
Julian know my email address and about my possible future
visits to Monaco? Maybe Andrei gave him these details
when he told Julian of his long-term plans. Mmm... or
maybe Julian knows a lot more than he has said in his email!

Ian pondered on this information and then decided to
respond as follows:

Hello Julian,

Thank you for your email. Yes, I do remember you. I remember Andrei saying that he also saw you as much more than just a good chauffeur!

If you let me have your mobile telephone number, I will let you know when we are next planning a visit to Harbour Heights.

Kind regards,

Ian Caxton.

Okay, thought Ian, let's see what that achieves!

Next morning Ian telephoned Bob Robins and informed him that a Mr Joseph Zhang had been employed by the Chinese buyer to make an inspection of *The winter bonfire gathering*. Ian obtained some dates and times convenient to Mr Robins and said he would email him back when he had spoken to Mr Zhang. Ian then telephoned Mr Zhang's office and was informed that Mr Zhang was away from the office. Ian eventually spoke to Mr Zhang's PA who said Mr Zhang was free on the following Tuesday and could be in Dedham for about 4 pm. Ian confirmed that was fine and stated that he would also be at the meeting. Finally, Ian drafted an email to Bob Robins, with copies to Mr Zhang and Penny, confirming all these details.

At 11 o'clock, Viktor arrived at Ian's office, for his appointment. Penny joined them and they both sat down.

Viktor summarised the discussions he'd had with the Baldwins and outlined his plans to research further the painting's provenance.

"Well done, Vic," said Ian. "I think your approach was fine. Have you spoken to Mr Hopkins?"

"No. I wasn't sure how to approach him at this stage," replied Viktor. In reality he did not want to speak to Ian's boss until he had some better news.

"Okay. I have a meeting with him this afternoon. Do you want me to update him?"

"That would be great if you would. I would like to find out some good news first before I speak to him."

Ian and Penny both smiled.

"Give Mr Baldwin a couple of days to come back to you, but chase him up after that. He might just find some new information," suggested Ian. "By the way, if you have not already done so, speak to Penny about the Munnings course she went on. Find out when the next course is and book yourself on it."

Viktor nodded but Penny said, "We have already had a brief chat and I've got the dates of the next two courses."

"Good. Pick one of those dates, Vic and book yourself in. Also let me know if Mr. Baldwin comes back with any new information."

Earlier that morning, and just after Ian had left to go to work, Emma had telephoned her doctor's surgery and made an appointment for the following Tuesday afternoon. Since reading the positive result following her 'self-test' in Monaco, Emma was now having mixed feelings about the possibility of being pregnant. She and Ian had discussed this in the past, but had not made any definite plans. They had both agreed that it would be nice to have a child, or even children, at some stage, but as they were still both committed to their careers, it was not deemed an immediate priority. Emma did recognise, however, that her 'body clock was ticking'. Even so, it was still a difficult decision.

On the following Monday morning it was an excited Anne Baldwin who telephoned Viktor.

"We went through the boxes in the attic over the weekend and amongst a lot of rubbish we found a letter. Let me put John on the phone, he will explain better than me."

Viktor heard some mumbled conversation on the other end of the line and then Mr Baldwin spoke.

"Hello, Viktor." Viktor replied likewise before Mr Baldwin continued. "In one of the boxes of my father's papers there was a file of very old correspondence and receipts. Amongst the letters was a handwritten note dated April 1841. It's a little hard to read and torn in places but it looks like it says:

Baldwin,

Thank you for your interest in my paintings. The following works are for sale -

Three people bathing

Margate at early dawn

Line-fishing off Hastings

Margate beach and seascape

If you wish to purchase any of these paintings, contact my agent Henry Powell at Bigby & Co. He will advise the prices.

Turner.

"Oh, wow!" exclaimed Viktor. "Can you email a copy to me urgently and also take several photocopies of that letter for backup. Please take great care of the original note. It could be worth many thousands, if not millions, of pounds!"

"I will email you a scanned copy immediately. By the way, I visited my Uncle Tom and he says he remembers my father having to sell the original painting of *Margate beach and seascape* in about 1953. Something to do with paying a gambling debt! Anyway, Uncle Tom says my father got him to arrange for a local artist to paint a copy. My father was embarrassed about the debt and certainly didn't want my mother to find out! One afternoon, when my mother was out, Uncle Tom and my father swapped the frames over and

Uncle Tom remembers personally putting the copy on the wall. He also said that my mother never did notice the difference, or if she did, she never said anything. Apparently, I am the first person that Uncle Tom has ever told this story to!"

"Well, that clears up that mystery. No wonder the experts decided it was a fake three years later. They probably thought that if one was a fake then the other must be too. But who knows?" replied Viktor.

When the telephone conversation had finished, Viktor immediately telephoned Penny and told her the good news.

"Oh, that's excellent, Vic," replied Penny. "I'm really pleased for you. I'll let Ian know."

"I wonder if we've got enough proof now to overturn the 1956 decision?" wondered Viktor, excitedly. "I can't wait to see this note."

Whilst Ian was driving back up the A12 towards Dedham for his meeting with Bob Robins and Mr Zhang, Emma had just been called in to see her doctor from the waiting room. Ian was still unaware of Emma's initial test result and also her planned visit to the doctor, but at that very moment Ian's concern was with the volume of traffic in front of him. He checked his watch. It was 3.45 pm.

Five minutes later, Mrs Robins opened the front door and was surprised to see a tall, middle-aged Chinese man standing there. The Chinese man bowed and offered her his business card. Mrs Robins looked at the card and noticed the name Joseph Zhang. "Oh, hello, Mr Zhang. We are expecting you. Do come in."

Mr Zhang smiled, nodded again and brushed past Mrs Robins as she stood holding the door open for him. Mr Zhang waited in the hallway whilst Mrs Robins closed the door.

"Do go into the lounge." Mrs Robins waved her arm in the direction of the lounge.

As Mr Zhang entered the lounge, Bob Robins looked up and suddenly said, "Good God!" in surprise. He then got to his feet and walked over to shake hands. "Sorry about that. We do not get many Chinese people in Dedham!" Bob and his wife, who had now joined them, laughed briefly.

Mr Zhang shook Bob's hand, smiled and nodded.

Bob Robins was not sure what to say next. "Er. Mr Caxton has not arrived yet, but do you want to see the painting?"

Mr Zhang said his first words. "Yes, pliss, that would be kind."

"Okay, follow me. The painting is in the dining room."

"Would you like a cup of tea?" enquired Mrs Robins.

"Very kind, but thank you, no," replied Mr Zhang. He duly followed Mr Robins back through the hallway and into the dining room.

At that moment the doorbell rang and Mrs Robins went to open the door again. Bob could hear his wife talking to Ian and, a couple of seconds later, Ian walked through the dining room doorway. "I'm so sorry to be late, Bob, the traffic on the A12 was very busy."

"No problem," replied Bob. "This is Mr Zhang. Mr Zhang, please meet Ian Caxton."

The two men shook hands and Mr Zhang nodded and gave Ian one of his business cards. Ian put the card in the side pocket of his jacket and then from his top pocket, he produced his own business card and handed it to Mr Zhang. Meanwhile Mr Robins had now taken the Munnings painting off the wall and was laying it on the table. He pointed to the picture for Mr Zhang to start his investigations. Mr Zhang nodded again, which Mr Robins took to be a form of thank you.

Ian and Mr Robins stood aside whilst Mr Zhang opened

his small briefcase, pulled out various pieces of equipment and his paper notes.

Mr Robins whispered to Ian. "What's he going to do, operate on it?"

Ian smiled and whispered his reply. "Sort of, but don't worry. I don't think he's lost a patient yet!" Both men made stifled laughs.

After a few minutes, Ian stood closer to observe what Mr Zhang was doing. It was all very quiet in the dining room and the only noise was the ticking of the grandfather clock in the far corner.

Just as the clock made a single chime indicating 4.30 pm, Mr Zhang stood up straight and turned to the two other men. "It is good painting. Needs good clean but seems okay. Copies of provenances you sent me seem good too." Mr Zhang smiled and nodded again before repacking his briefcase. Bob and Ian looked at each other and smiled.

"When will your report be sent to your client?" asked Ian.

"Two days," replied Mr Zhang as he zipped up his briefcase.

"Thank you," said Ian, holding out his hand. "Very good to meet you."

Mr Zhang shook Ian's hand, smiled, nodded and then walked towards the door. Mr Robins quickly chased after him and said "Thank you," as he opened the front door. Mr Zhang smiled, nodded and exited from the building. Mr Robins closed the door and walked back into the dining room where he found Ian holding the painting up at arm's length, looking at it very closely.

"Has he damaged it?" asked Mr Robins, concerned at Ian's close inspection.

"No, no. Not that I can see. It all seems fine."

"That's good. So what's next?"

Ian put the picture back on the table. "Well, with your permission, I would like to take the painting back to our office with me this evening. There are a few checks we would like to do before the picture is sent on to China. I have brought some packing materials with me. They are in the car. I will give you a receipt, but please make sure you tell your insurers that the painting has left your house and will be kept at Sotheby's until it is sold and dispatched."

"Yes, fine, Ian. It will be a big relief to see it go. How long before we get the money?"

"That depends on how quickly Mr Zhang reports back to China, whether the buyer is totally happy with his report and of course our own checks. All being well, probably ten days, maybe two weeks. It's a bit quicker nowadays with bank transfers."

"Excellent, Ian, and thank you very much." Bob held out his hand.

Ian shook it and said, "It is a pleasure Bob, but obviously, we are not quite finished yet."

Chapter 19

It was two days later whilst Emma was driving to her last appointment of the day, that her mobile phone rang. As it was connected to her car's Bluetooth system, she only had to press the button on the steering wheel to connect and answer the call. She answered, "Hello. Emma Caxton speaking."

"Hello, Emma, this is Nurse Gibson from the surgery calling. We have received the test results back…"

"Just one minute, please, nurse, I'm driving my car. Just give me a few seconds to pull over."

Emma indicated, pulled up against the curb and parked behind a stationary white van.

"Hello, sorry about that, but I did not want to receive any shocks whilst driving."

"Well, I hope this is not a shock, but a nice surprise, Emma. We can confirm you are pregnant."

Emma was really not sure how to answer, but eventually just managed a "Thank you."

"Are you alright, Emma? Is that not the answer you were hoping for?"

"I'm not really sure, but thank you for telling me."

"Is there anything the matter?" asked the nurse. She rarely received such indifferent responses to this sort of news.

"No, I'm fine … really. It's, well, just beginning to sink in."

"Do you want to discuss this matter with me or your doctor?"

"No, no," replied Emma. "I am fine, honestly. Thank you."

"Okay. But if you do need someone to speak to, please call me, Emma. Please."

"Yes, yes, I will. Thank you again." Emma switched off the connection and just stared out of the window. Slowly tears began to trickle down her cheeks.

After five minutes Emma telephoned the client she was on the way to meet. She apologised, but said she had developed a migraine and would have to postpone their meeting. The client was understanding and suggested Emma ring back when she was feeling much better. They could then rearrange the appointment for another date.

Emma wiped her face and decided to head straight home.

It was 7.30 pm when Ian arrived home. He spotted Emma's car in the driveway and several lights were glowing in the house. After he let himself in through the front door, he called out, "Hi Emma, I'm home."

Ian changed his shoes in the hallway and when he didn't get a reply he walked into the kitchen and called again, "Emma." There was no Emma and still no answer. Ian decided she must be in the shower so he went upstairs and into their bedroom. To his astonishment, Emma was fully clothed, sobbing and curled up on the bed, clutching a soggy handkerchief.

"Emma? What's happened?" Ian sat on the bed and stroked Emma's head. "What's the matter?"

Emma did not move, but slowly said, "I'm pregnant."

"What!" cried Ian. "Wow, well that's great… isn't it?" Ian was confused.

"Do you mind?"

"Mind? What sort of question is that! Of course I don't mind. I think it's brilliant! I'm going to be a dad!"

Emma raised herself up and threw her arms around Ian. "Oh Ian, I do love you."

"I know… and I love you too. So why all the tears?"

"This baby is going to completely change our lives. Is that what you want?"

"Look, we've discussed this before. A baby will not change our lives, it will enhance it. We will have to adapt like all parents do, but… anyway, why the tears?"

"I'm not sure I want a baby."

"Wow. When did this come on? Why do you say this now?"

"It's stupid I know but I'm worried it will change you and me. I've heard about a number of families where when a baby arrives the husband and wife's relationship changes and eventually the marriage breaks down. I don't want that Ian, I love you too much."

"Hey, hey, look. The majority of families are able to overcome these hurdles and bring up lovely kids… together. My parents, your parents…"

"My parents are not a great example. Dad has a lot to put up with!"

Ian laughed. "Yes, he does, but I guess it all still works for them. Look, I know you will be a great mum and I will try my very best to be a great dad and we will both try, try and try to still be a great husband and wife for each other."

Emma was now feeling a little better. "Yes, we will! But I will need lots of reminding and reassurance."

"I can nag too, when I need to!" said Ian, noticing Emma's gradual improvement of mood.

"Swine!"

"That's better. Come on, I'm hungry and you… young

lady, you have now got to eat for two people, unless of course, it is twins!?"

"Oh my god, don't say that!"

Chapter 20

Despite John Baldwin promising Viktor that he would email a scanned copy of the Turner note to him 'immediately', it was two days later when the email had finally arrived in Viktor's inbox. He eagerly opened the attachment and looked at the copy of the well-worn handwritten note. It was exactly as Mr Baldwin had described, difficult to fully read and with a few ripped sections. Viktor made a mental note to look up the various ways Turner had signed his name to see whether there were any similarities with the signature on the Baldwin note. The rest of the note otherwise seemed plausible even if some of the letters in some of the words had faded over time. Viktor pondered. If this note could be accepted by the experts as Turner's writing, as he was hoping, along with the rest of the provenances and the forensic evidence, surely, we are almost there!

Viktor walked into Sotheby's library and then across to the Turner section. Here were stored a number of books, catalogues and some research papers, all specific to JMW Turner, his life and his paintings. Viktor searched through the research papers until he found a section on 'Turner's signature'. He was surprised that there were so many very small variations recorded. All the entries he looked at usually had the letters of JMW before the surname. On the note Viktor had received, it was just signed 'Turner'. He tried another folder of research papers. He was just about to give up when suddenly he came across a short report which stated that *Turner sometimes just signed only his surname, or the letter 'T' on some of the more informal notes and messages.* Great, said Viktor to himself. He removed his mobile phone from his pocket and photographed the relevant paragraph.

He continued through the report and whilst there were two examples of Turner's 'surname only' signature, neither of these matched the one on Baldwin's note. Oh well, sighed Viktor, a little bit more positive news. But even he had to accept that it would have been unbelievable to have found an exact match. Maybe it was time to discuss the next steps with Ian.

When Viktor returned to his desk, he telephoned Penny to ask if he could see Ian. Penny informed him that Ian had taken the day off as Emma was not feeling well.

"Okay. I'm sorry to hear that. I hope it's not serious."

"No, I don't think so, but Ian was concerned about leaving her alone. He did say if anything urgent cropped up he would take emails and telephone calls."

"No, it's not that urgent. It can wait until he comes back."

"Anything I can help with?" asked Penny. She had noted the disappointment in Viktor's voice.

"Maybe. Have you got time for a chat about Baldwin's Turner painting? I've got some extra information."

"Yes, of course. Why don't you come up? We can use Ian's room. I need to be close to his telephone in any case."

Ten minutes later Viktor and Penny were sitting in Ian's office and using the small table in the corner. Viktor explained about all the information he had now gathered together about *Margate at early dawn.*

Penny asked some questions and then she agreed that Ian needed to be aware of all these developments. She also suggested that possibly Professor Richard Jackson might be able to throw some more light on the signature issue. Viktor thought that was a brilliant idea, but then they both agreed it was probably not such a good idea to approach the professor before Viktor had spoken with Ian.

Ian, in the meantime, was at home, partly looking after Emma and partly finalising the report he had promised would be delivered to Michael Hopkins by tomorrow morning.

Emma, after a good night's sleep, was now feeling a lot better about the baby and the future. Ian had insisted, however, that she take the day off from work and he had telephoned Emma's PA to say she was suffering from a migraine and would not be in the office that day. A small 'white lie', but Ian had informed Emma that his conscience could cope with it! He wanted Emma to be in a happier frame of mind before going back to work. Emma was partly annoyed, but also very pleased with Ian's display of concern and caring.

By lunchtime Emma was beginning to enjoy her relaxing day. She was also slowly coming to terms with her pregnancy and by mid-afternoon had even decided to have a brief flick through a couple of baby clothes and products websites. This exercise, however, only served to remind her that 'people', at some stage, would need to be informed of the 'new baby'… and that, of course, included her mother! Oh lord!

In between typing the last few paragraphs of his report, Ian had earlier been popping into the lounge to check on Emma and to see if she wanted anything like tea, coffee or food. After a while, Emma, as kindly as possible, reminded Ian that she was not ill, so Ian took the hint and said that if she did need anything to just give him a shout. He had disappeared back into the home office and eventually was able to complete his report. At 4.30 pm, after fully checking through the document for the second time, he added it to a covering email and pressed the 'send' button. Within just a few seconds the email and report was delivered into Michael Hopkins' email inbox.

He now took the opportunity to check on his own email inbox. Mostly usual and routine entries, until he came across a new email from a certain Julian Jefford! Well, well, well, he thought. Now then, let's just see what he's got to say this time.

> *Good evening, Mr Caxton, and thank you for your email.*
>
> *My mobile and landline telephone numbers are at the top of this email.*
>
> *Please telephone, or email me, advising of your next flight and time of arrival and I will be waiting for you at Nice airport.*
>
> *It will be my pleasure to work with you and Mrs Caxton in the future.*
>
> *Yours Sincerely,*
>
> *Julian Jefford.*

Interesting, thought Ian. I think that has now answered a lot of my questions!

At the end of the working day, Viktor decided to send Ian a holding email about the Turner painting.

Viktor informed Ian that he had some more information and also some suggestions as to how he should proceed. However, before he did so, he would like to hear Ian's opinion first. Could Ian let him know when he would be available?

As Viktor was packing his briefcase and getting ready to go home, his computer pinged. Viktor opened up his email inbox to find that Ian had responded:

Vic,

   I am intrigued!
   2.30 in my office tomorrow afternoon.
   Ian.

Excellent thought Viktor. Now I've just got one more idea to explore this evening!

It was after a frustratingly long dinner with his parents, that Viktor was finally able to go to his bedroom and take the copy of *The Complex life of JMW Turner* by Professor Richard Jackson MBE from his bookcase. He tried to remember where in the book the information he was looking for was likely to be. He flicked through the pages until, after about five minutes, he finally spotted what he was looking for. Yes, Viktor my boy! he exclaimed, to himself. That's exactly it! Jackpot!

Chapter 21

The next day Viktor arrived at Ian's outer office at 2.20 pm. Penny was working at her desk, but when she spotted Viktor walking in, she stopped and spoke to him. "So, I gather you have come up with some more startling news for us!" teased Penny.

"Well, I think we are getting there. I am more convinced than ever that *Margate at early dawn* is not a fake. The main problem now, though, is to convince the experts, they will obviously be making the final decision. That decision could eventually be worth millions of pounds to the Baldwins!"

Ian could hear the conversation in the outer office, so he called Viktor and Penny into his office.

Penny picked up a pen and her notebook and followed Viktor into Ian's room.

"Well, Vic, your email last night was intriguing. Sit down, both of you."

After Penny and Viktor had sat down on their usual seats, Viktor summarised his latest meeting with the Baldwins, Mr Baldwin's conversation with his Uncle Tom and the newly found Turner note. He then went on to explain his latest discovery from the previous evening. "I remembered when I read Professor Jackson's book earlier that there was a photograph of a note that Turner had handwritten to the president of the Royal Academy. Turner was criticising the decision of the setting and location of his pictures for a particular exhibition. However, what I suddenly remembered was that the note in question had been handwritten by Turner! So last night I looked again at the photograph in the book and compared it to the signature on the copy of the Baldwin note, and guess what!? Both the style of the writing and the signature were almost identical!"

"Excellent work, Vic," said Ian, genuinely pleased that Viktor was now finding solid evidence to back up his earlier opinion that this particular painting was not a fake.

"That's really great news, Vic," said Penny. She too knew how many investigative hours he had spent so far, many of which were by using his own free time.

"So, what do you propose now?" asked Ian. He had his own thoughts but wanted to hear what suggestions Viktor had first.

"With your permission Ian, I would like to speak to Professor Jackson and get his thoughts on my findings. I think I would like to do that first before going back to the Baldwins," replied Viktor. He hoped Ian would agree.

"I agree. I think the eminent professor will be very interested in your findings and hopefully will be able to point you in the right direction. It's a good piece of investigation, Vic. Do you want me to ring Richard for you?"

"I think that would be a great help. As you know, I've only met him once."

"I'll give him a ring this evening. I'm sure he will say yes. By the way, take your copy of his book to the meeting. He will, I'm sure, be doubly impressed and hopefully will sign it for you at the same time."

"That would be extra special. I've thoroughly enjoyed his book. He really brings the character of Turner to life. It's also funny in places too. Nothing like most of the textbooks I've been used to," replied Viktor. He thought back to some of the books he had read for his old college courses. Excellent for putting you to sleep!

"He was like that in his lectures and seminars," replied Ian. "He has a gift for being able to engage people with whatever subject he is talking about." Ian's mind was wandering back to one particular lecture where the professor had his audience in fits of laughter. As a result, Ian could still recall most of the details of that particular lecture. Yes, definitely a gift… and a well-developed skill.

"He sounds like a really interesting man," said Penny. She was wondering whether she could accompany Viktor when he had his meeting.

Since Emma had announced her pregnancy, Ian had been trying to get home earlier in the evening. He was still concerned about Emma, but he recognised that she was slowly getting back to her old self. Emma, too, was cutting down on her working hours a little. She was feeling a lot more positive and optimistic, especially after meeting up with her elder sister for lunch two days previously. Her sister, Jane, was 'over the moon' for Emma and Ian and had made all the right comments and positive noises about the baby. She reminded Emma that when she was pregnant with her first child, she too had been worried about how things would change, not necessarily for the better. Yes, her and her husband's lives certainly had to adapt, and the addition of a second child into the family did have its challenges, but it also added a different sort of quality to their lives as well.

When Ian walked through the front door, he could immediately smell and hear that cooking was happening in the kitchen. Another positive, he thought. For the last few nights Ian had done most of the cooking. He changed his shoes and entered the kitchen where Emma was engrossed in putting together a large casserole. Once she noticed Ian, she put down her knife and walked over to give him a large kiss and cuddle.

"What's that for?" asked Ian, teasing.

"I thought you deserved it, for putting up with me!"

"I gather you are feeling a lot better now then."

"Yes, thank you. Can you give me a hand with the vegetables, please?"

Mmm, thought Ian. Yes, she does sound like she's getting back to her old self. "Can you give me five minutes? I just need to make one phone call."

Ian popped through into the home office and dialled Professor Richard's home telephone number. When Richard answered the phone, Ian explained about all the information Viktor had collected about the Turner painting and told him that Viktor would like to discuss the matter with him. Richard said he was flattered and could see Viktor at the Institute one lunchtime. They eventually agreed on a date and time and Ian said thank you and goodbye. He put the phone back on its base and returned to the kitchen to help Emma.

After dinner, Emma said she was feeling tired and would like an early night, so when she went off to bed, Ian returned to the home office and opened up his laptop. Oscar had obviously been up early that morning in Hong Kong because he had already sent an email about the Munnings painting:

Hi Ian,

> *Great news. All clear for the Munnings sale to go ahead.*
> *May Ling will send you the buyer's payment and delivery details later today.*
> *Don't forget my commission!*
> *The sign is now officially on my door, 'Gone fishing!'*
> *Cheers buddy,*
> *Oscar.*

Ian smiled at the last few words of Oscar's email, and made a mental note to read his email inbox first thing tomorrow morning. Things were certainly on the up!

Viktor met Professor Jackson in the reception area of the Courtauld Institute. Penny's plans to join them never materialised due to a prior engagement. Viktor was disappointed as he was a little overawed at the prospect of meeting the eminent professor just on his own. Even so, he thought, it was very good of the professor to give up his lunchbreak, so he had made sure he was fully prepared.

The professor reminded Viktor that he preferred to be called Richard. He recognised Viktor's nervousness so tried to make it easier and more relaxing for him. Viktor nodded and Richard led the way to the college refectory. He took the opportunity to inform Viktor about some of the college's facilities as they passed by different rooms.

After queuing and collecting their meals, Richard paid for the food and pointed to a table on the far side of the room. As the two men slowly ate their food, Viktor explained his findings about the *Margate at early dawn* painting. By the time he had finished his story, Richard had long finished his meal and Viktor's was still only half eaten.

Viktor tried to catch up with his food when Richard began to respond. "You have achieved quite a result, young man. I'm pleased my book came in handy. I see you have brought your copy with you. Remind me before we go and I will sign it for you."

"Thank you," replied Viktor, swallowing to clear his mouth.

"Interesting character, Turner," continued Richard. "Caused all sorts of issues in his day. I think towards the end some of his work was just a 'two finger' gesture to the art industry."

Viktor raised his eyebrows in surprise at Richard's comment. He swallowed the last forkful of his meal.

"So, what are you going to do with this revelation then, Viktor?"

Viktor wiped his mouth on a napkin. "I was hoping you might have some suggestions, sir. I'm not sure if I have enough evidence to convince the experts that the previous 1956 judgement was incorrect."

"What else do you think you need to do then?" Richard, as was his style, was trying to get the student to think of his own ideas, solutions and conclusions. He was not one who just fed them answers.

"It's difficult to say, because in my mind, the case is clear, but I think I would like a more definitive link. A link that somehow specifically proves that there was no Mrs Booth connection. That was raised as one of the reasons for calling the painting a fake."

"Okay. I don't think you need to get wound up about the Mrs Booth connection. Your client's note and provenances probably proves she was not involved. No, I think your next step is to try and persuade an eminent Turner expert. If you can do that, then that extra weight might just win the day."

Oh, thought Viktor. "But I do not know any experts to approach?"

Richard just sat back in his seat and folded his arms. He then gave Viktor a teasing smile.

Viktor stared at Richard for about three seconds and then suddenly it dawned on him what Richard was hinting at. "Do you mean you would support our case, sir?"

"On the evidence you have told me, I think I could make a couple of telephone calls. As I said earlier, you have achieved quite a result. A strong and compelling argument that suggests this painting always was a genuine piece of work completed by our friend, Mr Turner. The 1956 decision on this painting, like on some others from around that time, deserve to be overturned. They were just bad judgments."

"Oh wow!" exclaimed Viktor. "Thank you, sir. Wow."

"It's Richard, remember! Now I need to leave you in a minute, but before I do, pass me that copy of my book."

Viktor eagerly passed it over. Richard removed a fountain pen from his inside pocket and wrote a message on the inside blank page. He then handed the book back to Viktor and stood up. Viktor immediately responded and stood up too. The two men shook hands and Richard said he would be in touch soon. Viktor said thank you once again and Richard left. Viktor sat down again and took a deep breath. He then opened the book and read what the professor had scribed:

> *To Viktor,*
> *You have achieved quite a result.*
> *Good luck in your future career.*
> *Very best wishes,*
> *Richard Jackson.*

Chapter 22

It was a week later when the telephone on Viktor's desk rang. It was Penny. She suggested Viktor should pop up immediately as Ian had some news.

"Do you know what it is, Penny?" blurted Viktor, partly alarmed and partly excited.

"Come on up and see," teased Penny.

Viktor immediately put down the phone and made the journey to Penny's desk in record time!

"So, what's up?" asked Viktor, as he was trying to catch his breath.

"What's up is in here," replied Ian. He was standing next to an open filing cabinet behind the door that Viktor had just charged past.

Ian's presence and sound of his voice made Viktor jump. He obviously hadn't seen him when he arrived.

"Come on you two, into my room," said Ian, pushing the drawer closed.

Viktor and Penny followed Ian into his room and they all sat down on their usual seats.

"Professor Jackson telephoned me a few minutes ago..."

Viktor's heart rate suddenly shot up. "Oh!" he said excitedly.

"... he told me that he has recently spoken to two

colleagues who are both well respected Turner experts. In short, they would like to meet with you and the Baldwins, inspect the painting and view all the evidence you have attained to date."

"Oh, wow!" exclaimed Viktor.

Ian and Penny both smiled at Viktor's outburst.

"I've got their names and telephone numbers here." Ian passed over a sheet of paper to Viktor. "They are expecting you to ring them."

"Okay," said Viktor, now trying to calm down. "I'll do that this morning... and then I'll ring the Baldwins."

"By the way, where is the painting now?"

"Er. It's in our security vault. I put it in there after collecting it back from Tate Britain."

"Okay. In that case I suggest you invite everyone here for the meeting. The two expert's telephone numbers are both London codes. The Baldwins will have to travel up from their home."

"Do you think that Mr Hopkins can escort them here?" asked Viktor. He was not sure whether the Baldwins came up to London very often.

"That's a great idea, Vic. I will speak to Michael. In the meantime, you had better tell the Baldwins to keep that original note as safe as the Crown Jewels! It might just be worth a lot of money!"

Viktor used the rest of the day to finally agree on a date and time for the meeting. When he had finally spoken to the Baldwins, Mrs Baldwin was elated. Mr Baldwin was pleased, but emphasised that where so-called art experts were concerned, nothing was certain, yet!

The day of the big meeting duly arrived. Viktor, John and Anne Baldwin, Ian, Penny, Michael Hopkins, Professor Jackson and the two experts, were all gathered in one of the gallery rooms at Sotheby's. The painting of *Margate at early dawn*, was sitting proudly on an easel with two soft spotlights shining on it. The two experts spent about 20 minutes looking at every square inch of both the front and the back of the painting. Viktor then showed them the forensic report from Tate Britain, a copy of the Turner catalogue raisonné from 1953 showing the painting's entry, a copy of the 1841 note, the rest of the provenances from the Baldwins and finally the photograph of Turner's signature in Professor Jackson's book.

Questions to Viktor, the Baldwins and Professor Jackson were then asked by the two experts, and answered. The two men then moved to the far end of the gallery and discussed their findings. After a further ten minutes they returned to the rest of the group. They had made their decision. They agreed that the picture was not a fake and very probably a genuine painting by the hand of JMW Turner!

"Yes!" exclaimed Viktor. Everyone present looked at him and smiled. Richard gave him a congratulatory pat on the back.

The experts then confirmed that *Margate at early dawn* would be reinstated in the next edition of JMW Turner, a catalogue raisonné!

At the conclusion of the meeting, Ian asked if Viktor, Penny and John and Anne Baldwin would remain in the gallery. Michael Hopkins also joined them once the other guests had departed.

John Baldwin was the first to speak. "This young man here…" Mr Baldwin slapped Viktor on the back "… has done a fabulous job. We can never thank him enough for his dogged perseverance. I honestly didn't think we would get that 1956 decision overturned, but he did it! Fabulous job!"

Viktor was physically embarrassed. His face had turned a light shade of red!

Penny smiled at him and wanted to give him a kiss. She desperately tried to hold back a tear.

Michael Hopkins was the next to speak. "So, John, what do you propose to do with the painting now? It could be worth a few million pounds. Isn't that about right, Ian?"

"Yes, it is. It's an excellent piece of work and I'm sure there will be a queue of potential buyers."

"Well," announced John Baldwin, "Anne and I have already discussed this remote eventuality and we have agreed it is a lovely picture but far too valuable for us to keep in our house. What we would like to do is firstly, to ask if you would temporarily store the painting securely for us and, secondly, we would like it sold. If a reasonably exact copy could be painted for us we can then replace this original and put the new copy back in our dining room next to our painting of *Margate beach and seascape*. Quite appropriate really because ever since we inherited these pictures, they have both been deemed copies. Now they definitely will be!"

"What an excellent idea, John," said Michael, smiling at his friend and neighbour. "I'm sure Ian and Vic, here, will be able to sort all that out for you."

It was four months later to the day that the hammer finally went down on lot 32, *Margate at early dawn*, by JMW Turner. The final bid was £9.8 million!!

Chapter 23

Emma was getting noticeably bigger and she was finding the pressure of working and travelling to work more difficult to cope with. She was also struggling with morning sickness and that was not helping the situation either. She had advised her two fellow partners of her problems and, whilst they were sympathetic, they also reminded her that their company was just a small group and they were all under pressure.

Gradually Emma had been passing more of the outside work on to her PA, but although Andrew was technically very skilled, he did lack confidence when he had to meet with clients face-to-face.

Ian was concerned too and had advised Emma to try and cut down even more on her hours but she reminded him that, as a partner in a small business, she still had 33.3% of the responsibility. Even so, Ian was worried that Emma did not have her priorities right and that damage may be happening to the baby and contributing to the increasing mental pressure on Emma too.

During one of his Saturday morning telephone conversations with his parents, Ian had mentioned his concerns about Emma to his mother. His mother, who said she was one of the 'old school', reminded him that women are a lot tougher than you think. What would be far worse is for Emma to just sit at home counting the days until the birth! Maybe she should still carry on working, but work from home a lot more. That way she could be a lot more flexible with her hours, reduce her travelling stress levels, but still keep her mind active.

The more Ian thought about his mother's suggestion, the more it all seemed to make sense. If Emma could work from home a lot more, he was also convinced that her worries would reduce and she would still be able to make her full contribution to the partnership. The problem now, however, was how to convince Emma. Not the easiest job in the world!

Over the next week Ian kept drip-feeding the feasibility and benefits of working from home for Emma. He knew that if he just said his piece, Emma would just reject it and carry on. He had learned from her initial reluctance to go back to the Monaco apartment that she gradually did respond… over time!

Finally, after a further ten days, even Emma began to realise that what she was doing was failing on all fronts. She discussed with her partners the benefits she saw for her working from home. Eventually it was agreed that Emma's suggestion did make sense. With the use of the internet, broadband, mobile phones, laptops and all the technological advances of the day, she estimated about 80% of her work could easily be done from home… or indeed, anywhere! The other 20% could be shared, in the short term, by Andrew and the other two partners. If they had to employ a temporary member of staff, then so be it. Emma's drive home that evening was very different. She felt much happier and more relaxed than she had done for months and, when she looked in her rear-view mirror, she could not fail to notice the broad grin on her face.

Later that evening, when she told Ian of her discussions, plans and agreement with her partners, he gave Emma a huge hug and kiss... and took a deep sigh of relief.

"We could go back to the apartment for a few days if you want? I'll soon be too big and would not be able to obtain medical travel cover if we left it too long!"

Ian was totally stunned. This was the last sort of statement he'd expected from Emma in her current condition. "What!? Are you serious?"

"Oh, yes. It would be a nice break and a useful exercise in trying to 'work from home'."

"Okay then. It's a quiet period at work at the moment. Penny is on holiday until Wednesday, so after that, it should be fine." Ian was still a little shellshocked.

"Good. I'll leave you to decide when and how long we go for. It should be fun!"

"Yes, right." Ian could still not believe what he was hearing. It was not that long ago that Emma was seriously reluctant to visit the apartment at all, but now... well, okay let's get it all booked!

Two days later Ian had booked the flights, communicated with Harbour Heights and emailed the flight details to Julian. Mmm, he thought, it will also be a very useful opportunity to have a face-to- face chat with Julian.

It was two days after Penny had returned to work from her two-week holiday in Sardinia with her partner, Harry, when Ian and Emma flew out of London Heathrow heading for Nice. Ian had sent a second email to Julian advising their flight had been delayed by an hour. Within seconds Ian received a reply from Julian saying 'Thank you. I will be waiting for you in the Arrivals terminal.'

As this was only the second trip to Monaco that Ian had had to pay for himself, he decided to treat Emma and they both were flying First Class. As Ian put the cabin bags in the overhead locker, he heard Emma begin to giggle. He looked down and saw her holding the two ends of the safety seat belt. "What's the matter?"

Emma looked at him, held the two ends of the seatbelt up and laughed again. "I think I need an extra large extension!"

Ian laughed too and asked a passing stewardess for the extension. He looked across to Emma and thought to himself, I don't know what is going on, but it's great while it lasts!

Their flight landed at Nice airport at 5pm local time. True to his word, Julian was waiting in the Arrivals terminal. All three exchanged greetings and Julian said congratulations to Emma when he noticed her protruding stomach. Julian pulled Emma's suitcase and Ian carried his own carry-on bag. Once they had exited the building, Julian said he would collect the car from the car park and then pointed to a spot where he would pull up. He then walked briskly away, pulling Emma's suitcase with him. Emma and Ian stood watching the comings and goings of fellow travellers.

"I hope he doesn't disappear with my suitcase!" said Emma, jokingly.

"Are you okay standing? There's a bench over there," said Ian, concerned about Emma's earlier complaints of an aching back.

"No, no I'm fine. We've been sitting for quite some time. Nice to stretch a bit."

"I'm going to suggest to Julian that he and I have a meeting tomorrow morning. I want to discuss with him how much we pay him and what we might use him for. It will give you a chance to have a lay in."

"Okay. That would be nice."

Julian arrived back in a large black BMW 5 Series car. Ah well, thought Ian, not Andrei's Rolls-Royce but still very acceptable. Julian stopped exactly where he said he would and jumped out. He took charge of Ian's bag and held the door open whilst Emma eased her way into the back seat. Once again, she giggled when the seatbelt wouldn't quite fit. When Julian noticed Emma struggling, he got out of the car and went round to the boot where he removed an extension belt and handed it to her.

"A proper boy scout, aren't you, Julian. I probably need to carry one of those in my handbag!" Emma giggled again whilst Ian clipped the extension into place.

"I have a customer who is eight months pregnant, so I bought it specially," replied Julian.

That was quick, thought Ian.

During the journey to Monaco the conversation in the car was more of a general nature. When Andrei's name came up, all Julian said was that he hadn't spoken to him since he had left Monaco, but he had received two emails. One which said he was having a good time in Mexico and a second one saying he was travelling on to Canada.

As Julian's car pulled into the Harbour Heights reception area, Ian suggested to Julian that they meet the next morning at ten o'clock at the Harbour View cafe, which was very close to the apartment block. Ian explained that he wanted to discuss the car hire arrangements going forward. Julian said that was fine and jumped out of his seat and opened the rear passenger door for Emma. Slowly she managed to squeeze out before Ian arrived to give her a helping hand. Julian then removed the bags from the boot and asked if they wanted him to take them up to the apartment. Ian said no, but thank you. They then said their goodbyes... until tomorrow morning.

Julian climbed back into his car and left the Harbour Heights property. Fifteen minutes later, he had driven the short distance to his own apartment block, parked his car in the reserved space in the basement parking area and ascended in the elevator up to the 12th floor. As soon as he had entered his apartment he switched on his computer. Two minutes later he was typing his update message to Mr Sokolov.

Next morning Ian was awake at about seven o'clock. He'd had a broken night's sleep as Emma was obviously finding it difficult to get comfortable during the night and kept changing her position in the bed. He quietly shaved, showered, dressed and made himself a cup of tea. He then took his drink out onto the balcony and watched the early activity in the harbour and along the harbourside. He did enjoy this wonderful view. His eyes followed the shops, bars and restaurants all along the harbourside until he focused on the Harbour View cafe. Mmm, he thought, so what exactly am I going to say to Julian? He sat down on one of the balcony chairs and considered his approach and options. He did not want to give Julian any impression that he knew something was going on, but at the same time he hoped Julian might just say more than he had done to date. He sipped his tea and looked out into the Mediterranean Sea and pondered.

At 9.45 am, Julian left his apartment, descended in the elevator and walked out of the building and into the warm sunshine. He turned right and right again and could see the harbour ahead of him. The Harbour View cafe was partially in view and it took just a further couple of minutes before Julian entered the premises.

About the same time Ian had departed from the Harbour Heights building and was walking the short distance along the harbourside to the same cafe. As he entered, he spotted Julian sitting on the terrace sipping what he assumed was a large mug of coffee.

"Good morning," announced Ian. Julian immediately stood up and they both shook hands.

"Good morning. Please sit down," replied Julian.

Immediately the waiter came over and Ian ordered a cappuccino. Julian refused and said he had only just started the one in front of him.

"Do you know, this is one of my favourite places," said Julian. "I love to sit here and watch the world go by. When Andrei was away, I used to come here often."

"Do you miss Andrei?"

"Oh yes. Such an interesting man. We worked together for eight years. Now I have to earn a living working much harder!" Julian laughed at his comment and Ian smiled.

"So, what are you doing now?"

"Andrei knew a few people in Monaco and, before he left, he recommended my services to them. Strangely, a number of people here do not own or have the need for a motor car. It is a very small place with little parking… and taxis are plentiful. If they want to go to the airport or somewhere further afield, say France or Italy, then they will ring me."

The waiter returned with Ian's coffee and Ian said merci. "Tell me, how did you know my email address and why did you contact me?"

"It was Andrei's idea. He gave me your email details and I thought I could be of use to you when you visited Monaco. One can never have enough clients."

"You have a British name but I do recognise a slight accent. Have you always lived in Monaco?" Ian was feeling that he was not really getting very far.

"No. My father is from Scotland, but my mother is Swedish. My first twenty years were based in Sweden. My parents still live in Stockholm. I met Andrei in Berlin. I helped him there when he got into a spot of bother over some paintings. I had an old Renault car at the time but it got us through France and on to Monaco. Andrei thought I was a good driver and offered me a job."

"Sounds like Andrei. He's had quite a life!"

"Yes, and now he is travelling the world as a tourist and not as a busy art dealer."

Ian wondered if that was really the case. "Do you know of Andrei's long-term plans?"

Julian finished the last of his coffee. Ian offered to buy him another but Julian declined.

"All I know is what he told me and that he was going to travel and enjoy the world. I've been organising his travel plans, but I have to wait for him to tell me where he wants to go next. Sometimes it's very last minute. He said he would not be coming back to Monaco. I didn't really understand that. He also told me that he was giving you the apartment."

"Did that bother you?"

"No. Andrei bought me a lovely apartment just over the back here…" Julian waved his arm behind him "… seven years ago. He also purchased an annuity for me too, so I am not jealous of you, Mr Caxton. Besides, Andrei really liked you."

"Would you like to work for me?"

"As I said, I'm always looking for extra clients. What would you want me to do?"

Over the next ten minutes they discussed the role Ian saw of Julian and they agreed individual payments as and when Julian worked for Ian. They then stood up and shook hands. Julian left the cafe and Ian sat back down and drank the remains of his, now cold, cappuccino.

Now then, thought Ian, what do you make of that!?

Chapter 24

When Ian left the cafe, he decided to walk around the harbour area to think. The sun was now strong and he wished he had brought a hat and some sunglasses. If we are going to come out here more often, I need to make sure that I have the proper protection and the right clothing for it!

After about an hour he returned to the apartment and found Emma up, dressed and in the office.

"Hello, what are you doing here?" asked Ian, somewhat surprised.

"Working from home!" said Emma. "Isn't that what we agreed?"

"I see," replied Ian, somewhat surprised. "Does everything work?"

"Oh, yes. The receptionist told me how to link to the building's Wi-Fi and it's faster than ours at home!"

"Right." Ian was impressed and pleased to see Emma being so positive. "I've not had any breakfast yet. Are you hungry?"

"No. I'm fine. I had some toast earlier. Do you mind helping yourself? I'm working on a client's spreadsheet."

"No, no, that's okay. I'll just make myself some toast too," said Ian, leaving Emma in peace. As he walked through to the kitchen area, he reflected on what a very strange morning it had been.

When Julian arrived back in his apartment after the meeting with Ian, he noticed that he had two messages on his answerphone. One was from Mrs Harrison who wanted to use his chauffeur services to take her to San Remo, a town just over the border in Italy. The other message was from Marie. He ignored both calls for the time being and switched on his computer. For the next ten minutes he typed his latest update report to Mr Sokolov.

After he had eaten his toast, and as Emma was still 'working from home', Ian decided to go out for a walk. Instead of going down to the harbourside again, he chose to explore other areas he had not been to before. He followed the shady side of the streets. Without any particular plan, he just followed his nose! Eventually he walked into a shopping precinct. After window shopping at some of the men's clothing shops, he decided he would give them all a miss. Even London's West End prices, he thought, were not as expensive as these! He made a mental note to get a suitable sunhat when he was back in the UK.

As he was about to exit the precinct, Ian noticed an art gallery and in the window was displayed what looked like a snow scene sketch by Camille Pissarro. He walked up to the window and studied the picture more carefully. After looking for a few minutes, he noticed a male face watching him over the top of the same picture from inside the gallery. The face smiled at him and a hand beckoned for him to enter the premises. Ian stood back in surprise. Just a minute, he thought, I know that face! His mind quickly tried to find the connection from his past. The face still smiled and the hand still waved. In the end Ian decided to enter the gallery.

Back in the apartment Emma was enjoying her work more than she had done for many months. She had always enjoyed the technical side of accountancy and the interrelationships with her clients, but it was the daily pressure of commuting and office politics that had been wearing her down. Now she felt free of those headaches and was much keener to utilise the flexibility of her working hours that the new situation presented for her. She had fully updated the client's spreadsheet and also completed the accompanying typed report. After attaching both documents to an email to Andrew, she then pressed the 'send' button and eagerly watched the screen until the 'sent' message flashed up. She sat back and gently stroked her stomach. Was that a kick, she wondered, or just a reaction for sitting too long?

She switched off the computer and walked slowly into the lounge area. I wonder where Ian has gone? Did he say something before he went out? She couldn't remember, but then decided to make herself a cup of lemon tea. Five minutes later, she was standing outside on the balcony doing some gentle stretching exercises. The sun was still very warm and she used her hand to shield her eyes as she looked down at the activity on the harbourside. She then thought about Ian again and so went into their bedroom and collected her mobile telephone. She carried it out onto the balcony and sat down. She took a long sip of her tea and then dialled Ian's mobile number. Strange, she thought, his phone seems to be switched off.

"Well, well, well. Ian Caxton, what are you doing in Monte Carlo?" said the man, who was now more than just a face and a waving hand from inside the gallery.

"Bob Taylor. You are the last person I thought I would meet here. How are you?" Ian had finally put the name and history to the face. He had not seen Bob since they had both graduated in Modern Languages from St John's College, Oxford, all those years ago.

"I'm good, Ian, very good, thank you. And you? You have not changed a bit. Spotted you straight away looking at my Pissarro painting. I had hoped you would be one of our local billionaires!"

They both laughed. Bob was always the cheery character at college and often brought light relief when the pressures of studying became intense.

"No such luck," replied Ian. "You have a lot of pricey paintings here."

"Not all mine though. I'm just a minor partner, but it does pay the bills. Are you into art?"

Ian explained his career history and Bob was very impressed.

"Wow, you have done well. So, what are you doing here?"

"Just a short holiday. We are expecting our first child in a couple of months, so my wife suggested we take a short break in the sunshine before she became too big to travel."

"Tell me about it. I have two kids. Pregnancy is a strange time." They both smiled.

"Do you live here, in Monaco?" asked Ian. He knew how expensive even the smallest apartment was.

"Yes. Actually, we live upstairs! My wife's parents own this building and the ones either side. They live in France, so we live here and look after the properties too. Keeps me out of trouble!"

"How long have you been here?" Although Bob was always interested in languages, somehow Ian never really saw him using this talent and living abroad.

"Tommy Pickard, remember him?" Ian nodded. "Well, after college, he and I decided we would spend the summer on a sort of working holiday on the French Riviera. To cut a long story short, that is where I met Zoe. She's my wife now. She was on holiday with her parents and brother. We hit it off straight away. My French came in extremely useful!" Ian smiled. "When Tommy went back to the UK, I stayed on. I didn't have a job, or anything lined up, so I just decided to stay on for a while longer. Zoe's parents and brother went back to near Avignon, where they live, and Zoe stayed on with me. We rented a small cottage just outside Cannes. We had a great time and then Zoe suggested I came to Monaco with her. She said she had been living there for two months after her father had purchased the gallery and building. So, I did. Within the year we were married and Antoine, Zoe's father, had offered me a small partnership in the gallery. So here we are."

"What happened to all your plans back in the UK?"

"Never happened. Mum and dad have been over here several times, but I've only been back, what, three times! I don't even think about it. My life is very much here now. I love it!"

"Sounds as though you have fallen on your feet. Why don't you show me around the rest of your collection? It looks very interesting from here."

For the next 30 minutes Bob gave Ian the gallery tour and, at each painting where they stopped, both men gave their opinions about the artist and the quality of their work. After the tour they arrived back near the front entrance to the gallery.

"How long are you here for, Ian? It would be great if you and your wife came for a meal one evening. We could chat about art and old times and the ladies can exchange notes on babies!"

"That sounds really good. We will be going back in three days' time."

"Okay, what about tomorrow evening? We close here at eight o'clock. If you and… what's your wife's name, by the way?"

"Emma," replied Ian.

"So, if you and Emma call here about ten minutes before eight, we can then pop upstairs for a few beers and a meal."

"That sounds excellent." Ian looked at his watch. "I had better get back to Emma. I don't want her to think I've walked out on her!" Again, both men laughed. They shook hands and Ian left the gallery, waving back as he walked away.

"Where have you been and why's your phone switched off?" were Emma's first words when Ian re-entered the apartment.

Ian immediately checked his phone. "Yes, it's switched off. I wonder how that happened? Anyway, I went for a walk and, guess what? I bumped into an old college chum, Bob Taylor. We have not seen each other since graduation." Ian continued and summarised their conversation.

"Did you meet his wife?" asked Emma, when Ian had finished.

"No, but you can meet her tomorrow evening. They live only about a ten minutes' walk from here."

Chapter 25

On a small remote island, just a short seaplane flight from Vancouver, Andrei had just checked in to a 4* boutique hotel for a two-week stay. First impressions were very good and the novel transfer by seaplane was surprisingly smooth and comfortable. Earlier that morning he had been staying at the sister hotel in the centre of Vancouver. After packing his bags, they were collected and he was told that the next time he would see them they would be in his hotel room on the island. When he entered his new suite, sure enough, the suitcases were laying on the bed waiting to be unpacked.

Andrei had earlier enjoyed being chauffeur driven around the Canadian Rockies. He'd especially loved his stay in the Banff National Park. Here his highlights were the abundance and variety of wild animals. His favourite being a distant encounter with a large, golden, grizzly bear! From the safety of the parked car, he and his tour guide, Hudson, had watched the bear slowly crossing a nearby field. He had also seen a number of black bears, bald eagles and two herds of buffalo. Hudson had informed him that the correct name for the buffalo was the North American bison. The weather was very different to what he'd been experiencing in Mexico and indeed it was colder than winter in Monaco. Early in the morning the temperature was often below freezing, but by lunchtime it had risen by 20ºC! Other highlights were the lakes and snow-capped mountain ranges. The much-photographed Lake Louise and the incredible turquoise blue Peyto Lake were especially stunning.

Andrei had now been away for many weeks, but exactly how many, he had forgotten. However, what he had not forgotten was the recurring pain in his chest. For the last two years he had received occasional reminders, but the two doctors he'd visited both suggested a mixture of stress and possibly too much alcohol. One also suggested it could be the onset of angina. His heart had been checked and his blood pressure had not been found to be overly high, but it was suggested that it should be monitored more regularly. Now the periods between the attacks were slowly shortening despite the fact that he had deliberately changed his lifestyle to try and reduce or eliminate the attacks.

He had just returned to his suite from breakfast and sat down to look at the view through the large picture window. He looked down to the expansive bay where his seaplane had landed a week ago. Now he watched as another seaplane circled and then skimmed the surface of the water before landing with the faintest of splashes. The seaplane then proceeded slowly towards the hotel and finally stopped at the jetty just below his window. He watched as the six passengers disembarked.

He rose from his seat and removed a small brown glass bottle from one of his cases. With the help of a tumbler of water, Andrei consumed two of the white tablets he'd removed from the bottle. He'd never been keen to take any form of medicine and, until he hit the three-score-and-ten birthday, he didn't have any need to. He tried to keep himself fit with his exercises and long walks, but now age was slowly creeping up on him and he really didn't like it one bit!

Andrei removed his laptop from the room's safe and placed it on the desk. He waited to be connected to his emails. A minute later he checked his inbox. There were five new entries, but he went straight to the one from Julian. Julian's report gave a summary of his meeting with Ian. When he had finished reading the report, he sat back and smiled. Ten minutes later his reply was arriving in Julian's own inbox.

The next evening Ian was dressed and ready for their dinner date with Bob and his wife. He removed the bottle of champagne from the fridge and collected the box of chocolates sitting on the dining table. Both were placed on the small table by the door. Emma was still getting ready.

Ian kept checking his watch, but did not dare say anything to hurry Emma. He had already been told off for 'not liking a particular green dress'. Ian had retorted saying he did like the green dress, but he thought the dark blue one was much nicer. If she doesn't want my opinion, why ask? he thought.

Finally, Emma was ready and Ian said she looked fabulous. Emma said she was not sure, but decided to go with Ian's comment.

They arrived at the gallery at just after eight o'clock. Ian apologised for being late and introduced Emma to Bob. They both exchanged greetings and Bob suggested they go straight upstairs. Bob led them towards the back of the gallery and pressed the elevator button. The plate showed eight floors. Bob explained that they lived on the top two floors, the remaining floors were set up as an apartment, currently unoccupied, and the others were used as storage areas. The elevator arrived and they all got in. Bob pressed the 8th floor button and they started to ascend. As they travelled up, Bob explained that their bedrooms were on the

7th floor, because they had a partial view of the palace from the very top floor.

When the elevator finally stopped and the doors opened, they stepped into a large open plan area that contained the lounge, dining area and kitchen. Zoe immediately walked across from the kitchen to greet the guests. Zoe had dark hair, held in a ponytail, and a sun tanned, Mediterranean skin colouring.

Emma guessed Zoe was about the same age as her, but she was definitely jealous of her slim figure. She herself felt more like a bloated whale in comparison!

Introductions and greetings were exchanged and Ian finally passed on the bottle of champagne and Emma passed on the chocolates. As they chatted suddenly Emma was aware of two small faces peering around a door. "Hello you two," she said and wandered over towards them. The children took this as an opportunity to run across to the safety of their mother.

"These two," announced Zoe, "WERE supposed to be in bed!" Zoe had walked back to the kitchen area to continue the meal preparation.

Bob walked over to help Zoe. "This rascal is Robert and this princess is Isobelle."

"Hello Robert and Isobelle. So how old are you?" asked Emma, bending down a little towards them.

Neither child answered and Bob came to the rescue. "Robert is five and Isobelle is three. They both mainly speak French, but a little English too. Now you have seen our guests, it is off to bed you go. Come on," said Bob, in French to the children. He picked up Isobelle and Robert ran back towards the door.

"Sorry about that," said Zoe, in English. Her French accent was quite strong. "They were asleep when I left them."

"They are both so sweet," replied Emma. "You must be very proud."

"Yes, we are, but sometimes, well, you just wish they would do as they are told!" Emma and Ian laughed. This is what we've got to look forward to, thought Ian.

Bob returned from the bedrooms and offered his guests a drink. Ian asked for a gin and tonic and Emma an orange juice, or something soft.

Ian and Emma walked over to the large window which looked out across the tops of other buildings and, in the distance, they could see part of the profile of Monaco palace.

After the four drinks were poured, Bob handed a glass of white wine to his wife and then carried two glasses over to Ian and Emma.

"Lovely view," said Emma, as she received the orange juice from Bob.

Bob gave Ian his drink and said, "Yes. When we first moved in Zoe was already using, what is now, the unoccupied apartment downstairs. But we decided these top two floors were much better so we renovated them and then moved up here." Bob walked back to the kitchen area to collect his own drink. Emma sipped her orange juice and walked over to the kitchen area and started talking to Zoe.

Bob joined Ian and they sat on a large settee which still offered the same view.

"So, where are you staying Ian?" asked Bob.

"We're in an apartment in Harbour Heights. Do you know it?"

"Oh yes. Very nice property. We have sold some paintings to owners over there. We also, from time to time, bought pictures from a Russian chap who lives there too!"

Ian slightly choked and coughed as he was trying to take a drink.

"Are you okay?" asked Bob, with concern.

"Yes… fine. I think I swallowed some air instead of my drink!"

In the background Zoe and Emma were putting the starters on the dining table. "The food's ready, Ian," announced Emma. The two men picked up their drinks and joined the ladies at the table. Good timing, thought Ian.

The evening was quite a success. Emma obtained a number of tips about childbirth, getting her figure back and a growing baby. Ian and Bob reminisced about their Oxford college days and the art world. Ian also answered a number of questions about Hong Kong and described how much the former colony had now changed since the Chinese reoccupation.

"So, what's the future, Ian? Do you fancy moving on any time soon?" asked Bob, topping up Ian's wine glass.

"I'm not sure, Bob, to be honest. Sotheby's has been really good to me and I still think I owe them. Also, with our baby due very soon, I'm keen to try and keep the relative security we have at the moment. But long term, who knows? What about you? Are you looking to expand?" replied Ian. He sipped his very acceptable Chablis.

Bob offered both Zoe and Emma drink top ups, but both declined. He topped Ian's glass and then partly filled his own glass with the same Chablis before replying. "Antoine, Zoe's father, and I have been discussing our next steps, but, as you know, the art market is a funny business. It reacts much more wildly to world events than other businesses. It's great when countries' economies are on the up, but suffers more when the opposite happens. At the right time we might look to increase our capital. Alternatively, Antoine likes property, so we might move a little more in that direction."

"Would anyone like a cup of coffee?" asked Zoe, standing and clearing away the dessert dishes.

"No, thank you, Zoe. I think it is time we should be leaving Ian," replied Emma, who was now feeling quite tired.

"Yes, I agree. It's been a super time and we certainly don't want to outstay our welcome."

"It's been wonderful to meet up again, Ian," replied Bob. "I rarely see anyone from the old college days, so it was really good. We must do it again."

Emma whispered to Zoe about using the bathroom and Zoe pointed the way.

Once Emma had disappeared and Zoe was in the kitchen, Bob gently pulled Ian further into the lounge area and whispered, "keep in touch, Ian. I think there may be opportunities in the future for us to do some business together."

"What do you mean?" whispered Ian.

"Not now. Let's just keep in touch." Bob smiled and gently patted Ian on the back. "Keep in touch."

Chapter 26

Julian was waiting in the Harbour Heights reception area when Ian and Emma appeared from the elevator. He immediately collected the suitcase and Ian's carry-on bag. Ian and Emma both said their goodbyes at reception and then followed Julian out to his car. The weather was once again warm and sunny. During the whole of their stay, Ian and Emma had hardly seen a cloud in the sky, never mind any rain. Ian was certainly disappointed to be leaving and he believed Emma had enjoyed her stay too.

The conversation in the car en route to Nice airport was mostly of a general nature, but then Julian announced that he had received an email from Andrei.

"Oh," replied Ian, somewhat surprised. "So, what did he have to say? Is he enjoying himself?"

"He said he was coming to the end of his stay in Canada and was now getting up much later because the weather was too cold first thing in the morning. He had been touring in the Rockies and had seen a lot of wildlife. He was especially pleased to have seen a grizzly bear. Apparently, they are not that easy to spot. He will be moving on in about five days' time."

"Is that it?" replied Ian, a little exasperated.

"I think so. It was just a short email. He also wanted me to look into possible flights to Europe."

Ian and Emma looked at each other and Emma shrugged her shoulders. Julian looked in the rear-view mirror at his passengers and made a small smile.

As Ian and Emma boarded the aeroplane, Emma asked a stewardess if she could have an extension to her seatbelt. When they finally sat down in their seats in the first-class compartment, the extension belt duly arrived. The stewardess asked if they required anything else. Emma said no, she was now fine. The stewardess returned shortly after and offered them a selection of drinks. On her silver tray there were glasses of champagne, water and orange juice. Ian chose champagne and Emma an orange juice. They both then sat back and relaxed.

It was Emma who was the first to speak. "Do you know, Ian, that was a lovely break. I felt more relaxed than I've done in months. I even enjoyed the bit of work I did."

Ian was really pleased with Emma's comment. "Pity we won't be able to do it again until after the baby is born."

"Yes," said Emma, and immediately thought back to her conversation with Zoe. "You know talking to Zoe was really interesting. The French have some slightly different approaches to the whole baby thing and I learnt quite a bit."

"Zoe's nice, isn't she? Bob's, like me… a lucky man!"

Emma smiled. "Yes, you both are!"

"Have you made up your mind what you would like to do after the baby's born? I mean juggling the role of mum and work? I will obviously help, but have you any more thoughts since talking to Zoe?"

"I'm even more determined now to get the work–life balance right. I know now that I can do most of my work from home, but I'm not sure that my partners would be as keen on me reducing my hours further."

"Well, firstly, you are entitled to maternity leave."

"Yes, I know, but it's not quite that straightforward. I'm

not just an employee. I need to think it all through a lot more."

"Sir," said a passing stewardess to Ian. "Can you please fasten your seatbelt please? We will be taking off very shortly."

Ian duly did as he was told and looked at Emma who was smiling at him and pointing to the already clicked seatbelt in front of her.

When their aeroplane landed at Heathrow, it was buffeted by strong gusts of wind and driving rain!

"Welcome back to England," said Ian.

"Bit of a change from Monaco," replied Emma.

Fortunately, the aeroplane pulled up close to the terminal and they could walk straight into the building via a connecting tunnel.

Emma was beginning to struggle to walk long distances and one of the passenger-assist buggies gave them a lift to the entrance of the passport control area. Thankfully the queue was not too long. Once through there, Emma walked the short distance to the exit and Ian went in search of the suitcase. They finally met in the Arrivals Hall about 20 minutes later. Exiting the building, Ian joined the taxi queue whilst Emma sat on a nearby concrete bench. It was still windy but fortunately the rain had now stopped. When Ian got towards the front of the queue, Emma walked over to join him. Due to the weather, the traffic was much heavier and slower than usual and it was another 90 minutes before the taxi finally arrived in their driveway at home. Emma was exhausted and her back was aching. Ian was annoyed that the last leg of a lovely holiday had been so displeasing. Not for the first time, he wished he was back in Monaco!

After dropping his passengers at Nice airport, Julian returned towards Monaco, but instead of going straight back to his apartment, he went to another address. One he had been to many times in the past. He was expected at the house and was waved through the security gates. After parking his car in the driveway, he got out and stood and stared at the view out to sea. It was still as splendid as he had remembered. The sun was just beginning to set and was casting a light golden glow as far as the eye could see. A warm breeze had now got up and Julian took a long, deep intake of breath. The smell of a mixture of ozone and newly mown grass, fed deep into his lungs. Yes, thought Julian, Andrei certainly knew how to pick his friends and colleagues.

"Hello, Julian," said a female voice behind him from the direction of the house. "Have they gone back to the UK?"

Julian turned around and put his hand across his forehead to shade his eyes from the sun. "Yes, they have. I don't think they will be back now until after the baby is born."

"Fine. Come around to the terrace. I have some champagne on ice."

Penny had just entered her part of the office when she noticed Ian was already in his room. She walked past her desk and across to their adjoining doorway. "Did you have a nice holiday?"

"Hello, Penny. Yes, thanks. It was a lovely break, especially for Emma who seemed more relaxed than she has been for many months. So, what's been happening while I've been away?"

"Not a lot really. It's generally been very quiet. I left some messages on your desk, but none are vitally urgent."

"What about Vic? Did he enjoy the Munnings course in Dedham?"

"He said it was really good and has learnt quite a bit, especially about Munnings' evolving style over the years. Like a lot of people, he thought Munnings' best work was the time when he painted the gypsies."

"Good. I'll have a chat with him later."

"Mr Hopkins asked me yesterday when you were going to be back. I told him today and he just said 'fine'. He didn't leave a message or ask you to speak to him when you got in."

"Okay, thanks. I'll give him a ring later."

Penny left Ian to his thoughts and went back to her desk.

Ian looked through his messages once more and decided to telephone Paul Heslop at Christie's, Sotheby's main competitor. He dialled the personal number and Paul answered the call on the second ring.

"Paul Heslop speaking."

"Hello, Paul. Ian Caxton."

"Ah, hello, Ian. Long time, no speak. Thanks for coming back. Gather you are about to become a father at last. Congratulations."

"Thanks, Paul. We live in interesting times!"

"Yes, we do and something very interesting has cropped up here. I was wondering if you had come across the same issue?"

"I've been on holiday for a few days, so I've not really caught up yet. What's the issue?"

"Over the last few weeks, we have been approached by six different past customers, buyers who have been informed that their paintings are fakes. When these buyers were asked who had said they were fakes, there was a common organisation. A firm called Hedges and Watson. They have been advertising in a number of art magazines offering free valuations. Needless to say, a number of people have taken up their offer." We checked this firm out and, whilst it's quite new, the three main partners are well respected in the art world."

"I see. So this company is saying a number of genuine paintings are fake?"

"It's all rather odd because when we sold them, they had

the correct provenances and all were thoroughly examined and verified. We've checked through all our records. We are positive none of them were fakes."

"I've not heard anything here, Paul, but as I say, I've been on holiday. Leave it with me and I'll check and get back to you."

"Thanks, Ian. Cheers."

"Bye, Paul." Ian put his handset back on the base and called Penny. When Penny came into his room, he explained the details of his conversation with Paul Heslop.

"I've not heard anything, Ian," replied Penny, a little worried. "I wonder if that's what Mr Hopkins wanted to speak to you about?"

"Mmm. Good point. Can you see if he is free? I had better have a chat with him."

Chapter 27

Penny immediately telephoned Michael Hopkins' PA. However, she was informed that Mr Hopkins was out of the office until later that afternoon. Penny booked an appointment for Ian at 4 pm. She also decided to speak to other departments and sections in the organisation to try and find out if anybody had been approached by past buyers with similar complaints.

Only one person reported that they had heard a whisper, but that was because her husband worked at Christie's.

Penny went back to speak to Ian and she told him of his 4 pm appointment and the results of her telephone calls.

"It's all a little strange," said Ian. "We've seen similar incidents to these before. There can be a number of causes. Originals are sold or stolen and replaced by copies. This can happen for many different reasons. We saw that with one of the Baldwin paintings, remember?" Penny nodded. "Mind it seems odd that just one firm is involved. Could be the paintings were swapped when they were taken in for valuation. Alternatively, of course, the valuers might just be incompetent, but, somehow, I doubt it. My advice to Christie's would be to seek the help of the police's art fraud team. In the meantime, can you let me know if anyone in the office receives any new complaints?"

At 4 pm Ian arrived at Michael Hopkins' office. After discussing Ian's holiday and some general chatting, Mr Hopkins came to the point. "I've had John Hargreaves, from Christie's, on the telephone. He's concerned that there is a problem with fake paintings alleged to have been sold by Christie's. Do you know anything about this problem?"

Ian explained his conversation with Paul Heslop and that Penny had checked with our office staff. Nobody had reported that there was a problem with any of our clients."

"Well, that's something, but what do you think is going on? Do you think we need to take any more action at the moment?"

"I will have another chat with Paul Heslop. I was wondering if they were going to involve the police. Otherwise, I don't think there is anything else we can do at the moment. Obviously if we do start to receive similar complaints, then we need to investigate them thoroughly. It's as though someone has a vendetta against Christie's. If so... why?"

Immediately after the meeting Ian updated Penny and then telephoned Paul Heslop. He explained that Sotheby's had not, as yet, received any similar complaints.

"So, is someone deliberately only attacking our clients, I wonder?" pondered Paul.

"Are you going to involve the police?"

"I'm not sure at the moment. We cannot see any obvious fraudulent activity, but we are investigating each case on its own merits. Thanks for coming back so quickly, Ian."

"Let me know how it goes. In the meantime, we will keep our eyes and ears open and let you know if we come across any-thing suspicious. Good luck," said Ian, and he ended the call.

Emma had returned to work at her office for one day. She had a number of things she decided that could be better done with face-to-face discussions. She was pleased to be welcomed back by her two partners and Andrew, her PA, who thanked her for unravelling a complicated situation with one of her clients. Emma's depth of knowledge of the client's business history had come to the rescue.

By lunchtime, however, Emma had become very tired and her back was seriously aching. She really wanted to be at home and the thought of fighting through the commuter traffic, yet again, really depressed her. It was just after three o'clock that she finally decided to take the chance and try to get home before the main traffic rush started. She explained her decision to Andrew and also told him that when she arrived home, she would log on to her computer and pick up any important issues that had arisen.

Andrew promised that if any major issues did crop up, he would email her immediately. He also wished her a safe journey home.

Unfortunately, her best laid plans were thwarted by a serious traffic accident on the M25. The traffic ahead of her started to slow down. However, she noticed the next junction was only a mile ahead. She just hoped she could get there before the traffic came to a complete standstill.

This turn off was two junctions before her normal exit and she knew that if she could just reach it before the traffic stopped, she would be able to wind her way home via the A30 and the local roads.

The queue in front of her kept stopping and then inching forward a little bit more before stopping again. The turn off was getting closer but, frustratingly, was still out of reach. Her back was now feeling extremely sore, to the extent that she now started to feel quite sick. She wound down her window for fresh air, but could only breathe in the traffic's fumes. This is ridiculous, she thought. Why did I choose to come back to the office? All the work I've done today I should have done it from the comfort of my home!

The row of vehicles on the inside lane began to move again and just ahead she could see why. A lot of drivers were making the same decision as her and coming off at that same junction. Slowly she crept up to the III hundred yards to go marker then the II and finally the I, before finally exiting the motorway. The traffic ahead continued to move very slowly down the slip road but the pain in her back was now excruciating. Suddenly Emma realised she was beginning to feel faint. She just had to stop. It was unbearable. She tried her best to pull into the side and managed to stop, just having time to switch on her hazard warning lights before collapsing on the steering wheel. Everything had suddenly gone blank.

Just as Ian put down the phone after another conversation with Paul, Penny came rushing into his room and announced, "Ian! The police have been on the telephone. Emma has been taken to hospital. She's apparently okay, but the hospital is running some tests."

"Oh God!" exclaimed Ian, leaping to his feet. "What happened? Which hospital?"

"The Ashford Hospital!" shouted Penny, as Ian disappeared through the door.

When Ian eventually arrived at the hospital, he was lucky as he had managed to find a parking space quite quickly. He dashed into reception, gave his and Emma's name to the receptionist and the receptionist checked her computer. "Mrs Caxton is fine," she announced. "The doctor is just finishing checking her. Can you take a seat please, Mr Caxton, I'll get the doctor to speak to you."

"Can I see her please? She's eight months pregnant!"

"As I said, she is with the doctor at the moment. She is fine, Mr Caxton. Apparently she fainted. Ah, here's the doctor now."

Ian turned around to see a lady in a white coat walking over towards him.

"This is Mr Caxton, doctor," announced the receptionist.

"Hello, Mr Caxton. My name is Doctor Patel. Your wife is fine. She fainted, but fortunately, everything is alright. I'll take you to see her."

"Thank you, doctor." Ian followed her along two corridors and into a small room where Emma was sitting up on a bed. Ian quickly ran over and gave her a hug. "Are you okay!? What happened?"

Emma explained briefly about the car journey until the point where she fainted. The doctor then took up the story.

"Luckily for Mrs Caxton a doctor and his wife were in the car immediately behind her on the slip road. The wife was driving and stopped. The doctor got out of the passenger side and, because Mrs Caxton's driver's window was fully open, he was able to assess her condition quickly. At first he thought she might have had a heart attack because she was slumped over the steering wheel. However, Mrs Caxton gradually came to but then fainted again. An ambulance and the police were called and the doctor waited to make sure Mrs Caxton was alright. She came to again and was able to speak. The ambulance arrived and the doctor suggested she be brought here. The paramedics helped Mrs Caxton into the ambulance and the doctor followed. He was driving your wife's car."

"So, Emma's okay then. How's the baby?"

"Both are fine, Mr Caxton. We've carried out a thorough examination and a number of tests. All is okay."

"Except for my horribly sore back," said Emma.

"I suggest you take Mrs Caxton home and make sure she has a warm bath and an early night. We have given her a mild painkiller injection. I would also strongly recommend that she does not drive again until after the baby is born."

Just over 90 minutes later, and with the aid of Ian, Emma was gingerly climbing into a lovely, hot, soapy bath at home.

First thing the next morning, Ian telephoned Emma's senior partner at her work and told him of the events that happened the previous afternoon. The partner was shocked and wished Emma a speedy recovery. Ian also announced that Emma would not be coming back into the office for the foreseeable future.

Ian then telephoned Penny and told her the same story. Penny immediately said she hoped Emma would get well quickly and Ian finished by saying he would be working from home that day. He then telephoned his friend Billy, at the local garage, and arranged for Emma's car keys to be picked up from the house and her car to be collected from the hospital car park. Lastly, he telephoned Ashford Hospital and told the receptionist that the local garage would be collecting Emma's car and also asked if she knew the contact details of the doctor who had stopped to help Emma. The receptionist said it was normally against the hospital rules to give this sort of information out, but after Ian had explained why he wanted these details, she did give him the doctor's name and his surgery address, but emphasised that the information had not come from her!

Emma was still in bed, but not asleep, when Ian crept quietly into the bedroom.

"You have been on the telephone a lot. The extension here has been permanently engaged."

"How are you feeling?" replied Ian. He walked round to Emma's side of the bed and sat down next to her.

"I feel a lot better this morning, thank you. Even my back is not aching quite so much. Who have you been telephoning?"

Ian explained all his calls. The only slight deviation from the full truth, was that when he mentioned ringing her office, he told her that he had explained to the senior partner what had happened and that you would not be at work this week. Ian also passed on the get well wishes from the partner and from Penny.

"That's nice of them. Any chance of a cup of tea?"

"Of course. I'll bring you one up in a minute." Ian got up from sitting on the bed and headed for the door. "I suggest you stay in bed for a while. Probably get up for lunch?"

"Okay… and Ian… thank you."

Emma did get up for lunch, which was a light salad prepared by Ian. She then moved into the lounge and picked up a couple of magazines. However, she quickly got bored with them and went over to the dining table where she switched on her laptop computer.

Ian was in the study and had just arranged, via a local wine merchant's website, for a box of 12 mixed red and white bottles of Australian wine to be delivered to Dr Powell at his surgery's address. Also included was a brief message of thanks to both him and his wife, for sparing their valuable time and showing such concern and professionalism when they stopped to help Emma. He also mentioned that Emma was now at home and recovering well.

Whilst on the internet Ian opened his email account and, to his great surprise, immediately spotted in his inbox, an email from Vladimir Sokolov!

Hello my friend.

I hope you and Emma are keeping well and enjoying the apartment. I am so pleased to learn that very soon you will both become proud parents. That is excellent news.

I am thoroughly enjoying my long and well-earned vacation. I am currently in Canada, but will be moving on again very soon. I will either be going to Japan or Europe. Time is ticking on and my old body is not as healthy now as it once was, so I need to make sure I make the most of every minute.

I have plans to visit our good friend, the Laird and his family in Scotland soon. I need to check up on my investment there and have a few 'wee drams!'

An interesting business opportunity may present itself to you in Monaco shortly.

Best wishes my friend and please remember me to Emma. Vladimir.

After Ian had read the email, he momentarily stared blankly at it, before reading it through once again. He knew Andrei liked to use different aliases in written communications and Vladimir was one of his favourites to Ian.

Ian sat back in his chair and considered the situation. Andrei, he thought, is on the other side of the world and he still knows what's going on in our lives! What does he mean by a business opportunity? He is the most unnerving of people … such a bloody enigma!

Chapter 28

"Would you like your mother to come and stay for a while?" asked Ian, as he was just finishing getting dressed. It was the next morning and he was nearly ready to go to work.

Emma was still in bed but had just decided to get up and see Ian off to work. "No, I would not! What made you think of that suggestion?"

"Well, I thought you might like the company whilst I was at work. Help you around the house, that sort of thing… "

Emma cut Ian's sentence short. "You know what she's like and she would certainly put my blood pressure up!"

"Okay, okay. Sorry for mentioning it."

Emma got out of bed, put on her dressing gown and walked over to Ian and kissed him on the cheek. "I'm sorry, but a bit of peace and quiet would be much better for me at the moment. Besides, Jane said she might pop in this afternoon."

Ian was ready to leave. "Give my regards to Jane. You can have a nice, long, sisterly chat!" He kissed Emma on the lips and left the bedroom. Less than a minute later Emma heard the front door close. She started to do her gentle stretching exercises, but was interrupted when the telephone rang.

"Hello," she answered cautiously.

"Hi, Emma. Oscar here in Hong Kong. Is Ian there?"

"No, Oscar. Sorry, you have just missed him. He's just left for the office."

"Okay. I'll try him there later. By the way, how are you? Must be very close now for the baby."

"Yes, very close. Just a few weeks left. I certainly don't recommend pregnancy!"

Oscar gave a small laugh. "If men had to be the ones who carried the babies, the human race would cease very quickly."

"Yes, we have to put up with a lot!"

"Nice chatting, Emma. Hope all goes well with the birth. If it's a boy, Oscar is a great name!"

"I'll remember that. Bye, Oscar." Emma put down the receiver. Let's hope it is a girl then!

Viktor put down his telephone after he had finished his conversation with Mr Hepplewhite. Mr Hepplewhite was complaining about a painting he had purchased via a Sotheby's privately arranged sale three years ago for £1.5 million. He'd told Viktor that he had just had the painting revalued and the valuer had stated that his picture was not the original work, but a good copy! What were Sotheby's going to do about it?! Viktor took down all the details of the painting, the name of the valuer and Mr Hepplewhite's personal details. He then said he would investigate himself and promised to telephone him back very shortly. Ten minutes later Viktor was talking to Penny about the telephone call whilst they waited for Ian to come off the telephone to Oscar in Hong Kong.

"There's something very strange going on," said Penny, when Viktor had finished. "Ian has been talking to Paul Heslop at Christie's and Christie's have received several of these calls over the last few weeks."

"It sounds as though there might be something organised, but what?"

"Ah. Ian is off the phone now. Let's go and speak to him." Penny and Viktor walked up to Ian's door. "Ian," said Penny, "can we have a word? Vic's received a phone call similar to the ones you told me about that have been happening at Christie's."

"Hello, Vic. Yes, come in, both of you. Sit down," replied Ian. He was intrigued to know what Viktor was about to say.

Viktor repeated the same story that he had just explained to Penny.

"That's interesting, isn't it?" replied Ian, once Viktor had finished. "And you say the valuers were Hedges and Watson. What a coincidence that they crop up again. I'll speak to Paul Heslop and inform him that we also have a similar problem. In the meantime can you both do a bit of digging. Penny, will you find the complete file for this client and his painting. Vic, go back to Mr Hepplewhite and ask him what has happened to his painting in the three years he has owned it. More particularly, has it been out of his sight for other valuations, cleaning, exhibitions and the like? You know the sort of thing. Let's all meet up back here at two o'clock."

After Penny and Vic had disappeared, Ian telephoned Paul Heslop and retold Viktor's story.

Paul listened carefully and recognised all the similar elements. "We have started to investigate at our end, but with so many possibilities as to what could have happened to the original paintings since they left our hands, it is difficult to see a common factor, except of course, for the Hedges and Watson connection. We have one painting that we sold nearly 30 years ago!"

"Are you going to involve the police yet?"

"We've decided to complete our own internal investigations first." Paul then explained that he had suggested to his boss that involving the police would be a good idea.

However, his boss was less enthusiastic as he didn't want the situation to go public. The boss was worried about the effect it would all have on Christie's reputation.

"The only thing we are certain about," continued Paul, "is that every one of these pictures that have been reported to us were absolutely genuine when they left here!"

Ian could feel the exasperation in Paul's voice. "Okay. We will investigate our case and then compare notes later."

At 2 pm Ian, Viktor and Penny were sitting around the table in Ian's office. Penny was the first to speak.

"The painting *Friends on a beach* by Jules André, 1851, had an excellent provenance and was sold privately by a Mr A. Carter to Mr B. Hepplewhite, just over three years ago. Sotheby's negotiated on behalf of Mr Carter. The price paid and registered in our records, was £1.512 million. Our records state that we did our normal checks and we were completely satisfied that it was the genuine article. Not a copy or a fake!"

"Vic, what have you found out?" asked Ian.

"Mr Hepplewhite was quite annoyed when I went back to him as he was convinced that we were trying to push the blame back on to him. After I calmed him down, I told him it was all part of the wider investigation and we were not trying to pass on any responsibility or blame on him. Anyway, he eventually said that the painting had been hanging in his lounge since he bought it, except for the two times when he'd let it out of his sight – before the current valuation that is. The first time was when it was cleaned 12 months ago and the second time was for a three-day charity exhibition of 19th century French painters, six months ago. I also obtained the name and contact details of the picture cleaners and the charity organisation."

"Good work both of you. Any suggestions as to how we should proceed?"

Viktor and Penny looked at each other trying to decide who should speak first. Finally, Penny began. "The common denominator in all of this is Hedges and Watson. I think we need to investigate them first."

"Vic?" asked Ian. It was his turn.

"I agree with Penny, but we could also liaise with Christie's to see if the cleaner and charity Mr Hepplewhite used were common to any of their paintings."

"Okay. Penny, you take the Hedges and Watson route and Vic, try and find out more about the cleaner and the charity. See if there is any connection with Christie's pictures. I doubt you will find a connection, but we must show that we have eliminated them both from our investigations. I'll bring Michael Hopkins up to date."

After Penny and Viktor had left, Ian opened up his laptop. Good, he thought, Oscar has been as good as his word. Ian slowly read Oscar's email and then he read the two documents Oscar had attached. When he had finished, he sent a reply to Oscar saying thank you and that he would be in touch again shortly.

On the following Monday morning Ian, Penny and Viktor sat around Ian's table once again.

Penny explained, "Hedges and Watson were a small new partnership consisting of three equal partners. All three are well respected dealers in the art world. For the last nine months they had been trying to attract new customers by spending a lot of money on advertising. Specifically, they have been offering free valuations. From what I can gather this has generated quite a bit of interest and there is now even a backlog of about two weeks. I'm guessing a little here, but I think about 5% of their valuation exercises produce a report stating the painting is a fake."

Viktor then explained that from his investigations he

hadn't been able to find any common connection between the Hepplewhite cleaner, the charity and with any of Christie's paintings.

"Okay, thank you," said Ian. "Here's what I think we'll do now. Let's take up Hedges and Watson's offer and give them a picture to value. Not a really valuable one but certainly one worth valuing. Let's just see what that achieves."

After the meeting, Ian telephoned Paul Heslop and explained what he was going to do. Paul thought this was a good idea and, depending upon Ian's result, he might just do the same.

Michael Hopkins agreed to Ian's proposal and arranged for a small oil painting by Eugene Delacroix, titled *Woman with red hair* to be delivered to the Hedges and Watson gallery for valuation. This particular painting had been sold to a friend of Michael for £850,000 two years ago. Ian said it should be valued at about £950,000. The gallery promised the results of their free valuation in about two weeks.

Before the Delacroix painting had been delivered to Hedges and Watson, it was photographed from every angle, x-rayed and invisible marks were made on the reverse side of both the frame and the painting itself. The provenances were double checked and finally Ian agreed this was not a fake or a copy, but the real deal!

Only a very small number of people were aware of the plan, the selected painting and the painting's owner. Even Penny and Viktor didn't know the full details of the chosen painting. Ian advised Paul Heslop that a painting had been selected and would be delivered to Hedges and Watson sometime in the next ten days. Paul agreed that it was unlikely that anyone would be in a position to be able to tip off the valuers! It was now just a wait and see time.

Chapter 29

Emma was becoming increasingly impatient and irritable. She was fed up with her backaches, her inability to get a good night's sleep and the sheer uncomfortableness of having such a large bulge in front of her. She just wanted it all over and done with. The early depression followed by various levels of excitement, were now replaced by frustration. She was snappy with Ian and had even upset her sister, Jane. However, she did ring Jane later that evening with tearful apologies. She tried desperately to find positives about the impending birth, but at the moment, she just hated everything about her situation.

What Emma did not know was that Ian had listened to most of Emma's tearful apologies to her sister. He knew it was an extremely difficult time for her and he'd had to bite his tongue a few times when Emma, unfairly in his opinion, had 'had a go at him'.

When Emma had finished the telephone call to her sister, she told Ian she was going to have a bath. Ian took the opportunity to ring Jane himself and also offered his own apologies on Emma's behalf. Fortunately, Jane was very sympathetic as she remembered well the last few days before her first child was born. She confirmed to Ian that she would still pop over and keep an eye on Emma and try to help her as best she could during the last few days.

It was just two days later that Emma announced to Jane that she thought things were beginning to happen. Jane checked the time between each contraction and announced it was time to go!

Emma's bag was already packed and Jane helped her into her car and they sped off to the maternity hospital. Once there the medical staff took over and Jane made a telephone call.

"Hello, Ian. It's Jane. Emma's gone into labour!" said Jane, in a calm and matter of fact manner.

"What, when, where is she?" exploded Ian.

"Calm down, Ian. It's very early and nothing will happen for hours yet. I suggest you get something to eat first and then arrive here soon afterwards."

When Ian arrived at the maternity hospital he was escorted into a small room where Emma was lying in bed and Jane sitting on a chair at her side.

"Anything happening yet?" said Ian, arriving excitedly at the bedside and kissing Emma on the forehead.

Just as he had finished speaking, Emma gave out a loud contraction scream.

"This isn't a false alarm," said Jane, calmly. "The doctor and nurses have been checking on her."

Ian pulled up another chair and sat on the other side of the bed to Jane. He tried to calm Emma by wiping her perspiring brow and stroking her arm, but that resulted in Emma grabbing his wrist very hard and having another contraction.

One of the nurses now appeared and Jane thought this was a good opportunity to leave Ian and Emma on their own together. She walked over to Ian and whispered in his ear that she was leaving now and wished them good luck over the next few hours. Emma released her grip on Ian's wrist and he stood up, kissed Jane on the cheek and said, "Thank you. I'll call you as soon as we have any news." Jane smiled and waved at Emma and headed for the door just as the doctor arrived.

It was another four hours before the sound of a crying baby could be heard in the room. Immediately after the baby emerged it began to cry and was wrapped in a towel. The nurse announced the baby was a boy and she handed him to Ian. Ian held his son briefly and kissed him on the forehead before passing him on to Emma.

Emma smiled and cradled him in her arms. She felt shattered but just stared lovingly at her new son.

Ian counted the fingers, toes and other bits, before pronouncing that everything seemed to be in place! Emma gave a very tired smile. He knew she was obviously very exhausted.

During the next hour, Ian popped out into the corridor and telephoned Emma's mum and dad, Jane and also his own parents. All were absolutely delighted and said congratulations to both of them.

When Ian arrived back in the maternity room, the baby was asleep in a cot at the side of the bed. Emma too had dropped off to sleep. The nurse was sitting where Ian had previously sat next to the bed and she suggested that he should get something to eat and a good night's sleep. There was little he could do at the moment. Ian heeded the nurse's instructions and went home. Although it was very strange to be getting into his bed on his own, it was only a few minutes later when he too was fast asleep.

When he awoke it was 9.30! He quickly telephoned Penny and told her the details and also said he would be taking the next two days as leave. He showered, shaved, quickly ate a bowl of cereal and headed back to the maternity hospital. When he arrived, Emma was awake and feeding the baby.

She smiled at Ian and when he arrived at the side of the bed, they both kissed.

"So, how are you now? You look really happy," said Ian, as he watched his son feeding contentedly.

"I'm still very sore and very tired, but certainly relieved it's all over."

"Do you need anything from home?"

"No," replied Emma hesitantly. "I think I've got everything in my case."

"Jane is bringing your mum and dad to see you both this afternoon and my parents are visiting early evening. I hope that is all okay?" said Ian.

"Yes," said Emma. "It will give me a chance to really thank Jane. She's been fabulous."

"Now we have got to decide on a name for this little chap," said Ian, gently stroking his head. "Are you still happy with our original ideas?"

"Yes, I think so. It would be really nice to include both our father's names," said Emma, shifting slightly to get into a more comfortable position.

"So, it's Robert, Richard, Ian then?" asked Ian, just making sure he had the right order.

"The three men in his life. My father, your father and his own father. I like that!" replied Emma.

Whilst Emma and Ian had been talking, baby Robert had gradually fallen asleep.

"Can you take him and pop him in the cot, please, Ian?"

Ian leaned over and gently picked up his son as he slept contentedly. He gave him a kiss on the forehead and placed him in the cot. Robert immediately put his right thumb into his mouth. "Who do you think he looks like?" whispered Ian.

"He's certainly got a lot of your features and I think possibly a little of my father around the eyes," said Emma lying back in a more relaxed position.

"Lucky chap then," said Ian teasingly.

Emma smiled and closed her eyes. Yes, he is, she thought. "Do you mind if I sleep a little bit, Ian, please? Otherwise I might fall asleep when our guests arrive later!"

Ian leaned over and kissed Emma on the cheek. She was already starting to drop off to sleep. He looked at Robert to check if he was okay, then quietly lifted his chair back towards the window and sat down again. He removed his mobile phone from his pocket and accessed his emails. He was briefly interrupted by a nurse, who, seeing both mother and baby were asleep, quickly checked on them both. She then smiled at Ian and left the room.

Ian went back to his email inbox and opened an email from Oscar. This email was a follow up on their earlier email exchange and a telephone conversation. Oscar had confirmed the dates he would be in London and hoped Ian would be available for them to meet up.

Ian wrote back explaining he was now a dad of 14 hours and would love to meet up with Oscar again. Ian suggested that Oscar visit their house on the Sunday, in between the dates he'd given and Oscar could then also meet both Emma and Robert as well.

During their previous telephone conversation Oscar had confided with Ian on some of his plans for the future. He said he would tell Ian more specific details when they met, but the one thing Oscar had mentioned was that he had sold his apartment and was definitely moving on, and away from Hong Kong!

Ian checked through some of his other emails and opened the one from Paul Heslop at Christie's.

Hi, Ian. Congratulations! I hope all went well and you still have a large smile on your face. Your PA mentioned the birth when we spoke earlier.

With my first born, my smile lasted for over a week! Although your priorities are elsewhere at the moment, I thought I would let you know the results of our investigations. We had six paintings which were valued by Hedges and Watson that they deemed to be fakes. We have analysed each of the six paintings and their records carefully and our conclusion is that three are not the pictures we sold! They are indeed good copies, but still fakes! Two are genuine, despite what Hedges and Watson have reported and the remaining one has now been sold privately. We have spoken with the Met police art fraud team and informed them of our findings. I also told them of your similar case and they would like to hear the results of your findings before they progress the matter further. Both the police and my colleagues at Christie's think there is a criminal at work within Hedges and Watson. The problem now is, how to prove it!

Cheers, Paul.

Ian looked up when he heard Robert begin to stir. However, once his son had found his thumb again, he settled down and went back to sleep.

The nurse, who had entered the room earlier, reappeared and glanced over to Emma and Robert. Satisfied, she then, very quietly, checked if Ian was okay. Ian put his mobile phone into his pocket and walked over to the nurse and whispered that he was going to find a cup of coffee. The nurse let Ian pass by her and leave the room. She then walked over to check on Robert and adjust Emma's bed covers.

Chapter 30

Three days later Emma was back at home. Ian had taken Robert into every room of the house, introducing him to his new home. Emma smiled as she watched and listened to Ian's guided tour. She was determined to get something like her old figure back and had started to gently carry out some of the exercises that Zoe had recommended in Monaco. Zoe said she had been coached by a professional and as long as Emma took each day at a time, she would be pleased with the results. Emma had also checked with the doctor in the hospital who told her that she thought that the exercises would help, but she had also insisted that Emma should not rush things… and do everything very slowly and gradually build up.

Robert seemed to be getting bored with his tour and started to cry a little. Ian guessed rightly that a new, clean nappy was required. "Okay, young man," he whispered. "Daddy is about to change his first baby nappy, so I do not want any complaining." Ian found the nappy bag and laid Robert gently on the changing mat. Five minutes later Robert was clean and dry once again.

Later in the afternoon, whilst Emma was feeding Robert, Ian went into his home office and opened up his laptop. Penny had emailed a copy of the report provided by Hedges and Watson on the painting, *Woman with red hair* by Eugene Delacroix. She also mentioned that the painting was now temporarily back at Sotheby's. Ian began to read the report slowly and analysed every word. When he had finished, he knew for certain where the problem lay. He immediately typed an email back to Penny asking her to check the painting for all the marks and against the photographs he'd taken, prior to the picture being delivered to the valuers.

About an hour later Penny emailed Ian back.

"Hi Ian. The painting that has been returned is not the one that was sent to Hedges and Watson! The frame still has the invisible marks on it, but the rear of the picture does not. The frame is the original, but the painting has definitely been swapped!"

Ian smiled and said quietly to himself, "Got you!" He replied to Penny and thanked her. He also asked her to send a copy of her findings to Paul Heslop at Christie's. He then closed his computer and went off to find his family.

At 10.30 next morning, Ian received a telephone call on his mobile phone from Paul Heslop. After a brief exchange about Robert and fatherhood, Paul explained that the police had raided the premises of Hedges and Watson first thing that morning. They found a number of original paintings in a store cupboard, including *Woman with red hair* and Mr Hepplewhite's *Friends on a beach* by Jules André. Paul continued to say that the police had also recovered all the real paintings owned by Christie's clients. Two employees have been arrested and are likely to be charged later today. The police also think there might be a Russian connection for the onward sale and distribution of the original paintings.

Ian's mind immediately sprung to Andrei and Sergei. He

just wondered!

Two weeks later, on Sunday morning, Ian collected Oscar from his London hotel. Ian told him about the events of the last three weeks. By the time he had finished talking Ian was parking his car in the driveway.

"Wow," said Oscar, when he saw Ian's house. "This is a serious step up from your apartment in Hong Kong."

"Yes, it is. Emma was really the driving force behind getting it for us."

"Do you know, I don't think I've met Emma since I was last in the UK for your wedding!"

"Are you sure?" replied Ian, quite surprised.

"Each time you and I have met up in Hong Kong, since your wedding, you have been on your own."

"Thinking about it, I guess you're right. Come on, let's go in and find Emma and our new addition to the family." Ian put his hand on Oscar's shoulder and encouraged him towards the front door. As they approached, the door opened and Emma appeared with Robert in her arms.

"Well, well, well. What have we got here?" said Oscar as he peeked closer to Robert and stroked his face. "Hello, young man. Hello, Emma. Long time, no see." Oscar gently kissed Emma on the cheek.

"Hello, Oscar. It's so nice to meet you again. What's this I hear that you might be moving on from Hong Kong?" said Emma, standing back so that Oscar could enter the house.

"Yes, all done and dusted. Isn't that the English saying? It's a long story. Let me see this lovely house first and I will explain everything later."

Ian took charge of Robert and started to give Oscar a brief tour of the house. Emma went back to the kitchen to finish preparing the lunch. When they arrived in the lounge, Ian placed Robert in his day cot and he and Oscar both sat down on separate settees.

"Would you like a drink of coffee, tea or a beer?" asked Ian.

"No, I'm fine for the time being, thanks." Oscar looked at the paintings that were hanging on the wall. "I recognise that one. You had that in Hong Kong."

"Yes. I bought it in a gallery in Aberdeen harbour."

Emma joined the two men, checked on Robert and sat next to Ian. "Lunch will be about 30 minutes."

"Well, Oscar, don't keep us in suspense any longer. Why are you moving and where to?" asked Ian, once his wife had settled down next to him.

"It all started about 12 months ago," said Oscar, sitting back on his sette. "I'd become unhappy for a while, both with my career, and the general changing of life in Hong Kong. You going back to England, Ian, was not a happy time for me either. Plus, it all seemed so easy for you. You were going back home! But for me, well Hong Kong was my home. I didn't have a home to go back to."

Oscar stood up and walked over to the large picture window. He looked out into the front garden before continuing, "Hong Kong has changed so much and I decided I needed to move on. One day, when I was at lunch with May Ling, she mentioned that one of her clients was moving to Cyprus. I queried about visas, etc. but she said it was now becoming far easier to buy a passport from another country, legally! It would give you, a so-called 'global citizenship'. Immediately that afternoon, and for most of the next day, I did quite a lot of research and found that at least 13 countries were offering their country's citizenship… but, for a price! Europe seemed favourite, but Austria was really the only serious option available at that time, but it was very expensive. In addition, I'm not sure Austria is a country where I wanted to live. Their winters are cold and they have a lot of snow! A number of Caribbean countries, however, were offering the same opportunity but for much less money. And, of course, they have much better… much warmer weather!"

Oscar returned to his seat and carried on with his story. "A number of these Caribbean countries already qualify for visa free travelling to more than 120 nations, including the 26 European countries of the Schengen Area. I can still, of course, use my Hong Kong passport if I want to, or, if I need to!"

"You seem to have it all worked out," said Emma. "I didn't know it was legal to buy different passports."

"Oh yes. If you have the money, a legal passport is not a problem. You do not have to live there or even set foot in the country! The old seven years residency rule to qualify, or marry a local, well, those rules just do not seem to apply any more. It's all about money!"

Ian was sitting quietly and wondered if Andrei had heard of this new development. Knowing Andrei though, he thought, he was probably the instigator of the scheme in the first place!

"Conveniently," continued Oscar, "many of the same Caribbean islands are also offshore financial centres. Citizenship in low-tax countries such as St Kitts or Antigua means lots more income for the local economy."

"How does that work then?" asked Ian, trying to wipe thoughts of Andrei from his mind.

"Most Caribbean countries, like Antigua, are not wealthy. They do not have oil like Trinidad or Venezuela and they have to compete with all the other islands for tourism money. Anyway, this is all very much above board and is actually promoted by these countries' governments! The money received is supposedly ploughed back into infrastructure and local business developments. It is reckoned that in 2018 this 'citizenship business' was worth $3 billion a year worldwide – and growing! Antigua normally charges US$200,000, but when I applied it was just $100,000! I had to apply through a London-based agent, but after filling in lots of forms and being subject to lots and lots of checks, I was given my Antigua passport – and that's where I'm heading now!"

"Wow," said Ian, looking at Emma. They were both surprised with Oscar's story. "So, you are going to live in Antigua? Have you given up on Hong Kong altogether?"

"Well, as the saying goes, never say never! But yes, at the moment I am going to try my hand in the Caribbean. There are art galleries in St John's that I've done some initial communicating with and I'm hopeful I might be able to do some business with them."

"I hope it all works out," replied Ian, genuinely pleased for Oscar.

"Thanks… look, you have this lovely wife and now a beautiful son. I do not have any of these benefits or responsibilities. You have also worked abroad in New York and Hong Kong whilst you were single. I have always worked in Hong Kong. If I don't do it now, well I guess I might just age slowly into a sad old man living in a branch of communist China. I'm certain that Beijing will slowly force more changes on Hong Kong as the years progress, so I want to take my opportunity now, whilst I'm still young enough… and can afford to do it!"

Opportunity! thought Ian. It's becoming a very popular word to use!

"I know it's going to be a challenge," continued Oscar, "but I'm committed now and intend to make it a success."

Robert was slowly waking up and this broke the brief silence. Emma went over to the cot and picked him up. "I had better change and feed this young person first. Hopefully we can then have our own lunch in peace."

After Emma had left the room, Ian said, "So, who is going to be my contact in Hong Kong from now on then?"

"It's all changing, Ian. The wealth now is all feeding in from China. Your best bet is to link with May Ling. She's good and knows her market well – especially Beijing!"

"Good point. Thank you," replied Ian, but he had already thought in this direction.

"I can, of course, still be your new contact … in the Caribbean!"

Chapter 31

Two days later, Ian had returned to work for the mornings only. Although he qualified for paternity leave, Emma had suggested that she would like some time with Robert on her own. It was therefore agreed that Ian would call into his office for the next few mornings.

Whilst Robert was asleep, Emma took advantage of the quiet time to access her business email account. There were a number of congratulatory emails, two small queries from Andrew, but otherwise nothing much of importance. She was able to answer Andrew's queries very quickly, but suddenly she felt partly sad and partly disappointed. She wondered if she had been deliberately excluded from the main goings on in the office. Everything seemed to be carrying on as usual, regardless of her absence! Maybe she should take Robert into the office and evaluate the situation for herself.

That evening Emma asked Ian if, tomorrow afternoon, he could give her a lift to her office. She said some of the girls would like to see Robert. Ian did not want Emma driving again just yet, so agreed to the request. He also knew that Emma would also be missing what was going on in the office in her absence. Was she being missed?

The following afternoon, Robert was placed into his carry

cot which was then carefully and securely strapped onto the back seat of Ian's car and the Caxton family headed off in the direction of Emma's office. Emma had spoken to Andrew that morning and he had informed her that, as far as he was aware, most people would be in the office and would love to see both her and Robert.

Ian parked in Emma's reserved car parking space and said he would stay in his car and do some emails.

Just over an hour later, Emma returned with an unhappy Robert.

"He needs a change of nappy and a feed. I'll sit in the back for a few minutes," said Emma.

She gently climbed into the back of the car and started to undress Robert.

"How did it go?" asked Ian. He was concerned that Emma had returned to the car with a serious expression on her face.

"The girls loved holding and cooing with Robert. Andrew asked me a few questions, but the other two partners were both out on business. Do you know what? There was a very strange atmosphere in there."

"What do you mean?"

"Bar for a couple of business questions that Andrew asked, nobody wanted to talk about work. It was as though I was more of a visitor than a partner."

"Oh. Well, maybe most people deliberately avoided the subject of work because you are on maternity leave."

"Ian. I am not just a lower grade employee, I'm a partner!"

"I know… but even so…"

"I'll give it a week and maybe make an appointment with the other partners. There may be something going on in the background that they are not telling me about."

During the rest of the time that Emma sat in the back of the car feeding Robert, Ian thought about what Emma had just said. She had always been quick to pick up on strange or unusual changes in the atmosphere at work, something Ian had admired. People cautiously avoided saying what they were thinking or deliberately changed the subject. Also, the absence of her two partners from the office was probably significant too. Was that just a coincidence or a deliberate act? Did Emma have a long-term future in the partnership, or, indeed, did she still see herself in the same role with the addition of Robert? Time would tell, he thought. One thing was certain, Emma would make her choice and it would be his role to support that decision.

In the time that it took Ian to leave Emma's office car park, drive back to their home and for him to open up his computer in the office, he had received three new emails. One in particular caught his eye. It was from Bob Taylor in Monaco.

Hello Ian,

Hope all is well with you and Emma and you are also enjoying your new life as a father.

Zoe's father, who I think I told you about, is the main partner in our business. He has come up with some new ideas about expanding the business. The gallery here in Monaco is largely a front for our much wider art trading organisation which covers mainland Europe and some sectors of the Far East. We are now looking at opportunities further afield, including London.

I told my father-in-law of your experience and business contacts and, to cut a long story short, we are interested to know if you would be available to help us set up a UK agency?

We don't need an answer this minute, but please have a think about it.

Look forward to chatting more in the future.

Zoe also sends her best wishes to both Emma and your

new baby. She also wants to know if the baby is a boy or a girl and names.
 Cheers,
 Bob.

Here we go again, thought Ian. How did Bob and Zoe know about Robert? Is this the business opportunity Bob had hinted at when they met in Monaco? And Andrei, what role does he have in all this? He said in his last email to expect a business opportunity in Monaco! Was this it? Ian certainly began to feel as though he was now being teased by the word 'opportunity' and more seriously, being played with – like a puppet on a string!

After reading Bob's email again and reflecting on it, Ian wrote a brief holding reply, including asking some questions. Let's just see what Mr Taylor makes of those!

Whilst Robert was asleep in his day cot, Emma had collected together her paperwork and files pertaining to her business partnership agreement. She wanted to remind herself what had been agreed when the partnership was first established and also what were the wider terms, conditions and levels of compensation in the event of one partner leaving the business.

Some minutes later, whilst Emma was making notes from her investigation, Ian joined her in the dining room. He was very surprised to see the table almost covered in papers and red folders. "What's all this, spring cleaning?!" asked Ian, jokingly.

"I'm reviewing my partnership agreement papers. I want to be sure of all my facts before any possible next meeting," answered Emma, scribbling away.

"You really do think there is something going on behind your back, don't you?"

"It's all too strange to be otherwise."

"So, what's your next step?" Ian pulled back one of the dining table chairs and sat down.

Emma put down her pen, removed her spectacles and looked across the table to Ian. "At the moment, I'm making sure I know all the details of the partnership agreement, when it was first set up and the amendments that have been added since. Depending upon what I discover will dictate my next move. Either to be proactive and push for a meeting and clear the air, or to just sit back and wait for my maternity leave to run out."

"Mmm. I see. But in the meantime, what about your clients?" said Ian. He was also thinking that office politics was one thing, but abandoning clients is something quite different.

"They are all aware that I am on maternity leave and Andrew has covered well. Where he has been out of his depth, or lacks historical knowledge of a client, he has either contacted me or spoken to one of the other partners. The clients are not going to be punished or penalised. I would not do anything to jeopardise the firm's relationship with any of our clients!"

"What's your thinking at the moment then? Do you still see yourself holding down a full partner's role in the future?"

"Between you and me, the answer is no. During the last few weeks of my pregnancy, I was seriously coming to the conclusion that it was not possible to be a full-time business partner and be a proper mum for Robert. Don't get me wrong, a lot of mothers can do both and with the proper childcare help, they can still be successful. I'm not really one of them. I would still like to keep some of my clients, but I would also want to exclude all the politics, hassles and complications attached to being a partner."

"I can see that. Look, I'll let you get on with what you

were doing. The main reason I popped in here was to ask if you wanted a cup of coffee." Ian stood up and walked towards the door.

Emma smiled. "Yes please, that would be nice. Thank you."

It was during the following Saturday morning that Emma received a telephone call out of the blue! If the information given to her was true, it would definitely mean a review to her thinking and potentially a change in the direction of her career completely!

Emma eventually found Ian in the garage. He had decided that with a little extra time currently available, he would finally tidy up the garage shelves and throw away unnecessary clutter.

"Ian. Can I have a word?" asked Emma, standing in the garage side doorway.

Ian stopped and put down two old tins of paint and joined Emma at the door. "Of course. What's the problem?"

"I've just received a strange telephone call."

"Oh. Who from?" queried Ian.

"That's just it. The woman on the other end of the line wouldn't give her name. All she did say was that she thought I ought to know that my company, Murray, Caxton and Tyler, was shortly going to be taken over by William Jones & Co."

"Who are William Jones & Co.... and how did this woman know?"

"A much larger firm of accountants. She did not wish to say any more."

"So that's all this anonymous caller said?"

"Yes, but the funny thing is, I think I recognised her voice!"

Chapter 32

Viktor's period of training in Ian's department was nearing its completion, but he still had one further department to move to before his part in the graduate training scheme was officially complete. He'd really enjoyed his time with Ian and Penny and thought the three of them made a really good team. He knew he had been treated just like any other team member and he'd appreciated being included in many department discussions and decisions. He had a high regard for Ian and felt he had learnt a lot from his experience, depth of knowledge and, especially, his effective management style. He didn't really want to be moving on, but hoped the opportunity might arise for the team to be reunited sometime in the future.

Penny was just in the process of updating Ian's diary when her telephone rang. It was Ian himself! What a coincidence, she thought.

"Hello, Ian. How are Emma and Robert?"

"Hi, Penny. They are both fine, thanks. Robert is beginning to find a sleep pattern at last, so that helps our own sleep patterns too!"

Penny laughed. "Yes, I can see that it would."

"Which means I'm needed less at home now, so I will be back full time from tomorrow."

"Oh. Okay. I've just updated your online diary if you want to check it through. Let me know if you want to make any changes. Also, Vic finishes with us early next week."

"That's come round very quickly. I will need to do his final report. Can you put some notes together on your observations too?"

"Yes, I will. Quite easy this time." Penny had a high opinion of their latest trainee.

The doctor looked anxiously at his patient laying on the examination table. He had spent the last 60 minutes completing a thorough examination of the septuagenarian in front of him. He now leaned back in his chair and pulled the stethoscope from his ears. "Well, Mr Petrov, all done. You can get dressed now and we will then have a chat." The doctor walked back to his desk, sat down and jotted down some notes.

Although the doctor's Canadian accent was very strong, Andrei had managed to understand most of what had been said during the meeting. Where it was not clear, he had asked the doctor to repeat or clarify his words.

Andrei climbed off the couch and put on his shirt and jumper, but left his heavy jacket on a coat hook on the wall near the door. He then sat on the remaining spare chair next to the doctor.

After a few seconds, the doctor looked up and removed his spectacles. "You are in quite good shape for your age, Mr Petrov. Heart rate is a little on the high side, but just okay. Blood pressure is a little on the high side as well. Weight is fine. We will know a lot more once we get the results of the blood and urine samples back plus the scan and x-ray results. I must admit I'm concerned about these recurring chest pains. As you've already been informed, they could be related to stress or alcohol, or both! But, as you said earlier, you have changed your lifestyle in recent months. I'm therefore hoping we will see a positive reflection of this action in these test results. If not, then my advice would be to be checked over by a specialist heart and chest consultant. I know an excellent one in Toronto."

Andrei had listened carefully to the doctor and had nodded repeatedly to inform him that he understood. "When will you have the test results?"

"They will probably all be here in about three days' time. So, should we say Friday at the same time to see you again?"

Andrei was booked to leave Canada in a week's time. He hoped he didn't need to start changing his plans. "Yes, doc. Friday is fine. Thank you."

Julian was just finishing preparing his early morning breakfast of freshly squeezed orange juice and a bowl of fresh fruit, when he heard his computer ping. He carried his food over to the table where his laptop sat. He ate a spoonful of fruit and opened up his emails. There were several new entries, but his immediate attention was caught by the one from Mr Sokolov.

> *Hello Julian,*
>
> *I'm not sure at the moment, but my plans to leave Canada next week may have to change. I will know better on Friday.*
>
> *Have you spoken with Marie recently? If so, is she happy with my request?*
>
> *VS.*

The Virgin Atlantic flight from London to Antigua and Barbuda had just finished banking as it adjusted its levels again for, what Oscar hoped, was the final approach and landing into V C Bird International Airport. He sat quietly, slightly perspiring and glued to the view through his cabin window. The airport suddenly came back into view for the third time. Whilst the very strong cross wind was not hurricane force, it nevertheless was having its impact, and challenging the skills of the pilot in charge. The plane dropped lower and lower and whilst intermittent strong gusts buffeted and tipped each wing, this looked like a definite landing, finally, this time. Oscar, up until the last hour, had thoroughly enjoyed the flight. He had treated himself to an upgrade to Upper Class, but he was now wondering if, whatever class you were flying in, whether we were all going to land safely – and in one piece! He tightly gripped the leather covered arms of his seat as yet another strong gust hit the side of the plane. The airport was getting closer as the plane was lowered. Oscar willed the plane to get down, this time. Finally there was the familiar bump as the wheels hit the runway and a loud cheer of relief from most of his fellow passengers. The plane still hurtled down the runway, fighting against the powerful gusts of wind, but then the pilot firstly applied the air brakes and then the wheel brakes, and gradually the plane almost came to a stop before turning and slowly taxiing towards the terminal. All passengers and most of the crew must have given a deep sigh of relief. Eventually a stewardess announced in a calm and collected manner, as only a British stewardess would in such circumstances, "Welcome to Antigua. The local time is now 16.35."

When Oscar entered the passport control area, he ignored the queue snaking towards the 'international passports' booths, and, instead, headed for the booths saying 'local residents'. He produced his pristine new Antiguan passport and was waved through almost without a second glance.

Once he had collected his suitcase from baggage reclaim, he headed to join the queue for taxis. Five minutes later, he was heading towards St John's, the country's capital and the largest city of Antigua. With a population of just over 22,000, Oscar knew that Antigua was going to be a far cry from the many millions of humans and the tall skyscrapers he'd left behind in Hong Kong!

Oscar checked into his pre-booked hotel for an initial two weeks stay. He decided to use his Hong Kong passport here, to avoid any possible confusion. He didn't want anyone in the hotel to query or wonder why a 'local Antiguan resident' was staying in a local hotel!

The hotel acknowledged Oscar's comment that he may need to extend his stay, and they assured him that it would not be a problem. After he'd checked into his room and partly unpacked his case, he quickly changed into his swimwear and headed for the hotel's pool. Although it was still early evening, the sun was already setting and gradually disappearing into the golden Caribbean Sea. The wind had now calmed down to a refreshing breeze, but the air temperature was still in the high 80s Fahrenheit and would, Oscar anticipated, hardly change for many months to come.

Oscar dived into the pool and slowly swam three lengths before arriving at the 'swim-up bar'. His heart rate had now fully recovered and the memory of his plane's troubled landing was thankfully fading fast. He watched the top of the sun finally disappear from sight over the horizon and then sipped his first rum and coke of the day. It tasted absolutely wonderful!

Bob Taylor and his father-in-law, Antoine, were sitting in the Monaco gallery and discussing the company's business. Whilst everything about Antoine said French, his use of the English language certainly didn't. Three years at Oxford University followed by six years working for two London art galleries, had certainly anglicised his accent. Despite moving back to France to join his own father's art trading and brokering business a number of years ago now, he still retained the same British accent when speaking the English language. Now, when he discussed matters with his son-in-law, it was simpler and easier for them both to speak in English.

Bob had shown Antoine the trading books for the last quarter and they had now moved onto plans for the future. Antoine had never been at all sure about Bob's expansion plans. He was keen for the business to remain stable, or even to be slimmed down slightly, especially as he was now nearing retirement. Bob, however, was more ambitious and often felt exasperated with Antoine's reticence. He was, and always would be, thankful for the business partnership opportunity Antoine had given to both him and Zoe, as part of their wedding present, but Bob still felt frustrated not to be able to make his own decisions. He had many more plans for the business.

However, just two months ago a compromise had finally been reached. Bob had agreed that the business would retreat from some of the smaller agencies, but in return, Antoine had reluctantly agreed to let Bob have his way with London.

Eventually, the discussion moved on to Ian's reply to Bob's earlier email.

"Interesting reply," observed Antoine. "I'm not convinced he is interested."

"I didn't expect a definite yes at this stage. However, I still think he will help us set up the agency. What I was really hoping for was that he might suggest someone who he could recommend."

"Well, this is your opportunity, Bob. I will help you with the initial financing but, after that, this will be your separate business." Antoine leaned back in his chair, removed his reading glasses and looked directly at Bob. "Let's hope you make the right decision and … a success of it."

Chapter 33

It was a week later when Emma marched towards the partnership's conference room. Although she was officially still on maternity leave, she was dressed in a grey suit and a white blouse. This was an important business meeting and it was her intention to treat it with the high level of respect it deserved. To do this, she decided, she needed to be dressed appropriately, thus demonstrating to her fellow partners the seriousness she attached to the meeting.

As she pushed open the conference room door and entered, she noticed Bernard Murray, the senior partner and John Tyler, the junior partner, were already sitting in their usual places. Susan Flewin, John Tyler's PA, was sitting slightly away from the partners. Emma walked towards her usual place and said a formal "Good morning" and sat down. Both Bernard and John had stood when Emma had entered the room and, before re-sitting, they gave each other an inquisitive glance.

"Hello, Emma," said Bernard. "You are looking well and how is young... Robert?"

"He's fine, Bernard. Thank you for asking." Emma proceeded to remove some papers from her briefcase.

Bernard and John exchanged glances again and raised their eyebrows.

"So, are you enjoying motherhood, Emma?" asked John, not really sure what to say. Emma seemed to be in a very serious and strange mood.

Emma looked straight at John, but did not answer his question. Instead, she looked from John to Bernard and said, "I have called this meeting because I have received some alarming information." Out of the corner of her eye she noticed Susan Flewin had looked down to her notepad. Her presence was normally required to take the minutes. "This information suggests that Murray, Caxton and Tyler is in the process of being taken over by William Jones & Co!"

"What!?" exclaimed John Tyler somewhat startled. "That's news to me! Bernard?"

Bernard Murray folded his arms and sat back in his chair. He didn't say anything for a couple of seconds.

"Well, Bernard," asked Emma, "Is this true?"

"About six weeks ago," explained Bernard, "Charles Jones, the senior partner at William Jones & Co, telephoned and invited me to lunch at his golf club. During the meal, he announced that his company had received an injection of money from a foreign investor and they were now looking to spend this money on acquiring one or two good quality accountancy firms. He asked me directly if we would be interested in being taken over! Needless to say, I was somewhat taken aback. I probably mumbled something asking about what terms he was proposing. Also, I said that I would need to discuss the matter fully with my partners, etcetera. He had certainly caught me on the hop. He went on to explain that he had identified three other firms and would be having a similar conversation with each of them before they made up their minds on who to formally approach."

It was John Tyler who was the next to speak. "So why all the secrecy? Why didn't you inform Emma and me?"

"Charles asked me to keep our conversation informal and personal for the time being. I had not committed us to anything and he promised he would come back to me once he'd sounded out the other firms. There was nothing really to tell!"

"So, you did not tell him that we were not for sale then?" queried Emma, now wanting to get to the 'nitty-gritty' of the matter. "What else has happened subsequently that you have not told us about?"

Bernard ignored the slight barb in Emma's questions. "Charles telephoned me early last week and suggested we meet again. I told him that I would need to speak to my partners first, but he said it was important that the fewer people the better who knew about their approach. He then talked about market sensitivity. And again, there was nothing concrete to say to you both."

"So, have you met Charles again?" asked John Tyler.

"Yes," replied Bernard. He looked at Emma. "Last week. It was the day you brought Robert into the office. I'm sorry I missed you both."

Emma ignored Bernard's apology. "Have you agreed to anything now?"

"No!" Bernard said emphatically. He was beginning to perspire a little. He knew he was appearing slightly deceitful in front of the other partners. "Charles wanted copies of our accounts, but I told him no, not until he was prepared to indicate what sort of terms he would be offering. That, truthfully, is where we currently stand."

Emma looked at John. She also noticed Susan Flewin deliberately trying to avoid any form of eye contact with her.

"Right, we all now know about this approach, so where do we go from here?" asked Emma. "I think before we discuss this matter it would be better if Susan was not a party to our further discussions. I don't think we want the rest of our discussions to be minuted." Susan took the hint and stood up to leave. As she walked towards the door Emma said, "Thank you, Susan." Susan briefly stopped and looked at Emma. Emma smiled back knowingly.

"So," said John, once Susan had left the room, "Are we for sale?"

"You tell me," replied Bernard. "You both now know about the inquiry. What are your thoughts?"

John was quick to answer. "I've worked damned hard to become a partner. I say we tell them to get stuffed!"

"Emma?" asked Bernard, still smiling at John's answer. "You have raised this situation to a debating level. What are your thoughts?"

"I would like to know the terms of any sort of deal before I can make a sensible decision. If they are prepared to make a substantial offer then I say we consider it. For Bernard it would help towards early retirement and, for you John, well, it would really set you up with your young family."

"But I would lose my job!" cried John.

"Emma's right, John," said Bernard, finally beginning to relax a little. "It would set you up. Charles thinks a lot about this firm so he is unlikely to just discard yours or anyone else's talents lightly."

"But what about our clients? Do they not get a say?" said Emma, being deliberately naive.

"The obvious answer to that is no," said Bernard. "But, of course, all would be negotiable." Bernard knew where Emma was aiming.

"Okay," said Emma. "Can we vote? I say we offer our accounts to William Jones & Co. and make our decision only when we've seen their final offer." Emma raised her right arm.

The room fell silent and John looked for leadership from Bernard.

Suddenly Bernard raised his arm. "I agree with Emma."

John looked across at his two senior partners. "Okay," he said, raising his right arm. "I guess there is nothing to lose at the moment. Let's get on with it."

"I'll speak to Charles straight after this meeting and get a set of accounts across to him," volunteered Bernard. "Mind, it is essential that Charles does not hear about this meeting. Our conversation has got to stay in this room. All agreed?"

Both Emma and John agreed. John also said he would speak to Susan to make sure she did not speak about what she had heard.

Emma smiled as she put her papers back into her briefcase. Seems your PA, Mr Tyler, already knows more than you do!

"By the way, John," said Emma, standing up, "To answer your question from earlier. Yes, I am thoroughly enjoying motherhood!"

"Before you go, Emma, can I have a word please?" said Bernard, still sitting in his seat.

John took the hint, nodded to Emma and left the room. Emma returned to her seat and waited for Bernard to speak.

"Thank you, Emma," said Bernard. "You hopefully can see it has been a difficult few weeks."

"Bernard. We have known each other for many years and I knew you wouldn't do anything underhand or be untruthful. I do not like, or applaud, Charles Jones' methods, but let's hope, no …, let's make sure … that the final deal he offers is exactly what we are looking for!"

Over dinner that evening, Emma relayed to Ian a summary of the partners' meeting, describing the discussions and the final conclusions.

"So, the anonymous telephone caller was accurate after all. I wonder how this lady knew?" said Ian.

"I recognised the voice immediately she telephoned me. After all, she worked for me for five years!"

"What?!"

"Susan joined me when I was a minor partner. She was a quick learner and we worked well together. We also became very good friends. However, when Harry Maguire retired and my role increased significantly, Susan asked if she could do a lesser job as she also wanted to reduce her hours. John Tyler was in line for promotion to partner and I recommended Susan to him. The rest, as they say, is history."

"Wow. But how did she know about the possible takeover before even her boss!?"

"Susan may not be as ambitious as some, but she is still very intelligent and has friends, who are also 'connections'. Hence she decided to tell me rather than her boss."

"This Susan is a very clever lady," said Ian. He was very impressed.

"Yes, she is and on Saturday, at her home, she will receive a Fortnum & Mason hamper with a nice 'thank you' card… anonymous of course!"

Chapter 34

When Andrei left the doctor's surgery on Friday, he was not a happy man. The results of all the tests were inconclusive. Yes, his blood pressure was slightly down again, but following his change in lifestyle of less alcohol and reduced stress levels, both he and his doctor were expecting this. Both blood and urine samples showed no obvious abnormalities, neither did the scan and x-ray results. The regularity of his chest pains was slightly less, but still there. In conclusion, the doctor recommended Andrei visit the specialist in Toronto for yet more tests. When Andrei had asked what would happen if he did not have any more tests, the doctor shrugged his shoulders and said that it was his choice, his life. Nobody was sure what was causing the chest pains, so really no obvious prescription could be made. He could live with a slightly reduced quality of life or he could take more positive actions and have more specialist tests.

Andrei said he would sleep on the doctor's comments. He paid the medical bill and left the surgery feeling no better… nor any worse than he had done when he first visited the surgery a week ago.

When he awoke the following morning, Andrei had made his decision. He would check out of his hotel in two days' time as planned and stick with the flights and arrangements that Julian had already organised and paid for. His next stop would be London and then on to Scotland to stay with his friend, the Laird and his family, to breathe in some lovely Scottish fresh air, check on his investment and partake in just the occasional 'wee dram'.

Andrei opened up his computer and sent an update email to Julian, informing him that he was moving on next week… this time to Scotland, as planned.

At the same time that Andrei's email arrived in Julian's inbox, Julian was driving back from Nice airport, where he had dropped off two of his regular Monaco customers. The rest of the day was unplanned so he decided to take the slower, but more scenic, coastal route back to Monaco. He stopped at one of his favourite viewing points, close to the town of Èze, and got out of his car. It was a lovely, warm and sunny afternoon. He immediately felt the sun's heat on his face and arms. The almost cloudless sky made the view seem bigger than he had previously remembered. On the horizon he could just make out the shape of either a cruise liner or was it a small oil tanker? Either way, the slow-moving ship and the smooth Mediterranean Sea gave a picture of peace and serenity.

Julian removed his mobile phone from his pocket and checked his text and email inboxes. He immediately spotted and opened the email from Mr Sokolov. After reading the message, he was once again worried about his boss. It was not what the message had said that concerned him, it was the tone. When there was a problem with Andrei, Julian could measure the severity by the seriousness of the words used in the email. When all was well, the message contained more jovial quips. There were no jovial quips in this email!

Julian switched off his emails and used the same flexible machine to telephone Marie.

"Bonjour?" announced the female voice at the receiving end of the line.

"Hello, Marie. It's Julian," said Julian, immediately pushing Marie to speak English.

"Julian! So good to hear from you. How are you?"

"I'm very well, thank you, but I'm still worried about Andrei," said Julian, with genuine concern.

"What seems to be the problem?"

"I'm not really sure, it's more a feeling that all is not well. He worries me. Did you sort out an answer to his request?"

"Yes, yes. I did that a few days ago. The gift should have arrived in Scotland by now."

"Thank you. I'll catch up with you again soon."

"Au revoir, Julian."

Julian switched from the telephone connection and back to his emails. He typed his new message to Andrei, wishing him a safe journey and a good time in Scotland. He confirmed that Marie had completed his request.

After Julian had sent his email, he put the phone back into his pocket, locked the car and started the 15-minute stroll to a little restaurant he knew, one of his favourites. The restaurant had a lovely shaded balcony overlooking the sea and was a favourite with the locals for its fresh seafood. Julian had not eaten since breakfast and he was particularly eager to find out what the restaurant's 'catch of the day' would offer this time.

Ian had put together a glowing, but fair, report of Viktor's time in his department. He had also included Penny's positive comments too. It was Viktor's last day and he was now sitting in front of Ian in Ian's office.

"Here's my report, Vic." Ian handed over a file which was a comprehensive appraisal of Viktor's time in the department. "I've also got a copy that will be given to Michael

Hopkins. In summary, I have been very pleased with your positivity, enthusiasm and commitment. Have a thorough read and come back to me with anything you disagree with or do not understand."

"Thank you, Ian. I've had a great time in your department and really feel you have treated me just like any other member of the team. I've especially appreciated being included in many of the department discussions and decisions and I know I have gained a much deeper knowledge and understanding, not only about paintings, but also about the wider art world as well. Your management style is quite refreshing and I have learnt a lot of positives from that as well! To be very honest, I am quite disappointed to be moving on. I really do hope we can work together again in the future."

"Thank you for that, Vic. You have contributed well and both Penny and I have enjoyed your opinions and enthusiasm. I guess we all learn from these times and yes, maybe we will work together again in the future,… who knows!? In the meantime, good luck with the rest of your career."

Ian stood up and walked around to the front of his desk. Viktor stood up and Ian offered his hand. Viktor grasped it firmly and both men shook hands enthusiastically.

"Keep in touch, Vic."

Viktor smiled back and headed for the door. He hesitated slightly but decided now was not the time. He walked over to Penny's desk instead.

"So how did it go?" asked Penny, genuinely interested.

"It went well. I've still got my report to read." Viktor waved the folder for Penny to see. "But, yes, he seemed pleased with my contribution. I'm really sad to be moving on. It's been great working with you two."

Penny leant a little closer to Viktor and whispered, "To be honest, I know Ian is disappointed to be losing you.

232

He does not say that about many of the trainees who pass through here!"

Viktor smiled. He was beginning to feel a little emotional. "Thanks for everything, Penny. See you soon."

As Viktor turned and headed for the outer door, Penny replied. "Good luck, Vic." She also had a small lump in her throat.

Chapter 35

Bernard Murray had sent copies of the last three years' accounts to Charles Jones and had subsequently answered some supplementary questions. It was a week later and early in the evening, after all the staff had gone home, that Bernard gave Charles a tour of all the offices. After the tour they returned to Bernard's office. Bernard offered Charles a drink and he asked for a whisky and soda. Bernard duly poured two drinks and they both sat down next to Bernard's meeting table.

"Here's to the future of Murray, Caxton and Tyler!" announced Charles and he immediately sipped his drink.

"I'll drink to that, Charles. Cheers." Bernard also sipped his drink. "So, what have you got to tell me?"

Charles leaned forward and placed his drink on the small table between them. "We would like to make an offer for your business, Bernard." Charles put his hand in his inside jacket pocket and pulled out two folded sheets of A4 paper. He also slipped on his reading glasses and read out the details of the proposed offer.

Bernard listened intently to every word until Charles had finished and then he spoke.

"My immediate reaction is twofold, Charles. Firstly, we, the partners, have not discussed or had a meeting to consider a possible sale of the business. I am not the only decision maker here and I will have to put those figures to my partners for their views. I am sure there will be a strong reluctance to accept. Secondly, I personally think this offer undervalues our company's current worth and our future growth projections. For the last five years our turnover has increased, on average, by about 7% per annum and we have budgeted for similar growth over the next three years."

Charles leaned forward, picked up his drink and sipped his whisky, before returning the glass to the table. "Okay, Bernard, maybe I need to speak with my people again."

"Do I get a copy of that offer to tell my partners?"

"No. I think we both agree it will not persuade them. So what do you think your company is worth?" asked Charles leaning back in his chair.

"Probably four times current annual turnover in cash. Plus, I would like guarantees for our non-partnership staff of at least 12 months' employment. Finally, we would need to agree what time constraints you would apply to any partner who leaves under the sale agreement.

"You mean from approaching existing clients?"

"Yes."

Charles smiled at Bernard and then nodded his head gently. "That's quite a deal! I don't think we can come anywhere near those figures."

Bernard shrugged his shoulders and sipped his whisky. He then looked directly at Charles and said, "Okay, but as I say, I will need a much stronger offer from you before I believe I have any chance of getting my colleagues to accept a sale."

Charles stood up, drank the last of the contents of his glass and said, "Bernard, nice chatting again. I hear what you say. I need to speak with my people and I will come back to you very shortly."

Bernard stood up and stretched his hand out towards Charles. They both shook hands. "Nice meeting with you again, Charles. Let me show you the way out."

The two men left Bernard's office and walked together towards the main entrance. They said their goodbyes and Bernard closed and locked the outside door. He walked back to his office and finished his drink. He then went over to his desk and pulled open the top right-hand drawer. He lifted out a small recording machine, pressed the 'stop' button and then 'rewind'. After about four seconds he pressed the 'stop' button again and then 'play'. Bernard listened to the clear recording of his conversation with Charles and smiled contentedly. He pressed the 'stop' button once again and then switched the machine off. He walked across to his wall safe and after opening the door, placed the machine on the top shelf... for safekeeping!!

It was two weeks later when Emma returned to the conference room. Although she was in a serious frame of mind, she also felt far more relaxed than on her last visit. Certainly, she was in a less confrontational mood. She greeted her two partners this time with friendly 'hellos' and smiles. After a brief exchange of baby comments, Bernard suggested they begin the meeting.

Since the initial meeting in Bernard's room, Charles had been back to Bernard several times on the telephone, discussing changes and different options. Two days before this current partners' meeting, Bernard had received, what he guessed, was William Jones & Co's final offer. He thought it was a reasonable offer and had called the partners' meeting to discuss all the details. He had photocopied the offer for John and had scanned and emailed a copy to Emma. All partners were now fully briefed of the offer currently on the table.

Bernard opened the meeting. "There is only one item

on the agenda this morning and that relates to the offer by William Jones & Co to purchase our partnership. I don't propose to have minutes taken at this stage. Firstly, we need to hear each partner's thoughts of the offer currently on the table. I might add that I've had further communications and another meeting with Charles Jones after I sent them copies of the last three years' accounts. Charles made his company's first offer, which he subsequently withdrew, after I said I would not be in a position to recommend the offer to our partners."

"Do we need to know the details of the first offer?" asked John.

"It is irrelevant as Charles and I have subsequently had a number of telephone conversations, which kept slowly improving on the original offer."

"Okay," said John, happy with Bernard's answer.

"So, we now come to the 'main event'. The latest offer. I have given you both advance copies." Both Emma and John nodded their heads. "Good. I personally think this will be William Jones & Co's final offer. It comes very close to what I was suggesting to Charles at our meeting two weeks ago and I recommend its acceptance. I'm open to questions and comments."

It was Emma who was first to speak. "There are one or two parts that I am not totally comfortable with, but there is enough here to get my vote."

"I'm not happy at all," responded John. "Essentially, I'm taking voluntary redundancy!"

Emma and Bernard looked at each other.

Eventually Bernard spoke, "Charles made it plain that they did not need the partners to stay on. That is why they are being reasonably generous with the lump sum they will pay each of us. It's probably worth about three years' salary, John, so it gives you ample time to start afresh. You are well respected and will have little problem obtaining a new position. You could even buy yourself a new partnership!"

Emma now intervened. "We don't need a unanimous vote on this, John. Bernard's and my share add up to 82%, which is well above our constitution's requirement of 65%. Also, if you wanted to stay on, I doubt they would offer you a partnership and you would be vulnerable in the future. This is definitely your best option."

"Why are you in favour, Emma? You have a lot to lose!?" asked John. He could not see why she would want out.

"With the addition of Robert to my life, I realise my priorities have shifted and, whilst I still want a future with my accountancy career, it is no longer my number one priority."

"I feel as though you have both ganged up on me," replied John. He was obviously unhappy.

It was Bernard's turn to speak. "We both think this is the best deal for the three of us. It's not what we had planned but life sometimes is not always as we've planned. I would prefer a unanimous vote, John. Do you want 24 hours to reconsider?"

For the next twenty seconds there was silence in the room. Eventually John reluctantly said, "No... I still feel stitched up, but I will vote for the offer."

"Excellent," said Bernard. In five years' time, John, you will look back and know you made the right decision."

"I hope you are right!" replied John, feeling somewhat brow beaten into submission.

"Right, let's just be clear," announced Bernard. "Let it be minuted now that we, Murray, Caxton and Tyler, after much discussion, agree to accept the offer in front of us, from William Jones & Co, to sell our partnership to the same William Jones & Co, subject to the full terms and conditions as set out in this document. All those in favour please raise their right arm."

Bernard and Emma raised their hands. John looked slowly from Emma to Bernard and then with great mental pain, raised his own right arm.

"Let it formally be recorded that this vote of acceptance is unanimous," said Bernard. "I will telephone Charles immediately after this meeting."

"Let it also be formally recorded that I still feel that I have been stuffed!" said John in frustration.

"Do you really want it formally so noted?" asked Emma to John.

After a pause, John stood up and started to walk towards the door. When he reached the end of the table, he stopped and announced. "No... just that I've been informally stuffed!"

When Emma returned to the car park, Ian and Robert were waiting in Ian's car. Emma opened the rear door and placed her briefcase on the floor. She glanced at Robert and smiled as she heard his gentle rhythmic breathing as he was sleeping. She gently closed the door and climbed into the front passenger side, quietly pulling the door to.

"A successful conclusion?" asked Ian.

"Just about everything I wanted. A good result. Bernard was really happy, but John thought we had ganged up on him!" replied Emma, pulling her seat belt across and clicking it into position.

"So, he refused to agree?"

"Initially, but by the time we all voted, the decision was unanimous. John still left the meeting saying he'd been stuffed!"

Ian smiled. "Oh dear. But he's good, isn't he? He can improve his career elsewhere."

"He doesn't quite see it that way at the moment. However, in time, I'm sure he will realise it was a good move."

"Will Bernard retire now?"

"I think so. I'm sure he's 62 and I know he and his wife have plans. Let's go home Ian. This office is now my past. My future is here in this car."

Ian leaned over and gently kissed Emma on the lips. He then started the engine and drove 'my future' out of the car park, however, he did wonder, was this really for the very last time?

On the journey home, Emma sat quietly and stared out the window. Ian wondered what she was thinking about. He also started to reflect on what had happened to both of them in just a short period of time. The Monaco apartment, the birth of their first child and now Emma leaving the partnership. In addition to these happenings there was still the Andrei situation and the opportunity the Russian had presented. Mmm, he wondered, who was it that first coined the phrase, 'May you live in interesting times'?

Chapter 36

Bob Taylor was not happy. He thought Ian would have been back to him by now. He knew Ian had his hands full with the new baby, but at the same time, this was not the ambitious go-getter he remembered from university days.

Had he made the wrong call, the wrong assumptions? He knew his father-in-law would be watching like a hawk, ready, at the first opportunity, to tell Bob, 'I told you so!' Maybe he needed to 'gee' things, and Ian, along a bit. Perhaps visiting London himself? He tried to remember how many years it was since he had last visited London. It was so long ago, he could not remember! Was his dream, just what, a pipe dream!? Bob had suffered enough years of frustration in France. He wanted some action in London. Finally, he decided, if Ian was not going to help, well that was not going to stop his own ambitions. He would go to London himself!

Oscar had slowly, very slowly, now accepted the Caribbean way of life. From the hectic, chase everything, competitive world of Hong Kong, it had taken him just short of eight weeks to understand that this was the 'mañana' culture. Gradually he had realised that the Antiguans were not going to change to suit Oscar Ding. Oscar Ding needed to change to be an Antiguan! He had found a small villa to purchase about ten minutes' drive outside of St John's. The property had been on the market for five months, but he was captivated by the wonderful location, the view of the Caribbean Sea, the lovely sunsets and the two minutes gentle amble to the golden sands of the beach. However, he soon realised that the wheels turned very, very slowly in this part of the world, despite offering the property's full asking price! Thinking this offer would 'fast track' the purchase, he eventually understood that he could have got the same property for about 15% less than the asking price! Offering the full asking price was little guarantee that it would have any influence on the speed of the contract exchange or indeed, the eventual sale!

In the meantime, he had moved out of his hotel and into rented accommodation, about a ten minutes' walk from his proposed new villa. He had now received the rest of his possessions from Hong Kong and had hired a small soft-top jeep. After six weeks enjoying his rest and holidaying, he finally decided he needed to sow some seeds for his future. Over a two-day period, he had visited all the art galleries on the island and had introduced himself. He tried to sell the sort of service he could offer and highlighted the levels of success he had attained in the past. However, he was reminded, once again, that everything here was relaxed and 'cool, man'. Indeed, his enthusiasm was certainly not matched by the laid back and easy-going way of life of the locals.

Oscar was certainly becoming a little deflated and wondered if he had made the right decision to come to Antigua and, indeed, buy a property here. Was the delay in the purchase a hint to him that he should not be here? One evening he was feeling particularly down and, after drinking more than his usual volume of rum and cokes, he decided to vent his feelings and sent a long and rambling email to Ian.

Ian picked up the email early the next morning. Robert had been unusually unhappy during the night and, by 5 am, Emma decided that Ian should take his turn to get up. Slowly Robert exhausted himself and eventually went back to sleep. Meanwhile, Ian was now wide awake and decided to do something more productive, but quietly! He therefore accessed his emails and that's when he found the message from Oscar. Immediately he smiled at the rambling writing from someone who had obviously been drinking to excess! However, reading between the lines, it was obvious that Oscar was not happy and was finding the culture change quite a challenge. He didn't mention wanting to go back to Hong Kong, just that he was not happy and frustrated where he was.

Ian had an idea and slowly put together an email reply, which he hoped Oscar would think seriously about. Ian pressed the 'send' button and closed his computer.

Andrei, meanwhile, had now arrived in Scotland. He had been met at Edinburgh airport again by Duncan, the Laird's driver, and, whilst Andrei was beginning to understand some of Duncan's strong dialect, he still found it difficult to have any sort of proper conversation when sentences were more than just a few words. Unfortunately for Andrei, Duncan was not a man of just a few words!

The weather was a lot warmer than Andrei remembered from his last visit and the daylight hours were certainly a lot longer. They arrived at Baltoun Castle at 7.45 pm and the sun was still shining brightly.

"Good evening, sir," greeted Jenkins, the butler who appeared through the castle's main gate door as the Range Rover drew up in the courtyard area. He opened the rear passenger door to let Andrei get out. "Welcome back to Baltoun Castle. I hope you had a good journey?"

"Yes, yes, good, thank you. The sunshine is lovely and

warm today," answered Andrei. He stepped from the car and walked towards the main entrance gate alongside Jenkins. Jenkins opened the smaller inner door and the two men entered into the huge entrance hallway.

Immediately Andrei felt a significant drop in the temperature of the hallway compared to outside.

Jenkins noticed Andrei's brief shiver and said, "Although it is summer, the inside of the castle rarely gets warm. We have therefore lit a fire in your bedroom, sir."

Andrei was relieved. "Thank you."

At that very moment, the Laird walked towards them from the side corridor.

"Welcome back, Andrei. It's so good of you to join us again." The two men smiled at each other and shook hands. "Come, let's go into the lounge. There's a large log fire burning there. Jenkins, can you bring the whisky to us in the lounge?"

Jenkins nodded to the Laird and disappeared along another corridor.

"It's so nice to be back, Richard. I hope you and Moira have been keeping well?"

The two men walked along the corridor and then into the large lounge. Andrei immediately spotted the roaring log fire and walked in that direction. He also spotted the large glass vase he had asked Marie to buy and send on to the Forsyth's.

"Yes, we have been keeping very well, thank you… and very busy thanks to your very kind investment. Ah, I see you have spotted your present you sent us. Moira was so excited when she opened the parcel."

"Excellent. I hoped she would be pleased. Your last email said you would be shortly finished with all the estate improvements. Is that still the situation?" asked Andrei, rubbing his hands close to the fire.

Jenkins came into the room and put the silver tray, containing a decanter of whisky, a small jug of water and two glasses, on the side table. Richard thanked him and Jenkins left the room.

"The builders think it will be another week. We have many bookings starting next month, so all should be completed by then. I will give you the tour tomorrow."

"That's excellent news. I look forward to that."

"Now, whisky, I'll leave you to decide on the water." Richard started to pour the first glass.

"Richard, just a small one for me, please. Doctor's orders."

"Oh dear. Not a problem I hope?" Richard put down the decanter and looked at his guest with genuine concern.

"No, no. I've just got to cut down for a while. Give my liver a chance!" Andrei laughed at his comment and Richard smiled.

Richard picked up the decanter again and poured just a small measure into the glass.

"Well, maybe a tiny drop more, just this time!" said Andrei with a smile.

Richard laughed and put another small measure into Andrei's glass.

Andrei took the glass from Richard and topped it with about the same measure of water.

"Cheers, my friend," announced Andrei, waving his glass towards his host.

"Good health," replied Richard, wondering how serious Andrei's situation really was.

"So where is that lovely wife of yours?" asked Andrei, taking a small sip of his whisky.

"Moira will be joining us shortly. She's just finishing off the dinner preparations. I have to warn you that she has been practising her Russian."

"Oh, excellent," replied Andrei. "She probably speaks better Russian than I do now!"

Both men laughed. The door was then opened and Moira entered.

"Ah dobriy vyecher, Moira."

"Rat teebya veedet, Andrei," replied Moira, smiling at her guest.

"I do hope she is not swearing at you, Andrei," said Richard, smiling and proud of his wife's quick response.

"No, no, my friend. She was just saying how wonderful it was to meet me again," responded Andrei, followed by one of his deep laughs.

"Is that what I said?" asked Moira with a knowing smile.

"Can we stick with English for the time being?" asked Richard. "You two can chat later when I have gone to bed!"

"Thank you very much, Andrei, for the lovely vase. As you can see it has pride of place in this room. It is a lovely present," said Moira, with feeling. She then leaned over and gave Andrei a gentle kiss on his cheek.

"I'm really pleased that you both like it."

"Anyway, dinner is now ready. Jenkins is waiting to serve. I think we should go through to the dining room," responded Moira, who was now leading the group towards the door.

As they walked along the corridor, Richard announced to Andrei, "There is also another log fire burning in the dining room and we have seated you closest to it."

"You are very kind, my friend. You know how to keep an old man's bones warm!"

When Andrei retired for the evening, he found his bedroom was cosy and warm. The log fire was now nearly burnt out, but the embers were still glowing red and creating warmth to the room. Jenkins had already unpacked his case and so, other than cleaning his teeth, he was ready for bed.

It had been a long day, but well worth it to, once again, be in the wonderful setting of Baltoun Castle... and to be back amongst friends. He was looking forward to tomorrow and anxious to see how well his investment had been spent. He also smiled at the thought of trying his hand at fly fishing once again!

Chapter 37

When Andrei awoke the next morning, he knew straight away that something was wrong. He assumed it was to do with his chest, but strangely there was no pain. His left arm seemed weak. No it wasn't weak, it was numb! He sat up in bed and realised he was sweating, despite the obvious early morning chill in the room. He rubbed his arm and tried to move it about. Gradually the circulation seemed to be improving and the strength very slowly began to improve. He was frightened and rubbed his arm more and waved it about. He stood up and was pleased not to feel dizzy. He walked into his en-suite bathroom and ran cold water into the basin. He washed his face and both arms. Slowly his arm returned to normal. What had caused that? He had no idea. Maybe he had slept on his arm for a long period during the night. That could trap the blood flow and result in a temporary numbness. He was pleased his body was responding, but frightened that different bits were now beginning to fail him. He had always been fit and trim and been lucky with general good health. Now in his mid-70s, all was beginning to change and he did not like it. For the first time in his life, he now felt mortal. He was concerned and a little frightened!

He shaved and showered and slowly became a little more

relaxed. He dressed into his casual clothes and after another session of rubbing his arm, he made his way downstairs to the breakfast room. There was no sign of Moira, but Richard was sitting at the table, eating toast with one hand and holding the newspaper with the other.

When Andrei walked in the room Richard folded his newspaper and put it on the far side of the table. "Good morning," he announced. "I hope you slept well."

"Yes, thank you. The room was lovely and warm and I slept through the night," replied Andrei, helping himself to orange juice.

"Good. We have a lot to do today, so I hope you're eager and ready to go!"

The last thoughts on Andrei's mind were 'eager and ready to go', but he was nevertheless keen to see what had been redeveloped on the land next to the two streams. "I'm certainly looking forward to seeing what you've been up to."

Andrei placed his glass of orange juice on the table and then helped himself to tea, toast and several rashers of bacon. He sat down at the table opposite Richard. Richard watched his guest make a bacon sandwich and begin to eat before he spoke again.

"The interior designer is calling later this afternoon. They want to start to dress the lodges."

"We are not too far away then?"

"No. I must admit I will be glad when all these people are finally gone and the work finished."

"I hope it is all going to be worthwhile. I can see you being swamped with new guests."

Richard smiled. "Well, we've certainly got more bookings already than I'd anticipated. The new website is definitely making a difference to the number of enquiries and bookings."

"This estate is in a fabulous setting. It's going to be

popular with walkers as well as anglers. Then there's the golf course for next year. That will attract even more people."

"Yes," said Richard. He was still not convinced about the golf course. Although the estate consisted of over 20,000 acres, the more fertile parts were currently used for the farming of venison, beef and cows for milk. The parkland area was mainly water meadow and subject to winter flooding. The rest was forest and streams. He couldn't see how just a 9-hole course could be fitted in. But then again, he was no expert.

Andrei had finished eating and was now sipping the last of his tea. "Well, I guess I'm ready."

"Good. Duncan is bringing the Land Rover over from the farm. That will make life easier for us along the stream banks. It's still quite wet in places," said Richard, now rising to his feet. "Shall we say we'll meet in ten minutes at the main entrance door?"

Fifteen minutes later, Duncan was driving Andrei and Richard through the first wooded area. Andrei spotted two groups of deer browsing in the undergrowth. As the Land Rover approached the first stream, it was clear that the ground was still very boggy.

"Of course, guests wouldn't normally come this way. We have built two new single-track roads that come in from the other side," said Richard, as the Land Rover lurched from side to side.

In the distance Andrei spotted another stream and three of the refurbished lodges. They looked splendid. The Land Rover exited the wood and joined one of the new tarmac roads up to the lodges. The builders were still on site, but Richard and Andrei were able to enter the first of the lodges. Even though it was still not quite complete, Andrei was nevertheless impressed. It was fully redecorated and had a modern kitchen and utility room fully fitted with cupboards and white goods. A new wood-burning stove was now installed in the open plan lounge/dining room area and the wooden flooring throughout the ground floor was finished. The two bedrooms had been reconfigured slightly and, whilst fractionally smaller, they now had their own en-suite bathrooms. After they'd completed the tour of the lodge, Richard took Andrei outside and showed him the new footpaths which led down to the stream. Richard pointed out the new access points to the stream for trout fishing. Suddenly, they were both momentarily startled as a flash of blue and orange flew past them. A kingfisher, Richard told Andrei. Andrei nodded. He had never seen one in the wild before.

For the rest of the morning and the early afternoon, Andrei was guided to the locations of all the other lodges. The original 12 lodges were now largely refurbished and the six new ones almost completed bar for the soft furnishings. Richard told Andrei that all the lodges would be finished to the same high standard as the first one they had seen. Duncan now drove the Land Rover with its passengers along both the two new roads. Andrei thought they had been laid well and the tarmac finish didn't detract too much from the woodland scene. Both roads now gave a much easier access to and from the main road. All visiting vehicles had to pass the new check-in cabin which had a small shop attached. Just after the check-in cabin there was a four-acre field. Duncan stopped here and Richard explained that this was the site for the planned luxury en-suite yurts. The field had good drainage and was a little higher than the surrounding land. It was also partly hidden by a dense area of a variety of mature trees. All ten yurts, when completed next year, would have a fully equipped kitchen and their own vehicle parking area close to the check-in cabin and shop.

It was just after 2.20 pm when the Land Rover stopped at the edge of a very large meadow area.

"I thought we would stop here for lunch, Andrei," said Richard as he climbed down from the vehicle. "We can go for a short walk whilst Duncan sets up our picnic."

Andrei climbed down from his side of the vehicle and joined Richard. The two men changed into wellington boots and walked onto the pasture land for about a hundred metres. Andrei thought the area was lovely. It was so peaceful and quiet, although somewhat wet under foot. They both certainly needed their wellington boots.

"This is the area that is earmarked for the golf course," announced Richard. "We are in the middle of summer and this field is rarely fully dry. Without a substantial amount of drainage and the building of flood gates, I honestly cannot see how a golf course could be built and maintained properly here, but then again, I'm no expert."

Andrei looked at his feet and could see the bottom half of each foot was standing in water. This is going to cost a lot of money, he thought. Probably a waste of a lot of money too. "Yes, I can see your point. We will have to rethink it properly."

The two men walked back to the Land Rover. Duncan had set up a table and two camping chairs. On the table were various salad foods, slices of venison pie, sandwiches and a bottle of white wine.

Andrei sat on the chair looking out to the pasture meadow. He declined a glass of wine, but accepted a glass of sparkling water instead. As he ate his meal, he thought a lot more about the challenges of the golf course option.

Later that afternoon, Andrei and Richard sat in the library with a pot of tea and a variety of biscuits. They were discussing the results of the day's tour.

"So, Andrei, do you think your money has been spent wisely?" asked Richard, whilst pouring two cups of tea.

"I think my investment is going to pay us handsome dividends my friend. I might try one of the lodges myself, you can almost fish from the veranda!" Both men laughed.

"Are you pleased with the new website?" asked Richard. He knew Andrei had seen it months ago but he was still concerned that it might need some more updating following the completion of the lodges.

"I've not looked at it for several months, I will review it again whilst I'm here, especially as I now have a better idea of the redevelopment. I hope the broadband connection is much better too?"

"Yes, I forgot to mention that. It is much better, thank you. The new system has been in place for about six weeks. The mobile phone reception is still patchy, but we are hopeful that improvements will be made over the next two years."

Andrei nodded and drank some of his tea.

"So what about the golf course?" asked Richard, with fingers crossed out of Andrei's view.

"Mmm. Yes. It looks a lot more of a costly exercise than I'd anticipated. Would you mind if we postponed the idea for the time being?"

Richard unfolded his fingers and made a fist in quiet celebration.

"No, Andrei. I think the long-term maintenance costs of such a project would always outstrip the income, unless we charged a very high green fee of course. We have checked on a number of the other local golf courses and their green fees are far more competitive than we could charge. Also, we would be reliant on holiday bookings only. There is very little demand in this area for extra membership golf. We do not have the population."

"Okay, we agree on that then. Do you have any other ideas or suggestions you want to discuss?"

"No, not at the moment. I think we need to see how the

lodges and yurts bookings develop over the next year and then review the situation. Your generous investment, Andrei, has been an absolute godsend. We have been able to increase the number of cattle and deer on the estate too. We've also refurbished the milking parlour so we can now milk more cows and far more efficiently. To be honest, without all your help, we would have been in a serious mess by now."

"I'm so pleased that I have been able to help, my friend. This estate is a wonderful part of the world. Which brings me on to a favour which I hope you will agree to."

Richard was a little startled and worried. "If I can, Andrei. I owe you so much!"

Andrei explained the details of his favour. Richard's worries quickly evaporated. "Of course we will do that for you, Andrei, but hopefully not for quite a few years yet!" Both men smiled, but Andrei was being very serious.

Chapter 38

Oscar had read Ian's email with some interest. It all sounded like a good short-term solution, so he quickly sent Ian a positive reply. It was not what he had planned for when he'd first landed in Antigua, but he was keen to give it a try.

Twenty minutes later, Oscar received a telephone call which he naturally assumed was from Ian. However, he was very surprised because it was from one of the directors of a large art gallery in St John's. "Hello, Mr Ding. My name is Wesley Fredericks from the Shell Gallery. We exchanged emails some weeks ago and you came into our gallery on Tuesday. I'm sorry I was out on business, but I would like to discuss some options with you if you are still interested."

"Yes. Yes, of course," replied Oscar. He was still trying to get over this surprise after his slow start in Antigua. "Do you want me to come to your office?"

"Would you be available at 11 o'clock tomorrow morning?"

"Let me just check my diary," said Oscar, knowing full well he had lots of blank pages currently in his diary. "Yes, that should be okay. I look forward to seeing you tomorrow."

Well, well, well, thought Oscar, after he had put down the phone. I wonder what Mr Fredericks wants? Things could be on the up... at last!

Next morning, Oscar arrived at the Shell Gallery. It was one of the top galleries on the island and he could quickly see why. After he had entered through the front entrance door he glanced at some of the pictures and immediately noticed the high prices of some of the paintings. A well-dressed young assistant came over to greet him. "Can I be of assistance, sir?"

"I have an appointment with Mr Fredericks," announced Oscar. He did not recognise this assistant from his earlier visit.

"Ah, you must be Mr Ding. Mr Fredericks is expecting you. Please, come this way."

Oscar followed the young man towards the back of the gallery. He glanced at some of the other paintings that were on display. They were mainly very bright and colourful modern Caribbean landscapes and wildlife, plus some portraits of, he assumed, Antiguan people. At the far end of the gallery the two men walked through a door and into a long corridor. The inside of the building, whilst only two storeys high, was nevertheless much larger and deeper, than it appeared from the outside. They stopped at the first door on the left, which was slightly ajar. The assistant knocked and a shout of 'come in' was the immediate response. Oscar smiled as he thought the loud bellowing shout might well have been heard all over the building! Both men walked into a large office, which must have been ten degrees cooler than the main gallery room. A large man rose from his seat and walked around his desk to greet Oscar. "Mr Ding. So good to meet you at last." The two men shook hands and Mr Fredericks said to the assistant. "Thank you, Worrell, that will be all." The assistant left the room.

"Please, Mr Ding, take a seat." Mr Fredericks pointed to a small table surrounded by three chairs, all on small wheels. Both men sat down and Oscar waited for Mr Fredericks to speak.

"I saw your emails from Hong Kong and was told you came into our gallery the other day, offering your services. Tell me, Mr Ding, what can you offer me?"

Oscar gave a potted summary of his career and emphasised the strong connections he had in South East Asia and Beijing. He also decided to take a little flier by saying he also had connections in London with Sotheby's.

"Very impressive, Mr Ding, so what brings you to our little island?"

Oscar explained that he was looking for a new challenge, new markets and new artists. The traditional markets were now saturated and he wanted to see if there were more potential opportunities in the Caribbean.

Wesley Fredericks leaned back in his chair. Being such a big man, his frame easily covered the seating area and, because the chairs were on wheels, his chair moved backwards a few inches as he began to speak. "We have a very small market here in Antigua, Mr Ding. We are not a wealthy country, but some of our customers are. We therefore have to make sure we can service their needs and also help to promote and develop our local artists. Traditionally, our customers have been from the Caribbean, with a few from America and the UK. What we see in the future is China, India and Russia. We currently have no representation in any of these countries. Do you have any knowledge of the Indian and Russian markets?"

Oscar suddenly felt a little deflated. "No, I'm afraid I have no connections there. My strength is the South East Asia area."

"Okay. Thank you for your honesty. What I am prepared to do is offer you, for 12 months, a commission contract to be our sole agent in China and the UK. If you want to include wider South East Asia, well that's fine too. What we want is our Caribbean talents exposed to these new markets. Do you think you can do that?"

"Well, yes, but I would need to see the quality of your paintings and artists we are talking about first, otherwise we could both be making a mistake."

"That's a fair point. I'll get Worrell to show you our collection. I would be particularly interested in your opinion of the 12 Tobar pictures."

"Tobar? I've never heard of him," said Oscar.

"Isaac Tobar was born in Barbados to two slave parents in the late 1700s. From a very young age he showed a great talent for drawing. The plantation owner, Mr Geoffrey Burns, an Englishman, became aware of the boy's talents and paid his parents extra money and gave them favours for Isaac to draw portraits of the Burns family. In addition, Isaac was given special privileges so that he could develop his talent. As he grew older, Mr Burns provided Isaac with both watercolour and some oil paints. Isaac adapted very quickly to these new mediums and again painted many of the Burns family. He was also encouraged to paint in the sugar fields and some of the wildlife. Mr Burns was thought to be one of the better slave owners and he wanted Isaac to capture his slaves working, but showing that the quality of their lives was much better than most slaves at the time. Over the next few years Isaac painted many pictures, adding to Mr Burns' collection. However, at the time of the abolition of slavery in 1833, Mr Burns was an old man and he, and his family, decided to move back to England. The plantation slaves were released and the estate was divided up and sold. Isaac's parents had, by now, both died and so Isaac moved away from the plantation. He disappeared and was never heard of again."

"So, what happened to the paintings?" asked Oscar. This all sounded like an interesting story.

"As far as we know, most, if not all, went with the Burns family back to England. They returned to their main home somewhere in Yorkshire."

"But you say you have 12 of Tobar's pictures?"

"Two years ago, a large former plantation house here in Antigua came up for sale. The owner was quite old when he died. The family didn't want to keep the property because it had been poorly maintained. It needed a lot of money spent on it to make it properly habitable. The family removed some of the more personal items but the house was sold with the rest of the other contents included. It was purchased by a British family and when they moved in they found boxes of old books and some old paintings and drawings in the attic. When they advised the previous owner's family about the property and items found in the attic, they were told they were not interested in any property found in the attic. They said it was part of the general contents of the house. Mr and Mrs Nash, the new owners, brought the pictures to us for our opinion and valuation. Fortunately, one of my colleagues had heard of Isaac Tobar and did some research. He found out about the story I have just told you."

"Interesting," said Oscar. "But it does not answer the question as to why these pictures came to be stored in an old plantation house attic in Antigua, when they were supposedly transported from Barbados to England, what, nearly 200 years ago?"

"Exactly, Mr Ding. That is why I would be particularly interested in your opinion of these pictures. After Worrell has shown you all our collection, could we discuss this matter again later this afternoon?"

It was just after 4 pm when Oscar sat down again in Wesley Fredericks' office. He had been very surprised by the sheer volume of pictures on the premises. He calculated that there must be only about 10% of the total collection on display. Most of the paintings were in several store areas about the building. About half of the total collection were owned by the gallery, but the other half were owned privately and placed in the hands of the gallery to sell on their behalf... including the Tobar paintings and drawings.

"So, Mr Ding, what are your thoughts?" asked Wesley.

"You have quite a collection. I was very surprised to see so many 19th and 20th century artists. I was expecting to see that most of your pictures would be more local and contemporary."

"Yes, we have quite an eclectic collection. It is mostly modern paintings on display because, locally, we are aiming for the local and expat market and they tend to like the bright and intense colours associated with the Caribbean. The more connoisseur buyer is looking for value and an investment. So, Mr Ding, which category do you see Mr Tobar's pictures fitting in to?"

"The Tobar paintings and drawings are superb. The portraits certainly appear to capture the personality, as well as the features, of the face. The landscapes are a little bit like a Caribbean Constable. You can feel the energy, sweat and toil of the slaves, but possibly in a slightly less inhumane working environment. Yes, the slaves are working hard, and of course, they are still slaves, but somehow, the atmosphere of the pictures convey a less miserable existence than some of the larger plantations operating at that time."

"That is quite perceptive, Mr Ding. Why do you say that?"

"The slave masters have not been painted by Tobar with whips or dogs. None of the slaves are being obviously restrained."

"Still not a very happy existence. After all, they are not free men."

"No, but would Tobar deliberately ignore these sorts of practices?"

"I guess we will never know, Mr Ding," responded Wesley. "I'm just glad that I didn't live in those times!"

"Judging history by today's standards is always subjective. I just hope we can all learn something from history and not just repeat our forefathers' mistakes." Oscar knew he was getting into hot water and just wanted to get back to discussing the merits of the paintings.

"Okay, so, Mr Ding, what would you value this collection at?"

Oscar wiped his now sweating brow. "As you know, I have little or no experience of your market. I can only compare them to the recent discovery of historical drawings found in Australia. Two artists on a Dutch voyage in the early 1800s produced attractive and highly artistic watercolours of Tasmanian Aborigines and early recordings of Western Australian landscapes. They sold for the equivalent of between £500,000 and £1 million each. I personally think Tobar's work is better."

"We valued the Tobar collection at US$13 million, Mr Ding, so we are roughly in the same ballpark!"

Oscar leaned back in his chair and decided that maybe the Caribbean will prove to be an interesting place afterall!

Interesting", replied Oscar. "Tobar's work is very good. He has the ability to capture the time well. The main problem I see is getting international recognition. I need to investigate the history more deeply. Can you give me any more information?"

"Tobar was a unique black artist. During a time when black men in the Caribbean were only seen and used as slaves, a white English family saw below his skin colour. They saw the person and Isaac Tobar's talent. Mr Ding, I too see the history and the talent. I also see an international market for these paintings. We are a small gallery on a very small island in the Caribbean. Do you think you can find an international market for such a talent?"

When Oscar left the Shell Gallery 20 minutes later, his

mind was spinning. He headed for the nearest bar, ordered a cold beer and sat under a slowly revolving ceiling fan. From his pocket he pulled out his notepad and pen and started to make a series of notes recording the key parts from his discussion with Wesley Fredericks. After about an hour, and a second cold beer, his conclusion was that Isaac Tobar just might, just might, be a very special find.

Chapter 39

Ian read Oscar's email reply with a smile on his face. It was obvious he was enjoying the Caribbean weather and the cocktails, but it was also a steep learning curve to understand and accept the new culture and lifestyle of Antigua. A lovely place to holiday, but after all the years in Hong Kong, it was obviously a shock to Oscar to be 'more laid back, man'! Nevertheless, he was pleased that Oscar had decided to take up his suggestion and he sent an email to Bob Taylor recommending Oscar to help set up the London agency. Ian was quite happy to be involved, but was less keen to get too close to his old university colleague.

Bob Taylor opened Ian's email. His conclusion was that it was an interesting response. Not what he had hoped for, but there were still some positive words. After a little thought, he decided that he wouldn't now need to rush off to London to set up the agency himself but would hold back until Ian was ready. He emailed Ian and suggested a meeting with him and Mr Ding, sometime in the next few weeks, possibly in London. That way Bob could also see what the local competition was likely to be for himself.

When Ian arrived home that evening, Emma was pottering in the front garden and Robert was watching her from his baby bouncer seat. It was a warm evening and both mother and son were enjoying the fresh air.

"Well, this is the life," announced Ian, as he walked into the drive. Emma immediately put down her trowel and walked over to give him a kiss.

"I could get used to maternity leave," responded Emma.

"Mmm. So, how's my little man doing today?" asked Ian. He walked over to where Robert was beaming a smile and kicking his legs. Ian put down his briefcase and laptop bag and picked up his son.

"We went to the park and fed the ducks!" announced Emma. "Also, I've received a lovely telephone call from Bernard Murray. The sale of Murray, Caxton and Tyner was completed earlier today! The money will be in the bank tomorrow and I... am... now... officially... unemployed!"

"Oh, wow," replied Ian, "so I'm now the official bread-winner for all three of us!"

"I think we might just scrape by," said Emma and they both laughed. Even Robert joined in with a toothless grin.

Later that evening, Robert had been put to bed and Ian and Emma were relaxing on the sofa in the lounge. They were finishing off a bottle of Chablis.

"Are you sad about the sale of the business?" asked Ian.

"Yes, and no, I guess the honest answer is," replied Emma. "I've worked very hard to achieve a partnership and yes, it's sad that it is now no more, but my life has moved on. Just look at the last two years. It's all been just unbelievable."

"Mmm, I know. Three years ago, who would have predicted our future? When you reflect back like this it all becomes a little frightening!"

"I know," said Emma. She had a slightly worried look. "What is really frightening is the next three years, the next ten years... fancy predicting those!?"

That same day, Oscar had been to the main St John's library. He tried to find out every last piece of information about Isaac Tobar, Mr Geoffrey Burns and his family. His research had achieved not much more than what Wesley Fredericks had told him. Accessing the internet did give him the family address in Yorkshire, England, as 'Helton Manor', but he had not moved on much further.

That evening, Oscar pondered on what his next move should be. He could try visiting Barbados, but he wasn't sure what that would achieve. He'd already been on to the Barbadian art museum's website and there was no reference to Isaac Tobar. Another dead-end. Even the registry of births, deaths and marriages had no reference to Isacc Tobar after his parents had died. Isaac, seemingly, had just disappeared! Oscar could not find any reference to any marriage or, indeed, his death.

He had one last thought. He opened up his computer and googled 'Geoffrey Burns Yorkshire England.' Strangely a number of responses came up. He looked at the entries, but most seemed to relate to a former cutlery and steel manufacturer in Sheffield. He then re-entered the same words but this time adding 'Helton Manor', after Geoffrey Burns. This time three responses appeared. Oscar read through each entry slowly and made some notes. In summary, Oscar established that the Burns family had formerly owned the Manor and 300 acres of surrounding land since 1532. A fire in 1899, however, had so seriously damaged the Manor that it was demolished and never restored. The land was subsequently sold off to a number of nearby farmers. Another dead end!

Oscar left his computer and went into the kitchen to make himself a rum and coke. When he returned, he noticed Ian had sent him a further email. Sipping his drink, he leisurely read the message. Okay he thought, so we might be having a meeting in London. Maybe I'll also be able to get some time to investigate the Burns family there and maybe establish if there are any more Tobar pictures still in existence. He finished his drink and decided to respond to Ian:

Hi Ian,

Looking forward to visiting London again and working with you and Bob Taylor. Should be interesting. Speaking of interesting, have you ever come across a 19th century, black, Caribbean artist by the name of Isaac Tobar? I'm desperate for any information!

Cheers,

Oscar.

Next morning Ian was sitting at his desk when Penny popped her head around the door and said, "Good morning."

"Ah, good morning, Penny. Come in, I've got a job for you."

Penny walked into Ian's office and sat down on her usual chair. She waited for Ian's next comment.

"What do you know of a 19th century artist called Isaac Tobar?"

"The name sounds Jewish. I don't think I've heard of him. Sorry."

"I'm not surprised, neither have I. Apparently, and according to Oscar, he was a black Caribbean artist."

"19th century. Mmm, that must have been about the time of the slave trade. Were there really black Caribbean artists then?"

"Well, that's today's job please. Can you find out anything at all about Mr Tobar? If Oscar is keen to find out more about this man, it must be worthwhile. Oscar has always had a nose for finding the occasional nugget of gold on a barren landscape!"

"Isaac Tobar, okay. I'll see what I can find out," said Penny, rising from her seat and leaving Ian's office.

Ian swivelled in his chair and looked out of the window. It was another lovely warm, sunny day, not Caribbean temperatures, but nevertheless very acceptable for England. However, Ian's mind was reflecting on Oscar's email. Who was this Isaac Tobar and more importantly, why was Oscar so interested!?

Just after 4 pm that same afternoon, Penny returned to Ian's office and asked him if he was available for an update on her findings?

"Come in, Penny, sit down. What have you been able to discover?"

Penny sat down and flicked through her notepad. "Most of what I have found out is from the internet and I guess Oscar would have already been there. However, in our archive records, I discovered two portrait paintings by Tobar. They were auctioned in 1898 and sold for 230 guineas and 189 guineas. They were sold by a Miss Agatha Burns. The buyer was the Framlington Gallery. The file notes also said that the Framlington Gallery was keen to purchase more of the Burns collection, but, apparently, the Burns family home of Helton Manor, somewhere in Yorkshire, was severely damaged by a fire less than a year later. It's thought the rest of the collection perished with the other house contents."

"Were you able to find any connection between this probable black slave artist and the Yorkshire Burns family?"

Penny explained that Geoffrey Burns had owned a plantation in Barbados until the time that slavery was abolished. It is probable that Isaac's parents were slaves there. After that, the information is not clear, but maybe someone in the Burns family saw Isaac's potential and helped him to develop his talent. The Burns family had also owned Helton

Manor since the 16th century, until it was destroyed by the fire in 1899. So, it is likely that they transferred the pictures back to Yorkshire at some stage before then."

"Do you know how many pictures there were?"

"No, but again, from our archive records, there might have been quite a few. Maybe Framlington's archives have a record?"

"Can you have a chat with them tomorrow and see if they can help? In the meantime, I think I had better have a conversation with 'our new representative in the Caribbean'. I think this could be much bigger than it appears at the moment."

Penny smiled at Ian's description of Oscar's new title. "I'll speak to the Framlington Gallery first thing tomorrow morning."

Chapter 40

Penny remembered that Peter Stones, who was now working in the 'The European Pictures 1300–1549' department, had joined Sotheby's from the Framlington Gallery just over a year ago. She telephoned his extension and told him that she was hoping to get some information from the Framlington archives. She also explained to him the details about Isaac Tobar. Peter said he would speak to a former colleague at the Framlington Gallery and try to obtain the information she was looking for.

Later that afternoon Peter Stones returned Penny's call and told her all the information he'd managed to acquire about Isaac Tobar and the Burns family. Penny thanked Paul and told him, "I owe you a favour."

Armed with this new information, Penny walked into Ian's office. Ian was working on his computer.

"Ian. I've got some more information about Isaac Tobar and the Burns collection."

"Excellent," said Ian, closing down his laptop. "Come and sit down. I'm all ears!"

Penny smiled at Ian's comment and sat on her usual seat.

"I asked Peter Stones this morning if he could recommend a contact at the Framlington Gallery. If you remember, he used to work there." Ian did not know but he let Penny continue. "I explained what I was looking for and he suggested that he might be able to get more information from a colleague that he used to work with at the Framlington Gallery. He's just come back to me with the following extra information accessed from Framlington's archives."

Penny flicked open her notepad and continued. "The Burns family, when they returned home from Barbados, following the abolition of the slave trade, brought back their remaining collection of drawings and paintings by Isaac Tobar. Framlington's records suggest that there might have been about 200 pictures in total, although it is thought that a number of these were sold to other plantation owners in the ten years before the Burns family returned home. The pictures were mainly portraits of the Burns family, but there were also some portraits of slaves too. Others were landscape paintings set in and around the sugarcane fields. When the Burns family returned to the UK, Mr Burns only lived for another year and Mrs Burns died soon after. That meant that the two daughters, Jane and Agatha, became the owners of the Helton Manor estate. Neither of the daughters married and Jane died in 1890. This left Agatha to deal with everything on her own. Both Agatha's parents were 'an only child' so there was no more Burns family to carry the line forwards. As a result, Agatha sold a lot of the estate land to surrounding farmers to help pay for the upkeep and maintenance of the Manor house. By 1897, Agatha was also selling some of the contents of the house and a number of the family paintings, including part of the Tobar collection. All sales, at this point, were made privately, usually in Yorkshire. A good friend of Agatha suggested that she might get a better price by auction. Apparently, there were some other nice pieces of artwork too. Sotheby's was recommended and an auction was carried out in 1898. Framlington Gallery bought the two Tobar paintings that were in the auction and approached Agatha directly to try and buy some more. Agatha agreed, but a day before the gallery's representative arrived to view the rest of the collection, a large fire devastated Helton Manor and most of the remaining paintings and house contents were lost in the fire. Agatha died three days later from severe burns and smoke inhalation."

"A sad story," was Ian's first comment. "So, nobody really knows how many Tobar paintings and drawings still exist?"

"No. There are probably still some in the Caribbean and maybe some remaining in the Yorkshire area from the private sales. But that would be guesswork. What do you want me to do now?"

Ian sat back in his chair and rubbed his chin. "I'm not sure. Why don't you look on the internet and look for websites of art galleries in Yorkshire. See if they have any Tobar's paintings for sale or have sold any recently. If any are for sale, then maybe there will be a photograph on their website … and a suggested sale price! I'll have a word with Oscar. I think it is fair to assume that he has unearthed some of the paintings that are still located in the Caribbean."

"Okay. But do you think these pictures are going to be valuable?"

"It's hard to say at the moment. Oscar obviously does and he is usually a good judge. Of course, we have not seen any of Tobar's work yet, so that makes it more difficult. Maybe if you find any of Tobar's work for sale in Yorkshire that might give a more accurate clue."

After Penny had left Ian's office, Ian drafted the following email to Oscar.

Hi Oscar,

I am trying to agree on some dates for the London meeting with Bob Taylor. Bob has suggested sometime over the next three weeks. How are you fixed?

Penny has found out some more information about Mr Tobar and the Burns family. She is following up on another lead. Will give you the full details when we meet. I assume you have seen some of Tobar's pictures in Antigua? He must be a good artist to get you all excited!!

Cheers,

Ian.

PS. We are looking for a good babysitter so you are welcome to stay with us for a few days!

Within the hour, Ian had received Oscar's reply.

Hi Ian,

I can fit in for the meeting anytime subject to being able to get a flight at short notice.

I've seen a group of Tobar's pictures for sale and they are very good. Pricey, but very good!!

Yes I'm really excited!

Just going for a cooling dip in the Caribbean!

Cheers,

Oscar.

PS. Love to babysit Robert. I'll teach him how to play mah-jong and use chopsticks!

After further emails to Bob Taylor and Oscar, a date was finally agreed. Bob said he was going to stay for three nights at the Hilton Hotel on Park Lane, opposite Hyde Park. He also suggested that the three of them should meet there at 10 am on Saturday morning.

Oscar flew into London Gatwick airport early on Friday morning, a day before the meeting. Ian collected him in his car and they set off for Ian's house in Esher. During the journey Oscar explained about the Tobar pictures that were for sale at the Shell Gallery and he also relayed the story Wesley Fredericks had told him. Ian explained Penny's findings, including the results of her Yorkshire art gallery investigations.

"So, Penny has found two of Tobar's paintings for sale," queried Oscar, seeking clarification.

"Yes. A gallery in Sheffield has two for sale. Interestingly, one is for sale at £15,000, the other is £7000. I've seen the photographs on the website and both are portraits. One is of a young white girl and the other is of a middle-aged black man."

"Let me guess, the black man is the most expensive."

"You're right. Why did you come to that conclusion?"

"My guess is the young girl is one of the Burns daughters. Looking at the pictures I've seen in Antigua, Tobar put more feeling into the drawings and paintings of the slaves than he did for the Burns family. Both would be good, but the black man would be a little more heartfelt piece of work."

"Interesting. Do you think that is the area where there might be the greater demand?"

"Yes, that and the landscapes. Shell Gallery has two landscapes and they remind me so much of Constable's style of work."

"How long has the Shell Gallery had this collection for sale?"

"Just over two years. They have had a couple of enquiries about some of the collection but none have sold to date."

"Why do you think that's the case? Are they asking for too much money?"

"For the market they are usually involved in, yes, they are asking too much money. I think six of the oil paintings, given the right promotion and marketing, could each sell for in excess of £2 million. I've seen similar sorts of work promoted in Beijing for that sort of money and these are better."

"Remind me, what is the Shell Gallery looking to achieve?"

"For all 12 pictures they are looking for about US$13 million, or about £10 million."

"What about the six that you have highlighted?"

"I think they might accept just over £5 million. Why? Are you thinking of buying them?" said Oscar, with a smile, but when he looked across at his friend, Ian had a very serious expression!

The conversation went quiet whilst Ian flicked the car's indicator and they exited the M23 to join the M25. Once the car had settled down on the new motorway, Ian broke the silence. "Fancy a trip to Sheffield on Monday?"

"Sheffield! Where's Sheffield?"

"It's where the art gallery is located that's selling the two Tobar portraits. I think it would be useful if we could both see these pictures 'in the flesh', so to speak."

"That sounds like a great idea. Sheffield, near London, is it?

Chapter 41

Ian and Oscar left Ian's house at just before 8 am on Saturday morning. It was a lovely warm morning, with just a hint of a breeze. Ian announced that it was going to be a hot day. The two men walked the short journey to Esher station and caught the 8.13 am train to London. At 9.45 am they were exiting the Underground station at Hyde Park Corner and entered the Hilton Hotel just a few minutes later.

Bob Taylor was waiting for them in the reception area and Ian introduced his two colleagues to each other. Bob suggested they sit in a quiet spot well away from the passing guests.

After they had a brief chat about Monaco, Hong Kong and the art market in general, Bob explained his thinking about his plans for an agency in London. Both Ian and Oscar listened without interruption. Once he had finished, both Ian and Oscar asked many questions about the gallery's location, the type of art to be sold and financing. The discussions continued amicably until just after 12.30 pm when Bob said he had reserved a table at a nearby restaurant. The three men set off and continued their discussions during their meal. At 4.30 pm they had finished their meeting. Bob had agreed to Oscar's fee and all three had agreed on the route forward. Bob walked with Ian and Oscar as far as the Underground station and there they said their goodbyes.

It was just after 6.30 pm when Ian and Oscar joined Emma and Robert in the back garden. Robert was splashing in his paddling pool.

"Have you had a good day?" asked Emma when she saw the two men walking across the patio.

"Yes, I think it has been quite productive. What do you think Oscar?"

"Certainly. There are possibilities for sure. A few loose ends to tie up, but certainly a possibility."

Emma passed Robert's towel to Ian. "Here you go. This little monkey needs drying and a clean nappy. I'll go and get his food ready." Emma left Ian in charge and walked towards the house. Ian lifted Robert up and started to dry him.

"Wow, you are domesticated," said Oscar, smiling at his friend.

"Have you ever changed a nappy?"

"Me!? This is the nearest I've ever been to a baby!"

Both men laughed and Ian laid Robert on his changing mat. "Okay, Mr Ding, here is your first lesson!"

Oscar concentrated as Ian stripped off the dirty nappy, cleaned Robert's bottom and fitted the new one.

"Quite easy, isn't it?" said Oscar, as Ian picked Robert back up again.

"Let's just say some are cleaner to deal with than others." Both men laughed. "Can you pass me his clothes next to the paddling pool please."

Oscar picked up the small pile of clothes and walked over to join Ian who was now sitting next to the patio table. Oscar placed Robert's clothes on the table and sat down next to Ian. He was fascinated and watched in silence as Ian slowly dressed Robert.

"I thought you two would like these," said Emma as she

joined them carrying two glasses of white wine. She put them on the table. "Let me have Robert and I will give him his dinner."

Both Ian and Oscar said thank you for the drinks and Robert was taken by Emma back to the house.

Both men picked up their glasses and Oscar said 'cheers', as the two men clinked glasses.

"Cheers to you Oscar too. So, tell me, what did you think of Bob Taylor?"

"He seems like a nice guy, knows his art, but also sounds a bit frustrated with his life in Monaco. Looking to establish a little more control over his business life, I guess. Mind, I'm not sure that London is the right place to start a new venture straight from scratch. I would have thought it was swamped already. Are there opportunities here?"

"I've been thinking about that. I think there could be a very interesting opportunity for the three of us. It all depends on what we find on Monday in Sheffield."

Much further north from Esher, at Baltoun Castle in Scotland, Richard, Moira and Andrei were standing in the warm sunshine outside the main doorway to the castle. They were waiting for Duncan to bring the Range Rover to take Andrei back to Edinburgh airport.

His flight to London was timed to depart at 21.05.

"Many thanks to you, my friends, for a lovely stay. You have once again been very generous hosts. I do envy your life here, especially with this warm sunshine."

"Unfortunately, this lovely weather is not typical for Scotland. It's been wonderful to see you again, Andrei. We are pleased you enjoyed your stay and approve the estate changes and developments. I'm really not sure where we would have been without your most generous investments," said Richard, grasping and shaking Andrei's hand.

Moira leaned over and gave Andrei a kiss on both his cheeks. "Please come and see us again soon, Andrei. You will always be very welcome here. Do have a safe journey."

"Thank you, both of you. You are so very kind. Ah, here's my driver."

Duncan arrived in the courtyard and parked the vehicle directly in front of Andrei. Richard opened the rear door to let Andrei climb aboard and Duncan loaded Andrei's bags into the boot. Within a matter of seconds, the Range Rover sped away with Andrei, Richard and Moira all waving their hands for their goodbyes.

"I hope you enjoyed your stay, sir?" asked Duncan, looking in his rear-view mirror for Andrei's facial reaction.

"The Laird and Moira are lovely people and most generous hosts. Baltoun Castle is definitely one of my most favourite locations," replied Andrei, looking out through the side window. Through the trees and in the distance, he could just glimpse one of the new lodges. He hoped his investment would work and bring many more guests to experience this beautiful part of Scotland. As the Range Rover exited the estate and headed towards Edinburgh, Andrei winced slightly and not for the first time that day. He rubbed his chest and his arm.

Viktor had been working in his new role, the last leg of his graduate programme, for five weeks. However, he was finding the new department both less exciting and less stimulating. So much so that he seriously wondered whether his long-term career should be with Sotheby's at all. He liked the buzz of the art world, despite all its flaws, but wanted to feel less restrictive and to be able to be more adventurous, entrepreneurial, similar to his father's good friend, Andrei. However, he also remembered his father's wise words, some time ago, when he had told Viktor not to put Andrei's wealth success on a pedestal. Before we escaped from Russia, his father explained, our successes were achieved due to hard work and very lucky circumstances. Also, he continued to explain that much of Andrei's subsequent riches were achieved outside the law. Sergei certainly didn't want Viktor to follow a similar route. He wanted Viktor to follow a much more sensible and stable career path.

As Viktor was leaving Sotheby's that evening, he received a tap on the shoulder. Looking behind him he saw a smiling face. "Hello, Vic. I hardly recognised you. Where's the usual skip in your step?"

"Hi, Penny," said Viktor, suddenly his morose mood temporarily lifted when he saw Penny. "How's things with you?"

"I'm fine, but you look as though you have the weight of the world on your shoulders. What's the matter?"

"Do you fancy a drink at The Grapes? It would be great to have a chat. You know I've always rated your opinions and advice."

Penny smiled again. "Come on, I'll buy you a pint."

Over the next hour, Viktor explained his feelings to Penny. She listened without interruption until he'd finished.

"Mmm, I see," said Penny. "The main problem is that there was a lot going on when you were working in Ian's team. It's not always so full-on, you know. Often it is… well … fairly routine."

"Even so, I really enjoyed the excitement and now… well… it's not exciting anymore and maybe it will not be in the future. I'm still young enough and would like to take a chance or two."

"I don't think you should do anything rash in the short-term. At least finish the graduate course. You have, what, about three months left? That should give you some breathing time to consider all the options for the future. A lot of people at Sotheby's have a high opinion of your potential and enthusiasm."

"I shan't do anything rash, Penny, I promise, but… I'm still not sure Sotheby's is my long-term future."

"Do you want me to have a word with Ian?"

"I'm not sure. Look, Penny, I'm holding you up. I've enjoyed our chat and what you say makes sense. I'm not going to do anything in the short term. Maybe we could have another drink sometime soon."

Penny followed Viktor's lead and also stood up. "Vic, I'd love to have a drink and a chat with you. Come on, you can walk me to the Underground station."

Chapter 42

On Monday morning, Ian and Oscar were up, dressed and on the road by 6.30 am. Ian told Oscar that even by this god's unearthly hour, the M25 would be very busy. Oscar did not believe him, but once they passed the M3 junction, heading towards the Heathrow airport turns, Oscar understood why Ian had made this comment. Although there were several stop/start incidents, they eventually turned off the M25 and joined the M1 heading northwards. Oscar asked Ian how long it would take to get to Sheffield.

"If the traffic flows okay, then it will be about four hours. If it's slow, then it may be nearer five."

"You are kidding me, right?"

"Oscar, this is England. It's not Hong Kong or Antigua. Sheffield is over 150 miles from here. It's not like travelling from Kowloon to Lantau."

Oscar eased back in the passenger seat and slowly closed his eyes. "I hope this is all going to be worth it."

"I hope so too." Ian put his car into cruise control and settled back himself. Fortunately, they were heading away from London. The traffic travelling towards the capital had already come to a standstill and Ian watched until the cars at the end were still moving. He looked at his wristwatch.

7.45 am and already the queue heading into London must be about four miles long!

Two hours later, Ian spotted a sign for a service station. He switched off the cruise control, signalled and began to slow down. This was the wake-up call for Oscar. "Are we there?" asked Oscar, hopefully.

"No, Oscar, about halfway. I thought we would stop here, stretch our legs and get a cup of coffee."

Oscar sat up in his seat, yawned and rubbed his hands over his face. "Good idea. I could use the bathroom."

Thirty minutes later they were back on the motorway and continued heading northwards. Oscar looked out of his side window. He could not remember seeing so many trees and green fields, cows and sheep. It was all just another world.

Whilst parked at the service station, Ian had inserted the address of the Sheffield gallery into his sat nav. After a few seconds the directions appeared on the screen and that's where they were now heading.

Slowly the fields and trees began to be replaced by rows of houses and industrial buildings. "This reminds me of Beijing," said Oscar.

"We may be an overpopulated country, but fortunately nowhere near Beijing levels. Welcome to the outskirts of Sheffield."

"It's very hilly. Interesting how the houses seem to follow the contours of the hills."

"It's a lot cleaner than it used to be. Lots of steel manufacturing used to go on here, but most of it has now gone."

"To China, I guess."

"That's right."

Ian now followed the signs to the city centre and the sat nav said, '1 mile to destination.'

Five minutes later they pulled up opposite the art gallery. It was just after 11.45am. Ian said he would get a parking ticket from the machine and they would then go into the gallery together. Oscar got out of the car and stretched his arms and legs. It was another warm day, but not as warm as in Esher. When Oscar mentioned this to Ian, Ian smiled and his response was, "We are nearer the north pole up here!"

"No kidding!!" was Oscar's amazed response.

The two men entered the gallery and wandered around separately looking at the various paintings on view. Oscar spotted the Tobar portraits, but stood to the right and pretended to look at the nondescript painting in front of him. However, his eyes were focused on the black slave portrait. Yes, he thought, this is one of Tobar's. Excellent piece of work. Suddenly a man appeared at his side.

"This is one of Grimsdike's best pieces of work. Don't you think he captures the industrial Sheffield so well? Quite a talent."

Oscar wondered what the man was talking about, but he then realised it was the painting straight in front of him that the salesman was referring to.

"Yes. Interesting. I'll look at some others."

Ian took the hint and wandered over to view the two Tobar paintings for himself. He glanced at the portrait of the white girl, but then switched his attention to the portrait of the black man. Oh yes, he thought, these are very good. Typical of Oscar to find another gold nugget. Suddenly the salesman was now at Ian's side. "Isaac Tobar. Caribbean artist. Not sure of the full history but we think it was painted during the slave trade era."

"Indeed," replied Ian. "What's it doing in Yorkshire?"

"Local family. They were out in the West Indies and brought back both of these pictures."

"Well £15,000 seems a lot of money for an artist I've never heard of."

Oscar walked past the back of the salesman and nodded his approval to Ian.

"Are you interested in purchasing the picture, sir?"

"I could be, but not for £15,000."

"What would you be prepared to offer then, sir?"

"Mmm, not really sure … £8000, maybe."

"No, I'm sorry, sir, I could not go that low."

"Okay, I'll look around at your other pictures." Ian wandered off and the salesman went back to his desk where he looked at his computer and checked his records.

After a couple of minutes, the salesman caught up with Ian and said, "I could sell it for £12,000, sir."

"Let me take another look." Both men walked back towards the painting. Oscar was already there making a much closer inspection of both the Tobar paintings.

"So, Oscar what do you think?" asked Ian.

"It's a nice piece of work. Would look nice in your dining room."

The salesman smiled and waited for Ian's response.

"Maybe," said Ian, also taking a closer look himself. He then switched his attention to the lesser priced Tobar painting of the young girl. After a few seconds Ian said, "Okay … final offer 10k… and 5k for the second one, £15,000, my final offer. Debit card."

The salesman's smile suddenly disappeared. Ian and Oscar both looked at him waiting for his reply.

"Alright, but I think you've got a bargain," said the salesman, reluctantly.

Twenty minutes later Ian was putting the two wrapped paintings into the boot of his car and the two men then headed off back towards London. As Ian drove away both he and Oscar had a smile on their faces.

"I think you've got a good deal there, Ian. Two for the price of one!"

The salesman peered through the gallery window. His eyes followed Ian's car as it was driven away. Suddenly the smile gradually re-appeared on his face. Well, he thought to himself, £4000 profit is a good start to the week!

Chapter 43

After stopping briefly at the same motorway service station they had visited earlier that day, Ian raised the subject of Bob Taylor and the agency he wanted to set up. Ian asked Oscar if he had any initial thoughts? Oscar listed some of his ideas and reservations and the two men discussed various options.

"I think I know where the gallery could be based," said Ian. "There's a small unit near Sotheby's which is in a prime location. It just recently had a 'to let' sign put in the window. The rent could be pricey, but the location would be excellent. When are you going back to Antigua?"

"I fly out from Gatwick on Thursday evening. If you don't mind, I will come into London with you tomorrow and do some investigations. Maybe get a chance to look in on these premises."

"Yes, that's a good idea."

"By the way," said Oscar, remembering a comment Ian had made earlier. "Didn't you mention you had an idea for the three of us after we'd been to Sheffield? Are you going to tell me about it now?"

"The reason why I was a little guarded was that I wanted to see the Tobar paintings before I told you my thoughts. If I didn't rate the pictures and the artist, well my idea was dead. However, I was very impressed and, like you, I think there are excellent possibilities with this artist. Do you think you could negotiate a good price for the whole collection in Antigua?"

"They would be a lot more than the £15,000 you paid this morning."

"Come on, Oscar, don't duck my question."

"You know me, Ian. I will try to negotiate a good price, but I need to know what your top price is."

"I will put in £5 million for a cut of 65%. Can you negotiate a good deal for your 35%?"

"So, you are asking me to obtain the collection for, what, £7.5 million! Phew! Where am I going to get £2.5 million from?"

"If you did a deal below 7.5 million, it would cost you less, but over that… well, you would have to find the extra. Don't forget your commission!"

"No, I haven't." replied Oscar. He stared out of the window and watched the passing fields, trees, cows and sheep once again.

Ian kept quiet and let Oscar ponder on the maths and all the options.

For the next 20 minutes the journey continued in silence. Oscar then decided to ask Ian a question. "If we purchased the whole of the collection, are you thinking they would be sold via Bob's new gallery?"

"That and the internet. The gallery will obviously need a good website anyway. Between the three of us, we have enough experience and know how to be able to promote and market each picture to its best advantage… and of course, be able to get the best price!"

"Are you saying we cut Bob in on the deal?"

"That depends on you, Oscar. You could offer him a share of your 35%."

"I've already thought about that. Maybe I should at least offer him the option."

"After you have seen the premises tomorrow, give him a ring and chat through all the options. I think we can all make a good return on our investment... thanks to Mr Tobar!"

At about the same time that Ian and Oscar were heading back southwards on the M1, towards London, Sergei was in his home office and investigating several websites on his computer. His wife, Ludmilla, had seen an antique pair of solid silver candlesticks that she really liked in a small shop off Old Bond Street. Sergei was looking for similar items so that he could get a comparable valuation. Suddenly the telephone rang. He looked at the number displayed on his phone. He was surprised to see it was one of Andrei's mobile numbers. Well, well, well, he thought, what a nice surprise! He picked up the receiver and said, "Andrei, so good to hear from you. Where are you?"

"Hello, my friend. I am in London for a few days. I've just returned from Scotland. I was wondering if we could meet and have a chat."

"You sound very serious. Is there anything the matter?"

"Yes, there is, my friend and I want to explain, but not on the telephone. Can we meet?"

"Yes, yes, of course, but you are worrying me now."

"Please do not worry, my friend. I am staying at the Savoy hotel. Are you free for lunch tomorrow?"

Sergei was caught off guard. "Err, yes... yes! That should be okay. At the Savoy you say? What time?"

"I'll book us a table at the 'Grill' for 1pm. Would that be convenient?"

"Yes... yes that's fine. I'll be there at 1 pm."

"Thank you, my friend."

Sergei heard a click and the line was dead. Oh dear, he thought. I wonder if it's going to be bad news. He put the receiver back on its base and went back to his investigations on the internet. A few seconds later he abandoned his search as he was worried about his meeting with Andrei tomorrow. He had a horrible feeling…

The following morning, Ian and Oscar travelled on Ian's usual commuter train. After they had exited from the nearby Underground station, Ian pointed out the premises he had in mind for the new gallery. Oscar said he would have a look around the area and see what the competition was like. However, before anything else, he decided to telephone the estate agents who were advertising in the premises window. He wanted to know if he could get access to the premises.

Ian said he would leave Oscar to carry on with his enquiries and they agreed to meet up at The Grapes at six o'clock that evening, to review the day's findings.

Fifteen minutes later, Ian entered his outer office. Penny greeted him and asked if she could have a word.

"Good morning, Penny, you got my text from yesterday, I assume?" Penny nodded. "Good. Come into my room and tell me what you've got to say."

Ian and Penny walked through to Ian's main office and they both sat down next to the small meeting table in the corner.

"I bumped into Vic the other day," said Penny. Ian noted a small amount of emotion in her voice. "We went for a drink at The Grapes. He's really not very happy in his new role. We chatted for quite some time and I was able to point out the positives for his future, but he thinks a career with Sotheby's is not going to be as exciting or rewarding as he'd hoped. He kept referring to his father's friend, Andrei. I asked him if I should tell you. He didn't say no, but was rather indecisive. I'm a little worried he may do something rash. You know how keen and enthusiastic he gets."

"Yes. How long has he got to go in Ivor's department?"

"I think it's about another three months. Then he will have finished all of his graduate programme. I would hate for him to leave Sotheby's before he's finished. I don't want him to leave at all. He would be a great loss to Sotheby's future."

Ian pulled out his mobile phone and looked at his diary entries for the week. "I could have a chat with him on Friday. Maybe go to The Grapes after work. Do you want to check with him and see if that is okay?"

"Yes, I'll do that. Thank you."

Chapter 44

The Savoy Grill is one of London's great restaurants. Previous diners have included Sir Winston Churchill, Frank Sinatra and a plethora of other celebrities down the years. Even royalty have enjoyed the special menu meals cooked by some of the most famous chefs of their day. However, as Sergei and Andrei sat and sipped their cocktail aperitif, Sergei was almost oblivious to the wonderfully restored 1920 art deco surroundings. He was concentrating more on what his friend was going to tell him.

After both men had ordered their food and wine, Andrei began to speak. "My friend, I have to tell you that I am not well." He went on to summarise the chest pains he had been suffering from for the last few years, the visits to the various doctors and all the medicines he had been taking during that time. He stated that he'd been able to reduce his stress levels and had cut down on his alcohol consumption, which had certainly helped, but he now felt the problem was getting worse.

"Andrei, I had no idea," said Sergei, with genuine, heartfelt sympathy.

"I had hoped things would have improved once I'd stopped working, cut down on my alcohol intake and, to some extent, they did, but now my friend… well, age is not on my side."

"I do not know what to say!"

"There is nothing to say, my friend. I have had a wonderful life, made lifelong friends and now I am spending my money and enjoying travelling around the world. How many people can reflect back on their life and say that?"

"Well, yes, that is all true."

"We are very lucky Russians, my friend. Just think, we could still be living in Moscow!"

Sergei shuddered and shook his head at the thought.

"There is another reason I have asked you to lunch today. At the same time that I had all the legal documents drawn up to hand my apartment over to Ian Caxton, I also had my will legally updated." Andrei put his hand into the inside of his jacket and pulled out an envelope. He handed it to Sergei. "This, my friend, is a copy of my will. The original is held by my legal people in Monaco. I would be very honoured if you would consent to be my executor. In the will you will see that I have left specific legacies to a number of very special people. For Viktor, I have given him £10 million. After these specific legacies, my friend, I am leaving the rest to you."

"Andrei, of course I would be honoured to be your executor, but you don't need to leave me the balance of your assets."

"Yes, my friend, I do. Our friendship has been so very special. You have tolerated and supported many of my… 'adventures' should we say. And without your and Boris' help in the early years, we would not be sitting here today. I still hope to enjoy some more years travelling, but I am realistic enough to know that I might not wake up tomorrow morning! I wanted to tell you, to your face, before it is too late. Besides, my friend, I also have a feeling that one of my enemies will finally catch up with me and I wanted to make sure all my affairs are left orderly. Is that the right word?"

"Wow, Andrei, you really are serious! I do hope you have many more years left to enjoy yourself first though."

"So do I, my friend… ah, here is our food. Let's hope it is not my last supper!" Andrei laughed at his own little joke, but Sergei just had a worried stare.

Later that afternoon, Ian joined Oscar at The Grapes. Oscar was sitting at the table close to the window and had a pint of beer already waiting for his friend.

"Thank you very much," said Ian, sitting down next to Oscar. He picked up his glass and they both said 'cheers'.

"So, Oscar, how has your day been?" asked Ian. He took his first sip and replaced his glass on the beer mat.

"Quite interesting. After you left me, I telephoned the agent's number listed on the sign in the window and they agreed to send someone to show me around the premises at 2 pm. So, I had quite a bit of time to kill. I wandered around the area and found three art galleries fairly close by. I had a look at their collections. Some okay pieces of work, but nothing really special. I think the Tobar paintings, in this area of London, would certainly be something different. I walked up here for lunch – they do a nice seafood salad by the way – and then I met Mr Carter at the premises. We chatted generally for a while and I got the distinct impression that I was their first viewer. For starters, Mr Carter could not find the right key. Anyway, once we were in, I had a good look around. The space to let is only on the ground floor. There are third party offices above with separate entrances. What could well be the gallery show area is quite big. It goes back quite some way. Behind that are some storage areas and a separate sort of kitchen area. There is also a sizable room that could double up as an office and possibly, as a packing area. All in all, it looked quite good. Needs a good clean, painting and fitting out, but fundamentally it could work for Bob. There is also good security, with a reasonably new burglar alarm system. Mr Carter also gave me these sheets." Oscar passed the papers over to Ian. "They give the details of the terms of the letting and the measurements of the various rooms."

Ian flicked through the two A4 sheets, scanning quickly the information provided. "I'm sure we can get better rental terms than these, but still, it is early days at the moment."

"Mr Carter also gave me his business card and asked me to contact him if I had any further questions, or if I needed any more information. I was there for just over an hour. After that I had a walk along Bond Street and Piccadilly. Fortnum & Mason's shop is quite fascinating! Have you been in there?"

Ian smiled at Oscar's last comment. "Yes, Oscar, I've been to the Fortnum & Mason's shop! So, you've had a busy day."

"It's been very useful. What I thought I would do tomorrow is put my findings in a report and email them to Bob. I will then give him a ring later to answer any of his questions. I'll also take the opportunity to mention the Tobar collection and get his reaction on whether he is interested in taking on a share."

"That sounds good. Emma's cooking one of her special cottage pies tonight so I think we should drink up and head home. I've also got two bottles of Chablis chilling in the fridge, waiting for our attention!"

Oscar finished the last drops of his beer and immediately stood up. "Let's go!"

When the two men arrived back at Ian's home, Emma said that the meal would be about 30 minutes. Ian took Oscar into his home office and showed him how his spare computer worked. He also said that he could use this machine tomorrow to produce the report for Bob Taylor.

It was already connected to the Wi-Fi system so he could send it via email.

Oscar said he would also send copies of his report to Ian and keep a copy for himself. He then stated that basically he understood how the computer worked and would use his mobile phone to ring Bob later in the day.

"Right then," said Ian, leading Oscar back towards the kitchen. "Let's go and open one of those two bottles of Chablis."

The following day, Oscar completed his report, checked it to make sure all the information was included and emailed it to Bob Taylor. He also sent a copy to Ian and kept one for himself. Additionally, he told Bob that he would telephone him later that day, about 4 pm UK time. This he did. Bob confirmed he had read the report and was pleased with Oscar's findings. Like Ian, he thought the monthly rental costs were on the high side and asked Oscar to see whether he could get them reduced.

When Ian returned home that evening, Oscar was playing with Robert on the rear lawn. Oscar had a small soft ball and was throwing it gently to him in his bouncer.

Ian entered through the front door and was greeted with a kiss from Emma. "Come and see these two on the back lawn," suggested Emma, before Ian had even closed the front door.

They both walked through to the kitchen and over to the bi-fold doors, which were fully open giving immediate access to the patio area. Both Emma and Ian stood there for a few seconds whilst Oscar, laying on the grass, was chatting away to Robert. He held a small ball just above Robert, who was laying on his back and kicking his legs in the air. Oscar was explaining what the Cantonese word for ball was! Both Ian and Emma laughed and Oscar looked up.

"Hi!" said Oscar, when he heard them laughing. "I think

this guy might be a goalkeeper when he grows up. He keeps trying to grab the ball."

"I hope not," replied Ian. "I was hoping he would captain England playing cricket!"

Ian walked out to join them and picked up Robert, who immediately gave his father a big smile. "So, Oscar, how's your day been?"

"I finished the report for Bob and then telephoned him. Otherwise, I've been relaxing with Emma and Robert. Enjoying this nice weather." replied Oscar.

The two men and Robert went and sat around the patio table and Ian continued, "I read your email report to Bob. Did he like it?"

"Yes, he seemed very pleased, but, like you, he thought the rent was a little high. I will give the agents a ring in the morning and see if I can negotiate a better deal. I also mentioned the Tobar pictures and he seemed interested, but said he would have to think about investing in a share. I think he might go for about 10%, leaving me 25%, but he was noncommittal at this stage."

"Ok. Remind me, what time's your flight tomorrow?"

"I leave Gatwick at 8.20, tomorrow evening, but I would like to be there about three hours earlier. Emma has volunteered to drop me at the railway station just after four o'clock. I'm taking her and Robert out for a meal tomorrow lunchtime. She suggested a Chinese restaurant not too far from the station."

"Oh, I know the one. I'd be interested in your opinion. I'm sorry I cannot take you back to the airport myself, but I've got an important meeting at 3.30 and I really should be there."

"I know. You mentioned it before. It's no problem."

"Are you boys hungry?" It was Emma shouting from the kitchen. "Dinner will be ready in five minutes."

Later that evening, Ian and Oscar chatted more about the new gallery. Bob had already stated that he had an idea of the pictures he would be moving from Monaco and Oscar had suggested a particular location for the Tobar paintings … if he could get them for a sensible price in Antigua, of course!

Oscar told Ian he had advised Bob that he could finish all the new gallery negotiations and final details from Antigua. He would then send him his suggested final layout for the display area.

Ian promised that once everything was finalised, he would obtain the keys on Bob's behalf and would find time to liaise with the workmen that Oscar had organised.

All that was needed now was for Oscar to apply all his best negotiating skills to finalise the rent and contract terms for the new gallery premises and, of course, to negotiate a 'sensible' price for the Tobar collection in Antigua. No pressure then!

At the end of the evening, Ian told Oscar that he needed to leave for work very early the next morning so they said their goodbyes there and then. Both agreed it had been a very interesting few days and they hoped it was also going to be an exciting and very profitable next few weeks as well.

Chapter 45

Penny told Viktor about her discussions with Ian following their earlier conversations at The Grapes. Viktor was partly pleased and partly annoyed. However, on balance, he respected Ian's opinions so he agreed to meet his former boss on Friday evening after work.

As he walked towards The Grapes, Viktor was concerned about what Ian was going to advise him. It was a few weeks since he had last spoken to him and, whilst Viktor was still unsure about his future at Sotheby's, he was similarly unsure about his other options as well. He enjoyed working in the art world, but he definitely wanted to pursue a more exciting and challenging career route. Despite what his father had told him, he still thought enviously about Andrei's business world.

When Viktor entered the bar area of The Grapes, he immediately spotted Ian standing at the bar. Ian was in the process of ordering himself a pint of beer and when Viktor joined him he ordered a second pint for his colleague.

"Well then, Vic, I gather you are not finding life so exciting in Ivor's department," said Ian, handing Viktor his pint of beer. "Come on, let's sit down over there." Ian pointed to a vacant table and the two men walked over and sat down.

"It's certainly not as much fun, or as exciting, as working

in your team, Ian," said Viktor, placing his glass on the beermat immediately in front of him. "You gave me more opportunities, scope and the freedom to follow my own ideas. You trusted me. In Ivor's team it's, well, to be honest, it's boring. I'm just not trusted at all. You were never like that."

"Well, we all work differently. People will give you more scope and opportunities to demonstrate your abilities when you've finished your graduate course."

"I'm not sure that is what I want now, Ian. I enjoy the art world, of course I do, but I want to be less constrained." Viktor took a sip of his beer and wondered if he was being too negative in front of his former boss.

"What are you thinking of doing?"

"I don't really know. I look at Andrei's life and your career. You have worked in exciting places like New York and Hong Kong. I've only been out of the UK once... and that was a school trip to France! I am an only child and my parents have been so protective – probably because coming from Russia, they are always looking over their shoulders. I'm still living at home and I really do crave some freedom." Viktor shrugged his shoulders. "The problem is, I do not want to upset my parents or give them a lot more to worry about."

"You are now of an age, Vic, when most children have 'flown the nest'. No matter what you do, your parents will always be worried about you. Even when you get to my age, your mum will still think of you as 'her little boy'. That's what parents do. You need to think about yourself and what you really want out of life. My parents were worried about me going to New York and Hong Kong, but once they saw I was happy and successfully progressing my career, they were pleased... but they still worried!"

"Do you think it is time for me to move on?"

"Only you can decide that, Vic. As I say, you need to think about yourself and what you want out of life. You are the best person to be in control of that. Don't rely on other people to control your life for you. The one thing I would say is make sure you finish Sotheby's graduate course. It will be a good fallback position if you need it in the future. When you have completed that course, come and have another chat with me. You are bright, ambitious and enthusiastic. All admirable qualities that are in such short supply in our industry. I do not want to see them go to waste."

"Thank you, Ian. I was serious when I said I would love to work with you again. I really do value your thoughts and opinions."

"Well, my current thought and opinion is, get the course finished… with flying colours… and come and see me again and we'll have another chat."

Andrei arrived in Sydney after a short break in Dubai. Despite all his business travelling in the past, this was the first time he had set foot on Australian soil. He was excited but still somewhat apprehensive. He planned to stay in the Sydney area for a few weeks and then take a cruise up to Queensland and around the Great Barrier Reef. Then flying westwards to Melbourne and then on to Perth. That was the excitement. The apprehension was his constant concern for his health!

Julian was sitting in his car outside one of the most expensive ladies fashion shops in Nice. Mrs Chalmers, his client for the day, was currently visiting the third main fashion shop of the trip. Julian's car boot was already bulging with earlier purchases and if previous experiences were anything to go by, then there was still more to come! As he watched the main entrance doorway for signs of his client exiting, his mobile bleeped to indicate an incoming message. Julian accessed his email inbox and smiled when he saw it was from Andrei. The message was simple and short, stating that he had arrived in Sydney safely and would be staying there for several weeks.

Suddenly there was a tap on his driver's side window and an attractive lady was staring at him whilst clutching several parcels and bags. Julian quickly pressed the rear boot release button and got out of the car.

"Sorry, Mrs Chalmers. Please let me take those parcels from you." Julian quickly relieved Mrs Chalmers of her purchases and laid them gently in the final spaces in the boot. He then ran back and opened the rear passenger door allowing Mrs Chalmers to get into the car.

"Where do you want to go now, Mrs Chalmers?" he asked, once he was back in his driver's position.

"Back home to Monaco please, Julian. I've had enough for today."

"Okay," he replied. He was surprised but pleased with the curtailment of the shopping trip. He had some information for Andrei and wanted to get it to him as soon as possible.

Meanwhile in Antigua, Oscar was entering the Shell Gallery for his 10 am appointment with Wesley Fredericks. He was immediately spotted by Mr Fredericks' assistant, Worrell, who greeted him and led him through the gallery towards Mr Fredericks' office. As Oscar followed, he cast his eyes around the display area and was pleased to see the Tobar pictures were on display and still for sale.

"Come in," bellowed Wesley Fredericks, as Worrell tapped on his door. Worrell then pushed the door wider and invited Oscar to enter. Wesley Fredericks, on spotting Oscar, stood up and walked around his desk to greet him. They both shook hands. "Hi, Oscar, do you have some good news? Come, sit down here, man." The two men sat down in the places they had occupied at their last meeting.

"Well I hope it is good news, Wesley. I have a possible buyer for the 12 Tobar pictures."

"That sounds like very good news indeed, but why the hesitancy?"

"The possible buyer is in England and he already owns two Tobar paintings. He wants to add to his collection and is prepared to offer a cash deal of £7 million for your 12 paintings."

Wesley's smile disappeared. "I see. A lot lower than our valuation."

"I know," replied Oscar. He waited whilst Wesley pondered on the offer.

Wesley rose from his seat and went back to his computer to check on the range of prices the client had said he would accept. Two minutes later, he walked back to rejoin Oscar and said, "That offer is below the minimum I can accept from my client. Do you think there is any room for your client to increase the offer?"

Oscar leaned back in his chair. "I don't know him that well. But I may be able to get him to go to £7.5 million. I will have to telephone him first though."

"Okay, Oscar, you telephone your client and I will contact mine. I'm sure we can do a satisfactory deal for all concerned."

"Getting this deal done will be a great start for me in Antigua, Wesley. Can I suggest we meet again in two days' time?"

"Here for 10 am?"

"Thank you, Wesley. That's fine."

Chapter 46

When Julian arrived back at his apartment, after taking Mrs Chalmers back to her own apartment, he opened up his computer and started to type an email to Andrei. He then attached copies of the rest of the booking invoices for the cruise ship, later hotels and two internal flights, as per Andrei's planned programme of stays in Australia. Andrei had already received the booking details for the two hotels he was staying at in the Sydney area.

Julian read through the details of his email once again and when he was finally satisfied that it was all accurate and the correct attachments had been included, he pressed the 'send' button. As he did so he made a quiet wish to himself. 'Good luck Andrei, I hope you have an enjoyable and healthy stay in Australia. I miss you.'

When Oscar arrived at the Shell Gallery for his second ten o'clock appointment, Wesley was in the display area with Worrell. The two men turned around when Oscar walked through the door and Wesley walked over and gave Oscar a large smile and held out his hand.

Looks promising, thought Oscar, as he shook Wesley's hand.

"Hello again, Oscar. Come into my office."

Oscar followed Wesley into his office and they both sat down on their usual seats next to the table. Oscar wanted Wesley to open the conversation so remained silent and waited for a few seconds.

"I have spoken with my client," opened Wesley, "and I'm pleased to say that I have persuaded him to reduce his asking price. We are now looking for £8.5 million."

Oscar kept a straight face and replied, "My client has given me permission to increase his offer to £7.75 million, tops. I am prepared to reduce my commission by half to try and bridge the gap. I really want to do this deal, Wesley, and demonstrate to you that we can do plenty of business in the future."

"Oscar, I think we can do a lot of business together in the future! I also think I can persuade my client that £7.75 million is the best deal he is going to get." Wesley held out his hand and Oscar shook it. The deal was done!

"I can have the £7.75 million transferred within seven days if you can give me the bank details."

Later, back in his villa, Oscar emailed both Ian and Bob and told them the details of the deal that he'd negotiated. He also reminded them of the amount of money that each needed to transfer to his bank account in the next two days!

Once Oscar had pressed the 'send' button he put a bottle of champagne in the fridge and went off to his bedroom to change. He was going for a swim in the Caribbean! Tomorrow he would finalise the lease agreement on Bob's new London gallery and also agree a date when the internal alterations could commence with the builders. Finally, he would make his suggestions to Ian and Bob as to how best the Tobar paintings should be displayed in the new layout.

Suddenly Oscar had a thought! We will, of course, need someone to manage the gallery on a daily basis. How would I know who to employ!? Mmm, I think I'll leave that one to Ian and Bob to sort out!'

It was early on the following Sunday morning when Emma made the suggestion to Ian. She was still in bed reading a magazine. Ian had just returned with two cups of tea. As he put a cup on each of the two bedside tables, he said, "Isn't it quiet without Robert? I had a great night's sleep. I cannot remember the last time that happened."

"I know… and I've been thinking. Robert has stayed with my parents for a full day and with your parents for two days and overnight. He seems quite relaxed about the changes, so maybe we should leave him for a few days with your parents whilst we go back to Monaco. What do you think?"

"You know my mum dotes on him and would love him to stay for more days. When we go and collect him this evening, let's see what they say. It sounds good to me."

"It would be nice to go back to the apartment, just the two of us. I will miss and be worried about Robert, but I want us to try and rekindle the relationship we had before Robert came along."

Ian had climbed back into bed and picked up his cup of tea. "I'll ask mum tonight and see what she says."

Ian's mum and dad were certainly happy with Ian and Emma's suggestion. His mum, in particular, said that Robert was not a problem and seemed to thrive on all the extra attention. So, it was all agreed. Ian would arrange the flights and inform Harbour Heights and Julian of the date of their arrival.

Next morning, Ian checked his diary and chatted with Penny. Penny checked the airline websites for the suggested dates and booked the flights. Ian then emailed Harbour Heights and Julian. They would be off to Monaco again in ten days' time. Ian was really pleased at Emma's enthusiasm to go back to the apartment. She had even suggested that they ought to consider redecorating certain rooms!

Ten days later, Julian met Ian and Emma at Nice airport. For the first part of the journey, they talked in general terms about Robert and each other's lives since the last visit. It was only when Ian asked Julian whether he had heard from Andrei that Julian said that he had received two emails from him. The first was when he arrived in Sydney three weeks ago and a second saying he was just about to board the booked cruise ship that was heading for Queensland and the Great Barrier Reef.

"He's certainly seeing a lot of the world now. A proper tourist!" announced Emma.

"How long is he going to stay in Australia?" asked Ian.

"After his cruise I've already booked his accommodation and internal flights to Melbourne and Perth. That will mean he will still be there for at least another two months. After that I don't know. He will send his next instructions in due course. By the way, did you know he'd been back to Scotland staying with the Laird and his wife?"

Ian and Emma looked at each other in surprise.

"No, I didn't," announced Ian. "I know he has invested in some new developments on the Estate, so I guess he was just checking up on their progress." Ian, however, was wondering if there was something more going on.

Just as they arrived on the outskirts of Monaco, Emma whispered to Ian. "What about using Julian's services tomorrow and having a day looking around San Remo. We've not been there before and I would like to look around the town and in a few shops. It's not that far from Monaco, is it?"

"Good idea. No, it's just inside the Italian border."

"Julian," said Ian, leaning forward and closer to the driver. "Are you free tomorrow as we would like to have a day in San Remo?"

"That's not a problem. What time would you like to be collected?"

Ian looked at Emma and after a few seconds she suggested 10 am.

"That's fine. I'll collect you from reception at that time".

It was the next morning, at 9.50 am, when a member of the reception team telephoned the Penthouse Suite. Ian answered the call. The receptionist asked if it was alright for Julian to come up to the apartment. Ian was confused as he thought it had been agreed that the three of them would meet in reception at 10 am. Nevertheless, Ian assumed Julian must have a good reason for changing the arrangements slightly, so he told reception to send Julian up.

Five minutes later Julian pressed the doorbell and Ian opened the door. Julian was dressed in casual clothes, unshaven, shaking and had a very white complexion.

Ian was shocked by Julian's appearance. "Julian, are you alright? You look in shock. Come in and sit down. What's the matter? Emma, can you bring a glass of water!"

Ian helped Julian to the nearest sofa and sat him down.

Emma arrived with a glass of water and handed it to Julian. She looked at Ian and asked, "What's the matter?"

Ian shrugged his shoulders and waited for Julian to speak.

Julian took two small sips of the water and then looked up into the faces of both of them. Tears appeared in both of his eyes and then slowly trickled down his cheeks.

"It's Andrei. He's dead!!"

"What!" exclaimed Ian. "When!? How did he die?"

Julian lowered his head and covered his face with his hands and said, "I don't know!"

The story continues in

'THE DECISION'

Volume 3 of the Ian Caxton Thriller series

ALSO WRITTEN BY ROBERT CORT

THE IAN CAXTON THRILLER SERIES

Volume 1 - The Opportunity

DISCOVER THE FIRST VOLUME OF THE
IAN CAXTON THRILLER SERIES.

Ian Caxton is a senior manager at Sotheby's. After successful career moves to Sotheby's branches in New York and Hong Kong, Ian is now based in London and earmarked for the top position.

However, following a chance meeting with Andrei, a very rich Russian art dealer based in Monaco, Ian suddenly reassesses all his plans and ambitions. Even his marriage is under threat.

The Opportunity charts the tumultuous life and career of Ian Caxton as he navigates the underbelly of the art world, one of serious wealth, heart-stopping adventure and a dark side.

The big question is, will Ian take **The Opportunity?** And if he does, what will the consequences be, not only for him, but also for his wife and colleagues?